The Last Bazaar

(Matt Drake #12)

By

David Leadbeater

Thriller, adventure, action, mystery, suspense, archaeological, military, historical

Other Books by David Leadbeater:

The Matt Drake Series

The Bones of Odin (Matt Drake #1)
The Blood King Conspiracy (Matt Drake #2)
The Gates of hell (Matt Drake 3)
The Tomb of the Gods (Matt Drake #4)
Brothers in Arms (Matt Drake #5)
The Swords of Babylon (Matt Drake #6)
Blood Vengeance (Matt Drake #7)
Last Man Standing (Matt Drake #8)
The Plagues of Pandora (Matt Drake #9)
The Lost Kingdom (Matt Drake #10)
The Ghost Ships of Arizona (Matt Drake #11)

The Alicia Myles Series

Aztec Gold (Alicia Myles #1)
Crusader's Gold (Alicia Myles #2)

The Disavowed Series:

The Razor's Edge (Disavowed #1)
In Harm's Way (Disavowed #2)
Threat Level: Red (Disavowed #3)

The Chosen Few Series

Chosen (The Chosen Trilogy #1)
Guardians (The Chosen Tribology #2)

Short Stories

Walking with Ghosts (A short story)
A Whispering of Ghosts (A short story)

Connect with the author on Twitter: @dleadbeater2011
Visit the author's website: **www.davidleadbeater.com**

All helpful, genuine comments are welcome. I would love to hear from you.

davidleadbeater2011@hotmail.co.uk

CHAPTER ONE

Kono Kinimaka placed her empty sandwich wrapper carefully beside her on the step and weighed it down with a plastic bottle of water. The sandwich tasted good. She'd prepared it before stepping out earlier and purchased the water on the way. The morning's walk to the Lincoln Memorial and Reflecting Pool was her compromise to a day off the gym and several hours of contemplative quiet.

Not everything was about top speed and sweat, although some guys she knew would disagree. Her years in Hawaii had taught her that peace of mind can be just as important as physical comfort. So she had tied her long, dark hair back, tucked it beneath a *Malcolm Reynolds* baseball cap, shrugged into a pair of joggers and a hooded jacket, then carried her small bag of food all the way down to Constitution Avenue. She hid her doe eyes behind blue reflective Oakleys. It was only after she set out that she remembered to convince herself that the camouflage gear was to ward off the sun and unwelcome male gazes rather than a dangerous stalker's eyes.

Kono had been living with the attentions of a stalker for some time now, culminating recently in an attack that was barely thwarted. Nothing transpired since, and Kono was starting to feel almost human again. It would be even better though when Mano returned from whatever mission the SPEAR team were currently undertaking. Kono had lost track of the madcap adventures her brother and his colleagues constantly accepted.

She had smiled at the cop outside her house and

wondered just how much longer the surveillance would stay. Yes, it made her feel safer but God it was so oppressing.

"Jim," she said in acknowledgement as she passed the parked car.

"Ma'am," he murmured as she continued on, the title making her both smile and frown at the same time.

Now she sat basking under the sunlight, a dozen steps down from Lincoln's immortalized feet, content to contemplate and observe and people-watch with the rest of the locals and the oft-bemused security guards. The Reflecting Pool lay ahead and below her, ever changing and yet so very still under the drifting clouds and sparkling sun. Kono tried not to gauge the eye of every passing person—it didn't help and that was what *they* wanted. And anyway, those days were over weren't they?

The first indication she had that something was wrong came from far away—a bright glint catching her eye. She remembered those movies where the target only knew they were under surveillance when sunlight caught a distant lens, but immediately shrugged it off. Tyler Webb liked his stalkings up close and personal—that had always been his way. Kono finished her sandwich and took a swig from the water bottle. Again the distant glint flashed across her vision. Of course it could be anything—a watch, a car windshield, a bottle.

Unable to help herself, Kono fished out her cellphone.

Then jammed it back in her pocket, breathing deeply and cursing that such an innocent incident could so easily ruin her morning. Brushing off and disposing of the sandwich wrapper, she rose and started the walk back to her apartment, sparing a last look for Lincoln.

Maybe tomorrow.

The return journey didn't last long; Kono was walking

fast. Jim looked surprised to see her, then resumed his cop's gaze and merely nodded. Kono strode past up to her front door and pushed the key into the lock.

Her cell rang. "Mano? I was just about to call you."

"Where did you go? I had you in my sights and then . . . *pshh*. All gone."

Kono stared at the screen as a rush of ice water flooded her veins. "What?"

"Where did you go, Kono Kinimaka?"

The screen read: *Caller Unknown*. The voice turned to laughter that was neither happy nor menacing—just . . . *neutral*. Odd. Weird.

Kono turned the key, glancing back toward Jim as she did so. The thought of police backup was suddenly much more comforting.

Jim's head sat on top of the car, his body still inside.

Kono screamed, unable to see the man that had murdered her bodyguard, unable to see anything but Jim's terrified, frozen, unseeing eyes. She barged open the door and leapt inside, only remembering at the last moment to reach around for the key . . . terrified that a strong hand might then close over her own . . .

It didn't. Kono slammed the door behind her, now remembering she still held the cellphone and the channel was open. The voice came again: *"Nice to see you made it."*

The words echoed strangely; both cellphone robotic and crystal clear as if . . . *as if the words were being spoken by someone standing right next to me* . . . Kono experienced shock like electrocution and staggered ungainly into the large front room. She flicked at her shoulders, her hair, her scalp, as if a tarantula had just landed there. She clutched her water bottle like a weapon.

And the man stared at her, chuckling, from the couch. "Good you could join us."

Us?

She spun. More figures stepped out of the kitchen. Too many to count. The front door—which she hadn't even locked behind her—swung open and another man stood there, black-gloved hands dripping blood.

"Tried a choke hold," he growled. "Head just came right off in my hands. I hear that can happen when you reach a certain age."

Kono backed away, a cornered animal staring between a dozen primed sights. The man still connected to her cellphone rose slowly, lips curling into an evil smile.

"Webb wants it done messy," he said quite amiably. "You gonna run, or what?"

Kono bolted before he finished speaking, hoping to gain even a fraction of a second, which she did. The stairs were at her back and she whirled, hitting them hard, expecting enemies to be lying in wait above but knowing she had no choice but to move forward. It would be a cold day in hell before she just lay down to die. With help, she had thwarted these attacks before. Now, alone, she could do so again. The knowledge was in her blood. To her disappointment and fear the men didn't stand around laughing and jeering as she had hoped—they pounded after her, grim-faced. A hastily thrown knife slammed into the door jamb she passed through, at head height, proving she'd be offered no quarter. Messy was just messy after all. She didn't have to be alive. Kono gained the top of the stairs and ground to a halt, panting, face and hair wild, posed with a terrible choice and no time in which to make it. Footsteps thumped hard behind her. Crazily, she recalled Mano regaling her recently with a story about the team's two new catchphrases.

One sprung to mind: *What would Drake do?*

The shit that just popped into your head . . . *well, what would he do?*

She had an advantage here, but it was a small one, easily lost. Before that could happen, Kono whirled and booted her closest attacker in the middle of the chest. As hoped for, he looked surprised, then staggered back, right into his colleagues on the narrow staircase, driving them all downwards. Not the domino effect she'd been hoping for, but a gain to her advantage. Kono now had two desperate choices—the small toilet or the bedroom. Only one of those places offered a way out.

Angling sideways she edged into her room. The window stood wide open, a welcome invite. She quickly decided that chancing a broken leg from the high jump was worth the risk. Once outside, her options opened wide up, and wouldn't just end with screaming. It was only as she started moving toward that avenue of freedom that she saw the small coffin on the bed.

"It's for you," came the quiet voice from behind her. "Yeah I lied about it being messy. He wants you all folded up and delivered to your brother. It's a bit small, but it's all we could get at short notice. Don't worry." He cracked his knuckles ominously. "We'll make some adjustments."

CHAPTER TWO

Kono staggered away as he grabbed for her, a finger grazing her arm. Fighting to stay focused, she forced the flooding fear from her mind. Debilitating terror was what these bastards worked to achieve. They would not beat her so easily.

"You think you're gonna get out that way?" The man nodded at the window, knowing her only exit. "Take a look. Hey, don't worry, I can wait." He studied his knuckles.

Kono inched over to the open window, enjoying the breeze on her hot skin. One look outside showed several craggy upturned faces. They were waiting for her.

"Just scoop you up and carry you back inside." The man's voice dripped malice. "Save us a job fitting you in that coffin though."

Kono prayed for inspiration. "Why are you all doing this?" Maybe help was on its way.

"Those guys downstairs? Well, they enjoy the payday. Me? I just love breaking beautiful things."

Kono shuddered. "Webb sent men before. They all ended up in the ground."

"Que sera." He spread his arms. "I don't care."

Trapped, out of options, Kono prayed for some luck. She broke for the window, expecting and receiving no reaction from the man taunting her. She climbed over the window sill, looking down into the blank eyes of those who waited. Then she did something totally unexpected.

She jumped.

Angling to the right, she caught hold of the water pipe with both hands. It took an enormous amount of courage to relinquish her hold on the window and dangle above the street but a moment later she was doing just that and crab-walking up the side of her own building, ignoring next door's small but functional balcony. Even if she gained entry she would be no better off and poor old Mr. Calabretta would end up dead too. The roof lay only a few feet away though and soon she reached for the gutter to help pull herself over the top. The metal felt thin and sharp, almost coming away with her weight. But Kono held on, breathing hard, feeling gravel scraping her belly as she squirmed over the top but knowing that meant she still lived.

Quickly, she glanced down. One of the men was speaking into a two-way.

Kono rose, suddenly screaming in shock as her taunter's face rose above the roof's edge. He had followed right behind her and now reached out with extreme confidence.

"It's a nice bit of exercise, sweets, but we're getting short of time."

"Fuck you."

Kono started to scream. The noise would send cops, she knew. Maybe they were already on the way. The roof of her apartment was flat, concrete, and empty. No outlets to run behind, no air-conditioning ducts. For a moment she paused, again a scared rabbit caught in the headlights of this man's smug proficiency, but then the sound of sirens split the morning air. She leaned over and vented her lungs.

Her heart leapt. She had a chance, the sound of sirens galvanizing her like nothing else could. And the man saw it. Determination replaced the superior set to his features and he quickly darted at her. For once, Kono anticipated it and jumped out of range. Her eyes swept the roof. *What would Drake do?* Again that phrase, keeping her alive, sharpening her wits. She would not panic. But catchphrase or not it offered a solution.

Jump.

Kono ran hard, the force of her launch spinning tiny bits of gravel out from the back of her heels. The edge of the roof came up fast, but there wasn't even a millisecond to spend entertaining doubt; she leapt across the gap, landing askew on top of the next roof. Pain exploded in her ankle and she tumbled. Thoughts of Mano and his absence flashed through her mind. She ended up against the far edge, crawling, groaning and then sitting up to watch her would-be killer make his leap perfectly and then approach.

"Too bad." The outer smugness was back, though the eyes were dead. "A millimeter either way, like me, and you'd still be running. *Pfft.* Into the horizon." He keyed his two-way. "Move around to the side of the apartment. I'll kick her off the roof."

And just like that this man decided her fate. The morals of it meant nothing. His principles were below gutter-level. To have lived for this long, experienced all that she had, harbored hopes and dreams and made plans—all for this. To be kicked ignominiously off a two-story roof.

"Wait." Kono held up her hands. "Dude, just . . . wait."

"Be quick with your pleadings." The man checked his watch. "I have someone else to kill at one o'clock."

"Oh, well," Kono had never pleaded in her life and wasn't about to start now. "If that's how it is . . ."

Without knowing exactly what she was doing she kicked out with her heels, aiming every ounce of power at the man's knees. It was all she had, all she could do. The movement itself sent trails of fire through her damaged ankle. The impact caused explosions. But it also produced a raft of emotions to finally emerge from the empty-seeming man—pain and hatred and several doses of anguish.

"You . . . you bitch!"

"Oh the temerity," Kono struggled to her feet despite her

own discomfort, "that the poor little victim should fight back.

The man stumbled toward her now, experiencing some agony of his own. Kono in turn stumbled away, the two of them performing an unusual dance. Inch by inch she backed away until the edge of the roof lay at her back.

"The good news is you didn't break my leg." The man grimaced as he spoke. "Bad news? You're still head-diving off this roof."

He leapt at her, trying to force her into a sudden step back, but Kono didn't move. Not at first, instead she waited and waited until the man was close enough to place his hands on her waist and just push. Their eyes locked together.

"You feel nothing?" she asked.

"Life gave me no conscience," the man said evenly. "You'd be surprised how many people it dealt similar gifts too. Right from the top of the food chain and downward, believe me."

"You think it is a gift?"

"Depends on your perspective." The man glanced over her shoulder. "Yours ain't so hot, right now."

"I pity you." Kono said. "I really do."

The man hesitated for just a moment. "And would you forgive me?"

"For killing me? That's possible. But for all the other murders you committed? No, for that you will rightly burn in Hell."

"Oh, well." The man laughed as he shoved her off the edge of the roof.

CHAPTER THREE

Kono grabbed the man's shirt and threw herself backwards as he pushed. Normally he might have pulled away, resisted, but his damaged knee refused to play ball and he went over with her. If the man had been watching carefully he might have noticed that Kono's fall wasn't exactly directionless; nor was it without power. She thrust herself in one direction, away from him.

Her fall ended abruptly when she landed on a top floor balcony, screaming in pain but alive. His didn't end at all until he smashed into the concrete floor of the alley below, his own scream cut off by instant death.

Kono groaned. The balcony was solid, railed and hid her from the eyes below. They would probably guess where she was and send someone up, but those sirens were awfully close now. Blue lights washed the walls of buildings. Would these killers risk capture?

Voices barked from the alley below.

"Sheeeyit! That's Tone. Did the bitch do this to him?"

"Boss ain't gonna be happy."

"We don't stop." Another disembodied growl drifted up. "That's the regimen."

"So we're cop killers now?"

"We are today."

Kono felt chills radiate from her heart to her brain. The first thing that struck her was guilt. No way would she allow any cop to die whilst she hid out of sight. But how the hell was she going to escape on her injured ankle? The only answer lay in the small avenue of movement open to her.

Kono used a small plant pot to smash through her

neighbor's French windows, not caring how much noise she made. Then she slithered through into the thankfully empty apartment, piercing her skin with shards of glass but barely noticing. She rose and limped over to the kitchen area, quickly grabbing a carving knife. Not that it made her feel any better, but now she offered a slight threat at least. In a world where it was a dozen trained killers versus one mostly retired surf queen, any weapon could make all the difference. Kono wondered how long it would take them to race around the building and encounter the cops. Not long. She had to get out of here.

On second thoughts . . .

A light bulb moment made her stop and study the room. Mano and his associates were probably over at the Pentagon. How long would it take?

Not long.

Kono knew the protocols. She had called her brother many times, sometimes in peril and often in anger. She blamed him partly for the death of their mother, but knew she herself had made the decision to run away long before that. She had deserted the family home. But that had been easy when you expected your mother would always be there, right there, waiting and breathing and living and alive. You always knew you could go back.

It never occurred to Kono, a young girl, that one day her parents might not be there. Even though they wanted to be with every beat of their heart, every ounce of eternal love in their souls. But parents were fragile creatures too, as fragile as they believed their children would always be.

Kono tapped out Mano's number and prayed for the big man to answer. He always did, of course, and this time was no different.

"Yeah? I'm busy, what do you want now?"

The brotherly greeting never changed. "I need you.

They're trying to kill me at my apartment. Jim's dead. The cops . . . I don't know. Help me, Mano."

Her voice was pitched low, but Kinimaka's came back at a high pitch. *"What? Your apartment?"*

The line went crackly; there was panting and pounding and incoherent shouting. Kono knew she couldn't hang around in one place so placed the receiver back in its cradle. Mano would either get here in time or he wouldn't. She couldn't change that, but it did make her feel good to have him on the way.

Maybe it was time to stop blaming her big brother for her own mistakes.

Yeah, maybe it is.

Kono approached the door and listened. The corridor outside was in silence. It occurred to her then that the door would be locked from the outside. She needed a key to exit. It took her another minute to find where the spare key was hung—next to all the other keys—and then to quietly and slowly unlock the door.

The corridor stretched away in both directions, quiet for now, but this was no time to linger. She limped out and pushed at the door that led to the stairs, cocked her head to listen. Again, no sounds. Three minutes had passed since her call to Mano. How long would it take SPEAR to get here?

Gunshots now echoed up from the street below. Kono inched her way to the staircase and put her face to the grimy window that looked outside. Her vision was limited, but part of the street in front of her apartment was visible. Jim's cop car still stood there with its nasty embellishment, but next to it now sat two other cop cars. Kono could see their occupants were kneeling and bobbing, engaged in a firefight. Clearly, the cops were under attack and even she, a civilian, knew that men such as the ones hunting her would only tolerate that as part of a deeper plan.

They were coming for her.

Kono hobbled painfully down a floor to help mix it all up, then poked her head around the exit door. The first floor was also quiet. Could her stalkers have taken the elevator? *Please, please be on the elevator.*

She turned back to survey the scene outside, staying low. Four cops knelt behind two cars with unknown assailants pinning them down from the side of the building and, Kono guessed, several other obstacles. It was a play for time that the cops wouldn't be expecting. As Kono watched and hoped and tried to keep her weight on one leg a sudden *ping* announced that the elevator had arrived.

And it stood right next to the staircase.

Questions hit Kono, quickly followed by doubts and second guesses. She was not a soldier who could make snap decisions. If she went up she would be trapped again and they might hear her. If she exited the building she would be exposed in the street. If she stayed here . . . only fortune would save her.

Don't overthink, just do. Kono chose freedom, placed her hand on the exit handle and pushed. Instantly, street noises flooded her ears. Shouting and shooting and men screaming into radios. What she hadn't counted on was the sounds being overheard by those who hunted in the corridor. There was a sudden banging and the door behind her smashed open, followed by a gun barrel. Kono hobbled out into the street.

Caught in the middle of a gunfight she suddenly wished she had thrown on a scarf or a hat or even a big overcoat. Anything to hide her identity. Because out here, now, the gunmen recognized her easily.

"Shoot her!"

Kono slipped along the side of the building toward the

cops. The glass window at her back exploded as men inside shot through, trying to take her head off. Shards attacked her exposed flesh. She ducked, the sudden movement buckling her ankle and sending her to the floor. A bullet slammed into the brick wall at her back. Gunmen were slipping out from behind obstacles to ensure she was properly in their sights. One whirled as a cop's bullet entered his chest. His cohorts stepped closer, uncaring.

Kono looked up. The sky was black.

At least I went down fighting.

Shots rang out, the ground around her convulsing with lead. She waited for the first deadly missile to enter her body, strangely impassive, knowing she had put up a good final battle. It was the heavily strenuous sound of gunfire that finally got through to her—no way was that coming from the gunmen. Looking around she caught her breath to see two black helicopters slowly descending, black-clad men leaning out and loosing endless salvos of bullets into the area where the gunmen had taken shelter. The volley seemed endless and louder than anything she had ever heard, the ground actually churning beneath its ferocity. Several bodies lay sprawled out, but more were returning fire, laying down an avenue of escape. Then rappel lines spiraled down toward the ground, quickly followed by men who unleashed compact sub-machine guns as they slithered to earth. Within seconds they landed, squatted and lined up their weapons. Two broke away to make a beeline for Kono.

"I . . . I . . ." she didn't quite know what to say.

Mano Kinimaka lowered his face helmet. "You okay, sis?"

"I . . . I think so."

Hayden Jaye checked her over quickly. "Nothing seems broken. Get after *them!*" she shouted at a black-clad agent who had been looking to cover them. He quickly veered toward the gunmen.

"All this firepower," Kono said incredulously. "For me?"

Kinimaka shrugged. "Dead men don't shoot back," he growled. "At least not until the Russians or Chinese fuck up in some laboratory somewhere."

Kono stared at him, but Mano only smiled. "It's good to see you, sis."

Hayden pointed to the wall. "Let's get something solid at your back. Are there any other gunmen?"

Kono nodded. "In the apartment block. First floor staircase." It occurred to her then that only two members of the SPEAR team were present. "Where's the rest of you guys?"

"Friggin' Drake took 'em all on some kinda track day." The big Hawaiian shrugged. "Go figure."

Hayden radioed in the potential hiding place of the remaining gunmen as Kinimaka reached down for Kono. At first she tried to stand and hobble around, but her brother was having none of it and he scooped her up in his arms.

"Let's get you to a hospital. Get that looked at."

Hayden fell in alongside as they headed for a chopper. The original cop car still remained in place with its grisly adornment, a terrible reminder of what Kono had faced.

"I have to say," Hayden said morosely. "You've handled a terrible ordeal, Kono. And you came out alive. How did you do it?"

Kono thought about all that had transpired that morning, all she had survived. The initial memory of Drake's catchphrase that had galvanized her into action and survival, and now the second little slogan she associated with the SPEAR team entered her head.

"Drake made me do it," she said with a weak smile.

Kinimaka groaned. "Oh no, don't you start with that too."

Hayden clucked at him. "Hey, whatever works, right?"

"I guess."

Kono buried her head in Kinimaka's shoulder. Her ankle throbbed badly but she would never say so. At least one good man had lost his life today, and Kono would never forgive herself for that and never forget.

"Will it ever end?" she said as the chopper started to rise.

Hayden set her jaw. "It's ending already," she said. "The Pythians are falling apart. They're done. All we have to do now is catch Webb."

"And where is he?"

"Pretty soon," Kinimaka said. "He'll be sitting tight inside a black site, king of all the cockroaches."

Kono said nothing, painfully aware that her brother's answer revealed the real truth—that they had no idea where Tyler Webb currently was and thus, no way of ending his reign of terror. She ground her teeth hard as the pain intensified.

Hayden cursed as her cellphone rang. "Shit, can't I get a minute's rest?" She put it to her ear. "Yeah, what?"

Kono watched her face change as someone spoke fast. Hayden's demeanor suddenly transformed into an expression of absolute shock and then pure determination.

"We're coming in!" she cried. "Call the troops. This is big. Get everyone together and prepare a plane. Fully loaded. No way can we miss this."

Kinimaka inclined his head questioningly.

Hayden clenched her fists. "The terrorists are gathering," she said. "It's time to go kick some radical ass, Mano. And I mean *all of it.*"

CHAPTER FOUR

Matt Drake sat with one foot pressed hard down on the Porsche's gas pedal, the other hard down on the brake. Torsten Dahl's voice came through the two-way radio.

"Stop revving the bloody nuts off it!"

"It's called launch control," Drake said a little huffily. "Something ole Aunty Aston probably never heard of."

"Bollocks."

Alicia stood to the left of the start-line, having borrowed a checkered flag from one of the track day organizers. She raised it up until it fluttered high in the air and then waited until all eyes were on her.

"Ready?"

Drake nodded. Dahl revved his engine.

Alicia mouthed: *"Three, two, one . . ."* and then brought the flag down swiftly.

Drake released the brake pedal, allowing the Porsche free rein of its howling engine, and felt his head pushed back into the seat as the vehicle surged forward. Black asphalt stretched away ahead, rising slightly, and he was aware only of the racing line that would take him to the first corner and the speeding car to his right. The Porsche was already ahead, but barely. Dahl had drawn the inside line, which would give him the advantage for the first corner. Drake flicked at the paddle-shift, gaining another gear and another few inches on the Swede. Alicia was already a speck in the distance, waving at their rearviews.

The first corner hit and Drake swung in hard, making it a few widths ahead of Dahl and almost cutting him off. Dahl veered to the right, huge in the Porsche's sloping rear window. Drake knew a badly timed gear here would result in an accident, but more importantly a race loss. Corners two and three materialized fast and seemed to merge together. Drake felt the Porsche's back end twitch as he accelerated out of the third and toward the fourth, but caught it as it slewed back into line. Dahl's Aston used the slight mistake to gain ground, its front grill now sneaking back into Drake's eye line.

"Fucking English," Drake growled.

"Through and through," Dahl said. "Made in Warwickshire."

"I meant you, ya knob."

"Oh, fuck you."

Both cars drifted around the final corner together, Drake concentrating hard to ensure he didn't miss a beat coming out of the last bend and crossing the line a meter ahead. His great cheer was lost as Alicia's voice blasted through the two-way.

"Get your asses back to the start line, boys. Some nice old man just leant me his brand new . . ." there was a pause as she reaffirmed the make of car. "Umm, Bugatti?"

Drake swore loudly. Trust bloody Alicia to get her hands on one of the best cars in the world. And trust Alicia to really start rubbing it in. He negotiated the turn-off and headed back to the start line, already dreading the sight of Alicia perched primly above the hypercar's imposing front grille. Dahl motored up behind, the Aston's exhaust note as intimidating as any starving predator.

Alicia waved as sweetly as she was able. The older man at her side looked decidedly uncomfortable.

"Hey guys, wanna race?"

"Always." Drake grinned up at her through the lowered window. "But does your new friend know what he's getting into?"

"Oh, Bob? He's cool."

"Umm, my name's George."

"Bob. George. Whatever. It all looks the same after fifty, right? Well, maybe fifty five in your case. C'mon, Bob, take me for a ride in your, um . . . Bugatti." Alicia's eyes flashed.

Drake could only smile and nod as the older man gave him a desperate, pleading look. Dahl thought even faster on his feet and stepped out of his rental.

"I'll lend you my Aston if you like," he addressed the older man. "I'll risk taking her round."

George grinned and jumped at the chance. Drake cursed his Swedish friend. "Nicely done, mate. Nicely done."

"Alligator," Dahl said, which Drake knew meant *see you later*.

"Not if I see you first, pal."

Drake lined up first, wondering which of his friends would end up driving. It would actually be an interesting contest to listen to, in particular now that George was questioning whether either of them should drive his two-million dollar car. He leaned over toward the passenger window just as his cellphone chirped into life.

X Ambassadors: Jungle.

This week that meant Hayden, and probably trouble.

With half an ear listening to his friends he punched the "answer" button. "Yep?"

"Matt? You guys really need to get back here."

Drake caught Hayden's urgent tone and tuned everything else out. "What's wrong?"

"Nothing. But we need to get to the Amazon rainforest double time."

Drake found that one hard to compute. "The Amazon *what? Why?"*

"Because we just found out that's where the terrorist prince, Ramses, is holding his last great arms bazaar, in two days, and anyone who's *anyone* in the murder for gain game is gonna be there."

Drake was momentarily lost for words. "That's bloody huge."

"Damn right. So get your asses back here."

Drake cut her off and shouted out the window. "Oy! You two! Time to go!"

Alicia looked up from where she had George in a playful headlock. "What? He's enjoying it."

"Work called," Drake said. "We have a job to do."

Dahl immediately focused. "Something big?"

"Something mega."

Dahl headed for his Aston and Alicia climbed into the Porsche. "We're taking the track day cars?"

Drake burned rubber as he swung the car's tail around toward the exit. "The world's safety is at stake," he said. "And may depend on our speed. I think we owe it to ourselves, don't you?"

CHAPTER FIVE

Ramses entered the bespoke elevator that would take him to the penthouse suite of his castle, barely noticing the gold-paneled interior, gilt buttons and plushy carpeted floor. The whoosh of the ascent was soundless and took only five seconds, the slowdown so smooth it went practically unnoticed. Ramses was a big man, almost seven foot tall and wider than some entrances, raw muscle upon raw muscle, with hands as big and deadly as a bird-eating tarantula and neck muscles that could crush Brazil nuts.

When the outer doors opened a guard greeted him with a nod which Ramses returned. He was an unassuming, quietly-spoken man for the most part, the menace, reputation and fear associated with him derived from what he had the power to do rather than what he actually *did*. It took very few examples to accrue that reputation. Ramses had initially cultivated a wide notoriety for violent fits of temper, though this was fabricated on purpose, or at least he thought so. All this said, Ramses hadn't gone soft in his thirty years as the Prince of Terrorism. He would order mass murder at the drop of a hat, sacrifice one of his sons if need be, and then turn to watch the big soccer match with a beer, a burger and a hearty laugh.

He entered his office, which was empty. He was under no illusions. Ramses was a man alone—at the top of this game there were no comrades. But the return was worth it. For thirty years he had been exacting nothing but cold revenge, and would continue for thirty more.

The castle—his home—sat high in the Peruvian mountains, perched halfway up a cliff face and overlooking a wide valley. Its foundations were as old as time, its stones weathered through centuries. Ramses had scoured the world for a fortress he might reside in, one where he felt secure and well-defended, one that had seen much in the way of history, one where he might live undetected. The drug dealers that had owned this gave it up without too much of a fight and now added to its rich history, part of the foundations.

Ramses turned his thoughts to today's itinerary. His schedule was quite full. Planning the world's greatest black-market arms bazaar wasn't easy and he refused to be dependent on any kind of help. Of course, it didn't help that the venue was in the heart of the Amazon jungle—coincidentally an area where he'd had to clear even more drug dealers and other undesirables out to make any headway. The local authorities had been a big help though . . .

Ramses rushed past the fact that he'd also had to uproot two indigenous tribes to utilize the area he wanted, not knowing nor caring in the least about their final fate. For six months he had been laying plans—now the final days were upon them. It wasn't the money or the notoriety he would gain from hosting the bazaar—it was mostly the small and large deals that resulted from it—many of which were made whilst it was underway and which otherwise might never have seen the light of day. When people came together, agreements and even detailed covenants were often made. The problem he faced, rather ironically, was the same problem posed by his enemies—security. The dark web was good for many things but even that was no longer perfectly safe. Email dropboxes were also out these days. Ramses found himself more and more frequently returning to the old fashioned ways.

Word of mouth, in particular. Face to face meetings in ancient rooms which were constantly swept and monitored for bugs. Underground caverns, impermeable to even the most sophisticated listening devices the Americans had. And here . . . the few places in the world where men like Ramses lived in anonymity. The logistics were awkward, but worth every discomfort.

Ramses stared over the valley, filled with a crawling mist, the air patterned by aimless, floating droplets. Distant trees hung heavy, their boughs indistinct and ephemeral. And the mountains that kept his small castle safe sat all around, watching over it all. From his vantage point he could gaze down onto the battlements and watch his guards shiver as they patrolled. He could see into the small courtyard, which at this time was empty. Plans for the great bazaar filled his mind, turning his focus inside for a while and he saw nothing. An old memory flitted through his thoughts.

Ramses had convened three arms bazaars in the past. The last had ended somewhat unsuccessfully due to a rather unfortunate and extremely noisy interruption—the team he now knew were called SPEAR. Like the Charge of the Light Brigade they had stormed his superior positions and totally routed his until-then highly productive event. It had taken years of recovery but here he was again—ready to lead the dark world to victory.

And thinking of the new dark world that was coming, Ramses now remembered his guest—the wealthy idiot that had thought he could create a new shadow organization that would control entire governments. Of course, the principles were sound—it had been done before—but the execution of those principles left an awful lot to be desired.

Ramses turned to his desk and pressed a button. "Send in Tyler Webb."

Before he had even taken his finger off the button an adjoining door opened and his elite bodyguard entered the room. Akatash was whippet thin, almost as tall as Ramses himself, and possessed of steel-cable like strength. His skills were unsurpassed, his worst deeds the stuff of dark legend, and quite fittingly his name the same as the demon that created evil.

Tyler Webb appeared through another door a few moments later, closely followed by his own bodyguard—Beauregard Alain. Ramses was very much aware of Alain's abilities and barely resisted a quick reassuring nod at Akatash. Tyler Webb, dressed impeccably, made Ramses boil inside. Here was a privileged, puffed-up, wannabe autocrat that had never known a day of hardship in his life and thought he could walk the same lethal line as a true radical, a true believer, and for that matter a real soldier, and then wondered where everything went wrong.

Ramses suppressed his hatred. "Welcome, my friend." His quiet voice, surprisingly for a man his size, was designed to put people at ease. A false promise if ever there was one.

"What do you have for me?" Webb offered no greeting, no good conduct and no etiquette.

Ramses sat back, distracted for a moment by the silent assessments passing between Akatash and Beauregard. It would be an understatement to say that the look between them bristled with daggers, more like ballistic missiles. Ramses could feel a sphere of tension blooming in the air.

"Remind me what it is that you need." Ramses said, deciding to give this American devil no assistance other than that which he might benefit from.

Webb sighed. "The suitcase nuke," he tapped a finger. "For starters. And, far more important to me, the scroll." He twisted a second digit rather nervously.

"Ah, yes." Ramses acted as if he'd just recalled an earlier conversation. "I have many clients. They want missiles or ammunition or chemical substances. They want body armor or even jet fighters. But never before have I been asked for a scroll?"

Webb tried to act coy in answer to the implied question. "Buyer's prerogative. My reason is my own."

"And you're right, of course. Well, the scroll will be there once the bazaar begins, of that I am certain. Our terms though—they have changed."

Webb allowed his entire body to puff up, it seemed, from his cheeks to his chest and probably to his toes. "I think not, Ramses. We *have* a deal, thrashed out many months ago. One suitcase nuke and one scroll. I am here, right now, prepared to take part and offer my support to this . . . this enterprise of yours, this *bazaar*, but I will not be hoodwinked."

Ramses sat back in his chair, then pressed a discreet button. "Coffee," he said, thinking *hoodwinked? What a quaint old term.*

Beside him he felt Akatash shift, the almost palpable fury coiled within him squirming to be set free. Akatash didn't take it well when other men and women questioned his prince.

Ramses considered unleashing the demon right now, but was well aware of Beauregard's fearsome reputation. So much so that he wasn't entirely sure of the outcome, though the conflict would surely be epic. But not here, not inside his home.

"It is a small matter," Ramses said evenly. "But an important one."

Webb sighed, clearly torn. Ramses could feel how much the other man desired that scroll. The need washed off him like stale sweat. At that moment the door opened and a suited man appeared, carrying a tray with two small cups, spoons and sugars. With a deft skill he sidestepped

Beauregard's watchful bulk and left them in the center of the table. Ramses indicated that Webb could choose his own cup.

"No, thank you."

Ramses shrugged, the gesture shaking the table that separated them. And of course, the cup looked tiny in his immense paw of a hand, something that was not entirely lost on Tyler Webb.

"What is it that you want to amend?"

"As I said, it is a small matter and related to the suitcase nuke. The one your colleague—I can't remember his name—has a plan for."

"Yes. His name is Julian Marsh and he's as committed as I am."

Ramses paused for one moment. "Really? The word is that the Pythians are dead."

Webb stiffened. "*I* am the Pythians. *Me.* I will say when they die."

"Very well, then. This man, Julian Marsh—he is well travelled?"

"Every week or so," Webb said. "DC. Tokyo. Israel."

"Good, then he will not be too obvious."

"He's not *flying* the nuke into the US."

"I realize that. But still, there is much travel involved is there not?"

"Yes. I guess."

"Your man's plan is to travel by circuitous route to America's greatest city and then ransom your puppet government for, umm, shall we say—precious goods? Eh?"

"You can say that if you like."

"But the whole exercise is a bluff, nothing more. The nuke is real; it has to be real to make the whole plan work, but he will never detonate. If they *call* his bluff he walks away with his tail between his legs."

Webb prickled a little. "They will never call the bluff of a man holding a nuclear weapon in the heart of New York City. Are you mad?"

"A little, yes. I find it makes life much more interesting. But listen—that small change I asked for? *I* want the nuke detonated. For real."

Tyler Webb stared as if all the blood-soaked nightmares of hell had just risen before his eyes. "What . . . are you . . . are . . . you can't *do that.*"

Ramses enjoyed the spectacle for a minute, then sighed. "Then I'm afraid there will be no scroll. Not for you, at least."

"But we made . . . we made a deal!"

Ramses was aware of both bodyguards shifting a little, most likely to achieve optimum attack positions.

"Marsh would never agree to it!"

Ramses allowed a sly smile to creep across his face. "But I thought *you* were the leader of the Pythians?"

Yes, yes, but we're talking a *nuke.* In New York! Only a fucking monster would condone that! You could be starting Armageddon."

The smile that then transformed Ramses' face was entirely genuine. "I know. And thank you."

"I need time . . ." Webb blustered.

"It's easy," Ramses said. "Do you want the scroll or not?"

"Of course!"

"Then it's settled. Let's shake on it."

Ramses leaned forward, hand outstretched. Webb regarded it like he might a predator's claw. At that moment Beauregard Alain coughed.

"I think it's better that you two stay apart, don't you think?"

Webb fought to think. Ramses could see multiple emotions warring inside the man's deviant mind—from complete acceptance to hard persuasion and from pretend ignorance to actual deception. Ramses knew even now that, in the end, both Webb and Marsh would try to betray him.

But that was fine. They were merely the dupes he needed to get the weapon inside the US.

Webb ignored his bodyguard, clasping Ramses' hand. "If I agree to this barbarity I get the scroll. No more changes?"

Ramses inclined his head. "In a few days after the bazaar has started. No more changes."

Webb shook.

Ramses gripped the man's pasty white, limp-wristed limb hard enough to grind bone. "You will not betray me, Tyler Webb."

Beauregard moved but Ramses sat back quickly, leaving Webb gasping but no worse for wear. Tears stood out on the Pythian leader's eyes but he waved Beauregard back. "No, no, I must have that scroll. *Must.* Do you hear? Everything depends on it." Then he closed his mouth, aware that he'd spoken aloud. Ramses wondered about the scroll in that moment, wondered greatly, but quickly decided that a scrap of paper was a madman's folly. Only power and force and immense weaponry could defeat the infidel and all its machinations.

"We are agreed?" he said.

"Yes, we are agreed. I will inform Marsh. But not too soon."

"Then I would start—quietly—to withdraw any holdings or connections you might have down the east coast." Ramses grinned. "Just a thought."

Webb shrugged it off. "When should I arrive?"

"At the bazaar? Oh, from the very start of course. Enjoy. There will be live entertainment, food, banquets twenty four hours a day. Only the best. Slave auctions, dancing men and women, shooting ranges, drug boutiques. Private tents, Sky TV and sports channels so you need not miss a single minute of your . . . favorite wickedness."

"You have got to be kidding."

"Of course not! And there's more," Ramses was enjoying himself now. "There's athletics. A daily hunt for crocodiles and other predators. Designer clothes stalls. Designer sunglasses and watch shops. Tents for secret meetings. Jet skiing down the river. Free Wi-Fi, of course, and secure connections. Any form of alcohol you might enjoy on a whim. And one extra special type of hunt—involving a live human."

Webb's face was a picture. Ramses wished he could take a photo, but that would just spoil the moment. Instead, he spread his hands. "Sound good?"

"So long as I get my fucking scroll you can keep your live hunts and jet skiing. But I will be there," he added quickly, "from the beginning."

"Excellent!" Ramses smiled. "In two days then."

Webb rose, and made a point of looking out at the startling Peruvian landscape. "This place complements you, Ramses. The cold and wet tempers whatever searing madness stirs within your black heart. You should stay."

"I might just do that. I do find it . . . soothing. Oh, and I guess certain parts of America will be a little *muggy* for at least a thousand years, eh?"

Ramses' belly laugh filled the room, overwhelming. Webb motioned at his bodyguard. No more words were said as the two men departed. Once they had exited the inner castle Ramses motioned that Akatash could depart too. The demon withdrew without a word. Ramses wandered over to his window and stared down at the courtyard, down upon Tyler Webb and Beauregard Alain.

How easily men could be manipulated. How easily even a mad megalomaniac could be turned to malleable jelly. All you had to do was find the thing they loved or needed—and *squeeze.*

First the bazaar, then the nuke business, and finally his revenge.

All of a sudden, Peru didn't look so lackluster after all.

He pressed another concealed button. "Let's begin," he said. "In the years to come the world will look back upon this moment, this day, and this place as a turning point in history. A fulcrum to ultimate change."

"So you're saying—let the games begin?"

Ramses laughed. "That I am, my friend. That I am."

CHAPTER SIX

The SPEAR team landed in Manaus, Brazil, a densely populated city forming the main entrance for visiting the wildlife and plant life of the Amazon rainforest. Once known as the 'Heart of the Amazon', it became more famous for its Free Economic Zone and cellphone manufacturing plants.

The team saw none of the colorful city as the plane landed at Eduardo Gomes International and then taxied to a stop near the smaller terminal normally reserved for regional aviation. They were met on the tarmac by officials who knew they were coming, locals firmly in the pocket of the local US agency way station, with instructions to let them pass. Of course, in theory this was easy but in real life nothing ever went to plan.

Before they left DC the team had been promised an utterly discreet passage and a final destination where they could equip themselves with all the latest weaponry—most of which they would unquestionably need—before being shown to a Manaus safe house. Drake trusted such seamless planning as much as he trusted most social media sites' privacy policies and the small links at the bottom of spam emails that read: 'click here to unsubscribe'.

The temperature was in the thirties and the ground looked as if it had recently received a soaking. Drake allowed Hayden to approach the authorities as he and the rest of the team fanned out to guard their flanks. He was also on alert for any kind of distant surveillance although actually spotting such a thing in any situation was even harder than it sounded. With the still grumbling plane at their backs and in the shadow of the terminal, the team could see only half a dozen windows overlooking them from a distant building and no activity in any of them. They waited until Hayden had produced the necessary credentials and then followed her through a small gate, passing two more smoking guards as they went. One of the guards blew smoke in the air, bored, whilst the other stared with deep interest at his belt. Drake guessed that this kind of thing happened all the time in this part of the world.

The Amazon rainforest, though known for many things including its great river, its immensc flora that formed over half the world's rainforest, its deadly creatures and biodiversity, had now also become a haven for drug dealers, arms smugglers and other similar scum-sucking types. Authorities were paid so little that they were always open to a little extra grease-money and those that weren't were often found decaying by the side of quiet roads or, in many cases, never seen again.

It has been said that the Brazilians had lost control of whatever small influence they had in the Amazon basin, but then eight other nations also claimed a percentage of it, and with every nation offering up a different policy, who could keep track of that? Drake knew it would be best to concentrate on their own small mission whilst they were here—a quick 'in-and-out' demolition of most of the leading lights in international terrorism—but found himself wishing there was some way to preserve such an innocent area of the world. Not everywhere should feel the touch of human boots, of human avarice and arrogance. The futility of his thoughts saddened him. Someone, somewhere, would always be prepared to destroy everything that stood in their way in order to accomplish their own goals.

Beyond the terminal and the security fence a feeder road curved away from the main airport, vanishing into the distance. Their own personal Brazilian customs official ushered them toward a black SUV, conspicuous by its detachment, ticking over at the curb. Drake headed for the passenger seat but Dahl pushed him aside.

"Relax, pal. Sit in the back with your new bird. The big boys can handle this one."

Drake steadied himself against the vehicle's door frame. "Bird? Big boys? Nay lad, tha's no need t' get yer knickers in a twist."

The Swede blanched at the Yorkshire accent. "Cut it out."

Drake opened the door for the others, a little unsure if Dahl was ribbing him or trying to subtly point out that he wasn't happy about what clearly might become a new relationship between Alicia and him. Subtle wasn't usually Dahl's strongpoint and, in addition, the Swede might also be warning him to stay focused. Who knew with the big lummox? Drake would find out when they grabbed a moment alone.

Hayden and Kinimaka took the back seats; Alicia, Yorgi and Lauren the middle set. Drake wondered if he might have to climb into the trunk. Smyth just growled.

Alicia patted her knee. "I'll take the smallest."

Dahl leaned over from the front. "See what I mean?"

Drake climbed in, leaving Smyth to wedge himself between Kinimaka and the window, not a pleasant task. Soon they were underway, tearing down the feeder road toward the airport's exit. The driver used an ID tag to raise the barrier and then filtered into morning traffic, saying nothing as he threaded them toward the center of the city. The team remained silent, each formulating their own thoughts and plans of how best to deal with the journey ahead. Soon, at the safe house, they would be able to discuss.

A brief, light shower coated the car's windows. Drake, who had jammed his body beside Alicia rather than risk the other ignominy, stared out at the passing streets, the bustling life. Manaus was an intense diversity, from the most orange and bright dockside he'd ever seen to houses on stilts arrayed along the riverside, to theaters, plazas and multi-million dollar football stadiums. Inside here, it was hard to believe one of the last great uncharted wildernesses lay just outside, and so in contrast with the last place they had faced down adversity. The Arizonan desert had been a vast wilderness, both hostile and stunning to observe and scoured by one of the worst storms he had ever seen. Even that phenomenon had been overshadowed though by the sight of the ghost ship itself, a part of the desert even after all these years, and a peculiar sadness now lingered that the American government were involved with excavating and removing it, and negotiating over its treasures. Such a mythical paragon ought to be allowed to remain in place, symbolic of what secrets this earth still had to yield. But men, power and greed trumped all that.

Their driver turned into a new road, leaving the main thoroughfare and heading across an area of flat wasteland. At the far side Drake spied a collection of dirty, rusting airplanes, parked haphazardly, wing to wing.

"An abandoned airfield?" Hayden questioned. "I thought our weapons cache might be more . . . state of the art."

Smyth coughed raucously. "When did that ever happen? We're lucky they didn't HALO-jump us into here."

Dahl nodded. "He's right. They could have just inserted us into the canopy and taught us how to sharpen sticks."

Drake grunted. "Sounds painful. Well let's hope they sell more than bows and arrows and blowguns in here."

The SUV stopped in between two of the larger planes, out of sight. The so-far-mute driver then nodded ahead and

Drake looked over to see an aircraft door being lowered next to some large blue lettering—*Skymaster*.

A man descended the steps quite slowly, sporting a limp. He wore a battered brown leather jacket and faded denim jeans. The team stepped out warily into the heat as the man blinked near-sightedly at them.

"Well, come on," he said. "It's hotter than Satan's scrotum in here."

Alicia leaned into Drake as they walked. "Do you think he knows where he is? Y'know . . . the Amazon?"

Drake followed Dahl, with Hayden and Kinimaka bringing up the rear. Smyth grunted that he would remain outside on watch, and Lauren chose to stay with him. Drake ascended the aircraft's steps lightly, staying close to the Mad Swede in case any surprises awaited inside.

The interior was dim, dingy, and dirty. Dust coated everything, traced through with finger marks and boot prints. Drake noted what he assumed to be droplets of sweat marking a trail along the aisle. Ahead, the leather-jacketed man stopped.

"So Jim's not my real name but that's what you can call me. What are your names?"

"James," Drake said, indicating himself. "And Buffy." He indicated Alicia, then turned to Dahl. "And this one's Dolph Lundgren, in the flesh."

Dahl shook his head. "Shall we get this thing done?"

Jim nodded enthusiastically. Drake sidestepped the flying sweat. Their host might be a breathing, festering pool of perspiration and his abode might stink to high heaven, but his wares were everything Drake could have hoped for.

"All this," Hayden said, "on a derelict airplane in an abandoned airfield?"

Jim shrugged. "Easy all around," he said. "And it's not exactly *abandoned*. Kick-ass security system and lotsa guns." He winked. "Surprised you didn't spot it. Oh, and believe me . . . in Brazil finding guns ain't a problem."

He turned away, leaving Hayden staring at Drake. The Yorkshireman cast it off with a sigh. "Okay, mate, so what we got 'ere then?"

"Heckler and Koch MP5, about a million of 'em. A few UMPs, its successor. These fire 9x19 Parabellum cartridges. The MP5s are the same and semi-auto. Take your pick and whatever ammo you need. Other goodies? Follow me."

Drake trailed him down the narrow aisle of the plane. Beyond the third row the seats had been taken out and replaced by long, flat tables. Weapons and other military necessities lay everywhere. The team ranged out a little, examining the wares. Kinimaka knocked a table of grenades over, but only Jim noticed. The rest of the team had known it would happen. They picked between flack-jackets, first-aid kits and field rations. The first-aid kits included more specialized antidotes than even Hayden could recognize, specific to the region.

"I wouldn't worry too much about getting bitten," Jim said without smiling. "Some of those creepy-crawlies out there'll kill ya before you even think the word 'antidote'."

Alicia shuddered. "I'm starting to rethink this mission."

"Ah, don't worry, love," Drake said. "No sand spiders here."

Jim looked at them strangely. "Sand spiders? No. But there are black caimans, jaguars and anacondas. Poison dart frogs, piranha and vampire bats. Parasites and disease vectors and fevers. Bullet ants, howler monkeys—"

Alicia spun around. "That's it. I'm outta here."

Drake watched her exit the plane. "Don't worry. She'll be fine."

Hayden continued to peruse the goods as if nothing had happened. Jim cleared his throat. "You guys wanna get a friggin' move on. This ain't a garden sale. I got places to be."

Drake picked up a military knife and a night vision scope. "Running for mayor?"

"Something like that. I'd take those other tents if I were you." He pointed to a pile beyond where Dahl and Yorgi were looking. "More protection from the insects."

"Oh, I am so looking forward to this trek," Kinimaka puffed.

"More predators out there than in any third-world shanty town. But luckily, you guys are the best, right?"

The sarcasm wasn't lost on Drake. "Just trying to make a difference," he said. "So the good folks can sleep easy."

"Oh yeah? Aren't we all?" Jim looked angry for a moment, but then his face slackened. "Listen, don't mind me. And is there anything else you need? Be warned, those fuckers out there may live in the fucking jungle—but they got fifty cals, RPGs, anti-tanks, you name it. Not to mention Range Rovers built specially for 'em. The chances of you beating them . . ." he shook his head sadly.

Drake took a final glance around. "We'll risk it," he said. "Believe it or not, we've done some weird shit in the last few years. And survived it all intact."

Dahl shoulder-barged him on the way past. "Well, your body at least."

"Oh, my body aches," Drake said. "Even my bloody bones ache. Every time you speak."

He imitated the rest of the team in choosing a Glock for his handgun and then adding as many spare mags as he thought it would be feasible to carry. Of course, they could get more ammo once they encountered their enemies, but it was sounding like this mission might have to be a more clandestine event than usual. It wouldn't do to crash the party before all the special guests arrived.

Drake exited the plane. The heat outside actually felt air-conditioned for a few moments as he descended to the asphalt. The military surroundings turned his mind toward Karin, and what she might be up against right now. At the end of the last mission he had eased her way into Fort Bragg, the home of American Special Forces, and into an intensive training program. Yes, she was British, he thought. But the commander hadn't batted an eye. Drake just hoped Karin might find some kind of peace in the strict regime of military education.

Now, the team congregated beside the SUV. Hayden surveyed the area, perhaps searching for the hidden security. After a minute she said, "Time for the next step. Let's find the safe house, break this stuff down and then find our pet official."

Drake glanced at the SUV. "Shit, so now we have to cram all this gear in there too."

"And under the tarps." Dahl nodded at the back end. "Don't want the local constabulary sniffing us out."

"Speaking of local constabulary," Alicia said as she worked. "Do we have a location for this official? And exactly how far can we push him?"

Hayden looked grim. "We know exactly where he goes and what he's into after his shift ends, so yes. And this is our shindig, remember? Most of the nine countries with a stake in the Amazon wouldn't like it if they knew we were here. Some of them are clearly facilitating the arranging of this bazaar. Some are protecting it. If it weren't for Beauregard . . ." she trailed off for a moment. "But yes, this official has clear ties to the terrorist, Ramses. We can push him as hard as needs be."

"All we need to extract is a location," Dahl said. "Apart from—the Amazon."

"Something narrower would be better," Yorgi agreed. "I

have never seen so much greenery."

"Seriously," Alicia spoke up. "I need an *exact* location. Something we can just drop in on. This creepy-crawly, caiman-frog, poisonous-disease thing ain't my cup of tea. C'mon, other horizons await, people."

"But you're not running anymore," Drake said seriously. "Remember? Take each day as it comes and enjoy it if you can. If not, face it anyway. Survive. Become stronger."

"That's what I'm doing."

"Then you have a future. Tomorrow could bring . . . roses?"

Alicia almost guffawed. "Oh, really? D'ya think they'll be poisonous?"

Drake did laugh. "Probably."

Hayden urged them on. "So let's get a move on. If my calculations are correct, our bazaar's about to start and the crown princes of massacre and destruction are already in town."

CHAPTER SEVEN

Ramses took his time climbing out of the chopper that deposited him in the exact location he'd demanded. Most of the time, his bulk came in handy for intimidation, as a deterrent and even in combat, but occasionally it could be an impediment. Like today—one wrong shift in muscle mass and he'd be paying his first visit to the hallowed turf of the Amazon jungle on his face. Akatash went first, of course, and Ramses waited until he nodded the all clear.

Outside, the saturated heat descended, an uncomfortable blanket. He concentrated on his reason for coming, and tried to forget he would be remaining here for days to come. The end result would be worth any discomfort. The canopy stretched above, completely intact, but the area he occupied had been cleared. His scouting party had no doubt found a small open spot and enlarged it as best they could. This was only a small part of the bazaar, and the construction crew were even now building stalls and erecting tents, wrestling with timbers and clearing undergrowth for just under a kilometer all around. A man would be able to walk an entire circuit of the bazaar in around fifteen minutes, but it was the diversity, delight and destructive capacity of the various commodities on offer that would make him linger for days.

Ramses walked the circuit slowly, taking pleasure in seeing the emerging skeleton of the dream he had created. The shops were small but well built, and currently being draped with fineries to hide any remnants of the jungle. Inside the larger pavilions, heavy-duty tables and crates were being positioned to display items like nuclear warheads and artillery. Refreshment stands were being installed. Staff were being trained, flown in sightlessly from various camps that Ramses owned. They would respect their new minimum contract—work hard or die—for obvious reasons.

Crates cracked and revealed their exciting possibilities as Ramses wandered around, the variety of goods he'd acquired lending a carnival atmosphere to proceedings. A nuke here. A prototype ray-gun there. A missile with guiding capabilities there; some sarin over here. Communications devices, passwords to dark web forums and the computers on which they were operational. Pounds of yellowcake. The list went on.

Ramses soon found another clearing, and here sat several great prizes for lucky customers. Attack choppers once owned by the Americans and one by the British, captured, repaired, ready for action. Akatash then took him toward the edge of the camp where a wide river flowed, the largest and deepest in the general area. This was a far tributary of the Jutai River, a twisting body of water whose extremes were largely unexplored. Ramses watched the river flow at a rapid pace, then turned to his bodyguard.

"This is where the barges will land?"

"Yes."

"We need a dock. A landing area."

Akatash nodded toward a new pile of timbers. "It will be ready in time."

A barge appeared as they waited, loaded down with more product, eager men ready to disembark and offload the floating vehicle. Ramses nodded. "All seems to be in order."

"It will soon be ready."

"I want to see the pond," Ramses said. "Is it where I specified it should be?"

"Almost to the precise inch," Akatash said. "The crew had to dig the hole, fill it with river water and then haul the—um, new residents—by hand."

Ramses laughed. "What fun. I hope nobody got eaten."

He followed the map in his own head now, the one he'd drawn by hand and expected to be able to follow on foot. Soon, he arrived at a freshly dug hole ringed by a high chain-link fence. Beyond, and deep down, the water churned.

Ramses stared. "Are they being fed human flesh?"

"Of course. As per instructions."

"Excellent. But I want them starved for the start of proceedings."

Ramses let his eyes linger onto those that stared back at him, unblinking. Black caimans were dark in color, carnivorous, and the largest predator in the ecosystem. They would make a good spectacle for his more jaded guests.

"Akatash," he said, "show me my tent."

"Of course, sir."

The bodyguard led the way and Ramses easily followed. He had employed the man many years ago now, and still shuddered a little when recalling his story. Born into privilege, Akatash had rebelled time and again until his parents could stomach the insubordination no more. With pure malice aforethought they explained what would happen, took him to some squalid warehouse and handed him over to slavers in exchange for nothing except the promise of future favors. Akatash grew up hard; old enough by then to know the difference between a life of honor and a life of adversity. Old enough to know what his indiscretions had cost him.

The lesson had been learned. But by then it was too late. Still, in later years, Akatash made sure he dealt out his own lessons. He was now the sole surviving heir of that family, though he could never set foot in the country again. At least, not officially.

Ramses entered his own luxurious tent, smiling at what he saw. All the comforts of home had already been shipped in: clothes, watches, oils, enormous TV, delicacies, guns . . . and much more. He could manage three days here, especially considering the diversions he had planned.

With a deep sigh of acceptance he turned once again to his bodyguard. "Security?"

"The men you call your 'legionnaires' have run every possible scenario, time and again. They are ready. Your own abode is under the usual scrutiny, no change there."

"No mercenaries? Not one?"

"Of course not, sir. These men are deserving of the title you give them."

"And the camp? The bazaar?"

Akatash never sugar-coated the truth. "This is the Amazon, sir. Dangerous and unpredictable by definition. I mentioned at the outset that we cannot control everything and we can't. But we're as close as anyone can be."

"Contingencies? Escape routes?"

"All in place."

Ramses thought about all they had accomplished. "It will be a grand occasion, Akatash. Good for us and for our brothers. The consequences of this day will alter the course of history. Do not underestimate this . . . pure beginning."

"I don't."

"We begin tomorrow. The last great bazaar will open for business, my friend, and the world will shudder in the aftermath."

"Hallelujah, sir."

Ramses blinked. "Hallelujah?"

"Isn't that what *they* say, sir?"

"Yes, hallelujah. What do they say in the Middle East?"

"How the hell should I know?" Akatash laughed. "I'm a terrorist, sir, not a cleric."

CHAPTER EIGHT

Drake and the rest of the SPEAR team waited for Yorgi to exit the seedy bar. Their vantage point was a narrow, filthy alley across the way where they could keep eyes on all the comings and goings. Yorgi had been chosen to reconnoiter the bar because he was the less European looking individual among them and more likely to pass with only a cursory glance. The Spider's Web wasn't among the most popular tourist traps in Manaus, though perhaps its name suggested it wanted to be.

Their target, a crooked official by the name of Almeida, drank here every night, bothering the local girls and the barmaids until it was time to move on to even less respectable neighborhoods. Almeida was a drunk and a drug-taker, and worked throughout the day only to feed his nightly habit. Known for his brutality, mercilessness and corruption, he was as much feared as he was abhorred, but so long as he continued to grease the right palms he would keep his position in the localized Manaus administration.

Drake crouched in silence, taking his turn at eyeballing the street. It was no secret that various American agencies had people in almost every major city around the world and much more. The team had purposely chosen Manaus as a destination because it was the closest city to the Amazon where the CIA and even less publicized acronyms kept a presence. Of course being the most populous city of the rainforest helped. He was aware of the others talking quietly behind him, planning the rest of the op. His gaze saw every movement, every coming and going and logged it, as his mind contemplated all the ways his life was changing. First, and most importantly, Alicia had reached a crucial turning point in her own life. No matter how it looked and no matter how much Dahl ribbed him, he would be there to help her. The motto 'so far, so good' was an overused one, but when it applied to Alicia Myles and her steady progress it was the most apt. That led him to Mai. The Japanese woman was currently overseeing Grace's recovery with help from her sister and Dai Hibiki. The best news was that Grace would almost certainly completely recover; the rather tricky news was that she didn't need Mai by her side to do it.

Would Mai return?

Was anything left of their relationship?

Drake didn't think so, but it wasn't as though Mai and he had discussed anything before she left. Or since, for that matter. The fluid, molten flow of their lives saw to that. Peace would be nice, he often thought. But they were soldiers. Peace might also deal them a slow death.

His eyes flicked around the entrance to the bar. The saving grace tonight was that the temperature had dropped at least three degrees, not exactly good old Yorkshire weather but a relief nonetheless. He watched a man with a brown weathered face enter the bar and then stiffened as Yorgi walked out.

The Russian thief headed away at first, ensuring he hadn't been pinned with a tail before doubling back.

"Any minute now," he said. "They're tired of him and want him to leave."

Hayden came forward. "Okay guys, be ready."

Yorgi pushed in next to Drake. "This is not a nice man. How far do we go with him?"

The Yorkshireman didn't move. "As far as we have to, Yorgi. But we're not judge, jury and executioner. Remember the old saying—cut off one head and another three shall take its place? Something like that."

"Is that a Yorkshire saying?"

"No. I think it was from *Jason and the Argonauts*."

They watched as the bar's door swung open once again and their target staggered out. Already weaving, he belched loudly, smoothed his black matted hair and then swung wildly down the middle of the street. When a car did come toward him he shouted at it loudly until it moved aside. Hayden split the team up to track his every step. They had already reccied up and down the street for the perfect abduction spot and it was now only twenty yards ahead.

Hayden keyed her throat mic. "Ready?"

"Ready." Affirmatives came back.

Drake, Lauren and Smyth pulled back, their jobs to ensure nobody saw the seizure. The only people in the street were two youths trying to gain entry to the bar and a couple now occupying their old alley, closely wrapped up in each other and paying no attention to the rest of the world. Windows lined the street and couldn't be properly verified, but everything Drake could see and control was acceptable.

"It's a go."

Behind them, Dahl rapidly closed the gap between himself and Almeida, Alicia a step behind. As a convenient alley came up the Swede pounced, dragging the Brazilian out of sight and clamping a huge arm across his windpipe. Alicia backed him up and then, seconds later, popped her head back out of the alley.

"All good. We have a homeless male down here but looks like he's asleep. Target is ours."

Hayden keyed her mic. "Mano. Bring the car."

Forty minutes later the team stood facing Almeida who was tied to a chair in the middle of an empty warehouse, head hanging down toward his own lap. Alicia brought over a bottle of water.

"Ready?"

Hayden grunted. "Do it."

Alicia emptied the contents of the bottle over their captive's head, then stood back as he revived with a splutter and a nasty curse. Alicia decided that was out of line and slapped him across the face with the empty plastic bottle.

"Language."

Almeida shook his head, droplets flying. "What have you done? Don't you know who I am?"

Drake crouched down so that they were at eye-level. "We know who you are. We know what you do. Now, if you tell us what we need to know, we're willing to let you keep doing it." He didn't add, *until the bazaar is over, then we're gonna make sure your degraded ass gets its just desserts in the worst Brazilian prison this side of Hell.*

Almeida laughed, as they had known he would. "Fuck off, American. You can't intimidate me."

Drake blinked hard as Dahl laughed. "What did you call me?"

Kinimaka moved into the man's eyesight. "If you think he's American then you're gonna struggle with me, brah. Now listen. We know you helped establish a huge arms bazaar somewhere in the rainforest. We know you were paid to look the other way whilst they shipped men and goods in. We know it's been underway for many months now. Don't look away—" Kinimaka reached out to hold the man's face in place. "All we're asking is for a location. An area. And a list of attendees."

The man spat on the floor. "How would I even know that? You think they would tell me that? Fucking idiot."

Kinimaka stared to squeeze. "You are a parasite, Almeida. You hear things. You make sure you hear things. It's how you survive. Your dirty little friends hear things. The game turns, the players going round and round. It has been months. I *know* that you have a list of attendees. You wouldn't be the filthy, lazy, bloodsucking fuck we know you are if you didn't."

Almeida's eyes bulged as his jaw was squeezed in an unbreakable grip. Drake could almost hear him wondering just how far the big Hawaiian would go. It was a little ironic that Kinimaka had stepped up to the interrogation, since he was probably the most laid-back person in the room.

Almeida clammed up, pretending not to be intimidated. Alicia then hefted a heavy bag of nails they had procured along with a claw hammer. The threat was obvious.

Almeida suffered in silence for a minute, then said, "I can't. They would kill me. Not just that. They would crush, chop, obliterate me. They could do worse than you. Much worse."

Hayden nodded. "That I can understand. Yes, they could because they are unconscionable psychopaths much like yourself. But how would they ever know?"

"I ain't telling ya, bitch. An' I ain't telling this big fucking whopper neither."

Kinimaka let go of the man's face. "Then you die," he said. "You die tonight. In that chair. With your hands tied behind your back and no hope. Are you ready to die?"

"Ah, fuck off with the flowery speech, man, and hand me one of those nails. If I stick it through my ears it might drown out your bleating."

Kinimaka bowed his head. "I tried," he said. "For you. I really did."

Almeida stared. "What are you taking about?"

Dahl and Smyth stepped forward at the same time. "Me," they said in unison, before glaring at each other. As Almeida stared, Drake watched Alicia step quietly up to the back of the chair, towel in hand. With one deft swoop she wrapped it around the shocked man's face and held it tight.

Dahl then stepped forward with another bottle of water and, without ceremony, upended its contents over the towel.

Almeida struggled soundlessly, inhaling the liquid until Alicia gave him a moment's respite. Then they started again; and again until Almeida buckled.

"Stop." He held up a hand, spluttering uncontrollably. "Please stop."

Hayden sighed deliberately. "You don't tell us when to stop, asshole. We tell you when we're ready to hear you start talking." Shc motioned at Alicia to continue.

Another three empty bottles hit the ground before Hayden ended it. Even then she only gave Almeida a few seconds respite before slapping his attention into focus.

"Here," she said. "Right here. Now do you remember what we want from you?"

"It's some kinda natural ground-clearing they're using and widening, right next to the Jutai so they can boat everything in. Even people. This guy's a major whack-job, thinks he can tame the jungle or something. King of Leopard, ha!" Almeida spent a moment spitting up water before continuing. "Coordinates are in my wallet. Please, please don't rat me out for this."

Dahl nodded grimly. "Not a problem."

"Good . . . good. Some of the people I have helped gain passage," even the hardened criminal blanched, "you should not even speak their names . . ."

"What?" Alicia flapped the towel ominously. "If you're about to say Rumpelstiltskin I'm afraid it's back to Water World for you, boy."

"No, no! There is Abdel Nour, leader of the Black Light; El-Baz, leader of The Dozen Death Squads; Boutros, ultimate boss of the world's biggest cartel; Ghannouchi, *leader* of the biggest crime family in the *world.* Not

America or Italy. The world. Al-Macabre, terrorist leader of Devil's Breath, and let's not forget Ramses himself . . ."

Drake listened as the man rattled on. For a man so reluctant to spill the beans they could now barely shut him up. The names he reeled off would be amazing scalps, even a single one could be a game-changer in the unstable war on terrorism. But ten or more? Drake saw havoc ahead.

"And they're just the ones arriving by barge, the ones I have facilitated. There are many more arriving by helicopter and other means. I don't know many, but one is Tyler Webb, the leader of the Pythians." Almeida stared at them as if expecting a pat on the back. "Y'know him, right? Most wanted man in the world?"

Drake steered him back to an earlier point. "Ramses," he said. "What exactly do you know of him?"

Almeida's eyes clouded over. "Crown Prince of Terrorism. Runs everything. Knows everyone. They say not a single attack passes that he doesn't have previous knowledge of, not a hit happens without his sanction. They say some of these terrorist leaders don't even know they work for him."

Drake waited. "Is that it? So you know . . . nothing?"

Almeida shrugged. "Man's a myth. I've heard whisperings that this is Ramses' last bazaar, but it's probably being run by some big cartel. They own most of the basin anyway."

"They don't *own* it," Drake said. "They're just squatting until a man with a bigger gun comes along. Or until the forest figures out a way to annihilate them."

Dahl nudged him. "Whoa, that's deep for a Yorkie bar. Have you been sneaking some of this guy's coke?"

"Well, let's hope it happens," Drake said. "Save us a job."

"You spoke of others arriving by chopper." Hayden turned to Almeida. "What others?"

Now, the Brazilian dropped his gaze cagily. "I shouldn't tell you," he said. "I shouldn't even know. It's not even definite, just hearsay, and sounds like a deep pile of shit to me."

Hayden shrugged. "Let me be the judge of that."

"And what happens to me then?" Almeida asked. "After I tell all."

"Then you can go. Free."

"Do I have your word?"

"You have this," Alicia barked, wrapping the towel around his face again. Almeida struggled and flapped his hands.

"Okay, okay!" he squeaked as the towel was removed. "I heard this from a dude I know, but like I said it could be complete bullshit." Again he hesitated.

"Speak!" Dahl cried. "Do it now!"

"Okay, okay. Keep yer trilby on. It was the CIA," he said matter-of-factly. "The CIA are coming."

Hayden, perhaps naively, immediately shook her head. "No way. We'd have heard about a joint op."

"No." Almeida grinned maliciously at her misunderstanding. "The CIA are here . . . as clients. Customers. They're fucking buying, lady."

Drake touched Hayden's shoulder as the ex-CIA agent gaped and then looked ready to explode. The truth was, the CIA had many shadowy arms as did most organizations. Black ops missions and black sites had to get their raw materials from somewhere. Maybe this was one of those places. But this was a revelation from which the whole team would have to take stock. Were they safe? Did this particular CIA entity know they were here? Or was it all, as Almeida said, complete bullshit?

"And the Big Dog," the Brazilian added. "He's coming with them."

Now Drake frowned. "Big Dog? What the hell are y' blathering about?"

Almeida seemed confused. "What?"

"Explain," Smyth growled.

"That's all he said," Almeida blurted. "My friend. The man I talked to who helped them with the choppering in. We spoke often," he admitted. "Compared notes in case there was someone we—" he stopped abruptly.

"Could blackmail," Dahl completed it for him. "Yeah, we know."

"He told me about a guy the CIA were bringing to meet the man of myth—Ramses. Called him the Big Dog. That's all."

Hayden turned to Drake, shock embedded into her features. "Surely not the director? The assistant director? The—"

"It could be anyone," Drake affirmed. "Let's not jump to any conclusions."

Alicia flung the towel at Almeida's head, making him flinch. "We done with this bottom-feeder? Can we fling him back to the sewer now?"

Hayden nodded. "Take him back. Keep his wallet."

As Alicia and Smyth led him away the SPEAR team leader regarded the rest of them. "That's some roster," she said. "And some target. Security will be absolute and top-notch. Are you guys ready for true jungle warfare?"

"Always," Dahl said.

"I do like to enrich my resumé," Drake said. "Bad ass is an easy label to achieve. But jungle bad ass? That's special."

"Then let's move."

CHAPTER NINE

Tyler Webb was as unhappy as he'd ever been in his life. He sat alongside Beauregard in the back of a luxury chopper, minutes away from landing at Ramses' ridiculous flea market, compelled to attend by the one thing he desired most of all in this world.

The scroll. The final piece of the puzzle on the path to Saint Germain.

Call it a life-revolution, a game-changer, a world-ender. It was all of those and yet didn't matter. It was the last thing he needed to lead him to the treasures of Saint Germain. It was a much-deserved redemption.

For now though he needed to temper those desires, almost impossible though that was. Their unstoppable itch ran in his blood. But even this close the scroll still stood a world away. *Just a little while longer,* went the mantra inside his head. *I'm almost there . . .*

The chopper descended. Webb clung on as the canopy rose toward them—a seemingly impenetrable bed of green. Beauregard sat like a statue beside him, unreadable. Webb choked and hyperventilated as the pilot deftly inserted them into the canopy, veering through stepped gaps and then deposited them with a bump onto terra firma.

Beauregard yawned. "Ready?"

Webb gulped hard. "Sure. Of course. Yes."

The Frenchman led the way, straight into an atmosphere of cloying heat. Webb stopped to stare into the surrounding jungle, a ruthless force barely held at bay, and tried not to hear the sounds of predators lurking and screeching within. The tents nearby were overhung with mosquito netting and other accoutrements but Webb dreaded to think what Ramses might have set up for him. The Pythian network was almost dead, their mercenaries unpaid and deserted, its leaders isolated and unable to communicate with their leader. Zoe Sheers? He hadn't heard from that woman in over a week. Webb's only requirement now was that Julian Marsh performed. The rest would be his to discover. Beauregard followed a safe but makeshift path cut through the underbrush, passing by overhanging trees and through lines of old trunks.

"What is this?" Webb grumbled. "The goddamn scenic route?"

"Just be thankful you remembered to apply the insect repellent," Beauregard returned petulantly. "And that I reminded you."

Webb knew the man had a point. He didn't deign to reply, but eyeballed several unmistakably obvious guards as he passed them by, oddly reassured by their presence. The path wavered for a while, eventually leading to a large clearing at the center of which stood a high podium. Arranged around the outside were a series of tall tents. Webb spied lines of sturdy wooden tables and more tents, even what looked like a pavilion further away near the bend of a quick-flowing river. More people were coming from that way, all shapes and sizes and wearing everything from cut-off jeans and leather jackets to turbans and sandals, from dark-skinned men to platinum blond women, and from several traveling alone to those who were surrounded by thick-necked bodyguards. The sound of quiet chatter filled the nearby trees.

Sunlight filtered down from between torn clouds, but Webb had been told to expect regular cloudbursts followed by baking heat. Apparently, Ramses had installed what he called a cool canopy, where you could relax whilst being sprayed by gentle mists, but Webb hadn't bothered to check the emailed guide to find its location.

Possibly a mistake.

The sound of another chopper landing made him peer into the trees. The place was filling up rapidly. Right then, the sound of loud music reached his ears, spreading through the forest and he saw a chain-gang of twelve half-naked slaves being led among the revelers. None of them looked happy, but that fact only made Webb take a longer look. Perhaps this bazaar wouldn't be so tedious after all. He wondered what other diversions might be available, wishing again that he'd studied the guide and read the itinerary. Beauregard stayed alert at his side.

"Let's wander," Webb said. "See what else is on offer."

Beauregard led the way along the path, circuiting the clearing and starting along another route. As they walked, they passed tents to left and right, their doors pinned open so the curious could peer within. Webb halted as a man with too much testosterone tried to barge Beauregard aside into the undergrowth, a jest for his companions' appreciation, only to find himself unceremoniously dumped on the tail-end of his spine.

"What the—"

"Stay down," Beauregard intoned. "Or it will be worse."

"We shall see." The man, a large olive-skinned individual, with golden teeth and fistfuls or rings rose and took a lunge at Beauregard. Webb barely saw the Frenchman move, but soon he was a lithe shadow across the path and the other man squirmed in his grip, blood already coating one half of his face. The man kicked. His comrades stepped to help but Beauregard twisted one more time.

"Any closer and it breaks. Is that what you want?"

Everyone paused. Webb was interested to see the

security guards looking on—it seemed scuffles had been expected to break out at an event like this. Most likely they would only intervene if proceedings got really out of hand.

Beauregard loosened his grip. "Are you calm?"

The olive-skinned man nodded, tried to collect his dignity and then continued along his way. Beauregard watched until all was clear.

"Are we safe?" Webb asked.

"For now," Beauregard said.

Webb snorted. "Don't fill me with too much confidence, Alain, will you?"

He inspected tent after tent, spotting arrays of weapons, communications devices, rocket launchers and super-computers. Pure yellowcake, used to process uranium. One gaudy tent held two dozen easels, to each of which was pinned the photograph of a rare supercar or utility vehicle the customer might be interested in. Bids were being taken, the most of which Webb saw were currently attached to a six-wheeled, midnight black Mercedes G-Wagon. He moved on, uninterested in most kinds of transport, came to the end of the row of tents and then stopped dead in his tracks.

"What on earth is that?"

Beauregard shrugged, uninterested, but Webb strode right up to the spectacle. A high wrought iron fence ringed a deep pit, at the bottom of which caimans thrashed to and fro. People were holding onto the bars, staring down.

"Do they do anything?" Webb asked a man with a goatee after a minute's perusal.

"Well, dude, I guess they might chew on ya a little if ya fall in. An' I guess they might drown ya if they're anything like crocs. But tricks? Illusions? Nah, I don't think so."

Webb shook his head. "I don't get it."

"The people they throw in every few hours do. They get it big time."

"Ahhh." Webb turned away, attracted by the intensifying dance music now and yet another large tent. Once inside, he was witness to what could only be described as a slaver's auction. Men and women were dragged up to a podium, turned back and forth, prodded, displayed, and then subjected to a bidding war waged by members of the audience. All manner of depraved thugs shouted enthusiastic numbers at the auctioneer, who was only too happy to comply with their demands to show off the current lot in a number of reprehensible ways. Webb decided the bidding was a little too downbeat even for him, his own stalkings were so much more thrilling, dangerous and psychologically tormenting, when a twenty-something blond women struggled up to take center stage.

Webb stopped in his tracks. A thick, terrible desire for ownership filled his heart, making his blood run hot. "Oh, dear."

Beauregard turned to see what had happened. "What is it?"

"I . . . I want her. I must have her."

"Why? Isn't your vice somewhat different?"

"Yes, of course. But I still must have her."

"Why?"

"She reminds me of my mother."

Some time later, after Webb identified several more potentials for new ownership, they went in search of food. Many mouth-watering meals were available, from fast-food stands to sit-down, seven-course banquets. Webb decided to kill some time by attending the more lavish set-up and got a little frisky with the whisky. Already, he had a feeling of wellbeing deep inside and he hadn't even started searching for the nuke yet, never mind the scroll.

That thought though, sobered him more than a little.

With a glance of regret he rose from the low table, settled the bill for his meal via pre-paid credit card, and exited the tent. Earlier, he had seen tents full of military hardware. Already, the vault above was starting to darken but he would not retire tonight without being in possession of a suitcase nuclear weapon. And there was so much more to explore. Webb decided it was going to be a very full and stimulating night.

And then tomorrow.

The culmination of all his days.

Beauregard dogged his trail, but Webb was feeling more and more confident by the moment. No Pythians to drag him back, no Matt Drake and Co. to thwart his plans. Not even an appearance of Ramses himself to drive home his terrible threat. So far.

No threats whatsoever.

Webb relaxed as he spotted a tent sporting a discreet nuclear waste symbol. That was a start. Happy, he moved among the hundreds of lethal people shopping, negotiating, plotting and playing at the last bazaar.

CHAPTER TEN

They came down through the low clouds, choppering in to around three-quarters of their journey's end. They figured the bazaar would have close-in security as well as several outposts dotted around to build up a more long-reaching picture, so they would start from afar, but not so far that it would take hours to traverse a narrow, meandering river. They all wore their backpacks and carried an excess of weapons and thick rubber boots to help with the rainforest's saturation levels. They left the chopper and approached the bank of a river where two large skiffs sat waiting, fishermen close by. Payment was made, the gas tanks filled, and then the team were putting out into the middle of the river. The sun was a haphazard affair, visible on occasion but always dappled and seldom welcome. The heat was like nothing Drake had experienced before.

It was late afternoon on the day before the bazaar was due to start. The team had chosen to depart today to allow all of the players time to depart and ensure Ramses' security teams would have their hands full. They were hoping to determine its location tonight and do a proper scout tomorrow. Drake soon became bored of the twisting river and its earthy banks overhung with wide-leafed branches, every square foot seemingly teeming with life. The air smelled marshy, one moment offering the scent of fresh greenery, the next the stench of decay. The two fishermen piloted the long skiffs with skill, grins rarely off their faces. Hours passed, and soon a perennial darkness started to fall. Two natives watched them from a flattened bank as they passed, nets clasped in their hands.

Alicia perched beside Drake. "This is the life, eh?"

Drake gave a low whistle. "Despite your recent life change, I just know that's a lie. Who you gonna piss off out here, Myles? A baboon?"

"Are you saying I live to upset everyone?"

"Nope. It just comes natural."

"Ah, well, speaking of baboons, have you heard from your tiny girlfriend?"

Drake paused as movement inside the jungle caught his eye, but it was only a passing monkey. "Nothing meaningful. I think Mai is a little lost."

"Any chance we'll be seeing her soon?"

"Why? Missing the provocation?"

"Nah. The Sprite's no match for me."

"I'm not too sure, Alicia. No doubt Grace will have a say in that."

"Did I hear a touch of bitterness there?"

Drake rolled his neck to ease the tension in his shoulders. "If you did I'm sorry. Grace deserves all the Mai-time she can get."

Alicia smiled at that. "And the world moves on."

The skiffs negotiated their way along the river, fanned by a blissful breeze. Drake dug into his rations and drank water. By the time the fishermen pulled onto a sandy slope and beached the craft it was full dark and the team were working by torch light. Dahl had kept hold of the GPS and assured them that the site of the bazaar was but a few miles of heavy slog away.

"This is a good place to stop," he affirmed.

"We're putting an awful lot of faith in a crooked official," Lauren said.

"It's a good lead," Hayden said. "You know as well as I do the enhanced satellite pictures show heavy disturbance in the area and unknown comings and goings. And the

Mingaloa cartel that held sway over the area haven't been heard from in months. The CIA thought they'd been absorbed by the Cinigan family."

"Ramses annihilated them," Kinimaka said, not without a hint of satisfaction.

"Maybe. Or maybe they're working for him now. It doesn't matter. The world's worst mass murderers are all about to arrive at the same place at the same time."

"And we're walking right into the middle of them." Alicia grinned.

Drake waved the two fisherman off and watched as Dahl and Smyth set about the tents. The ground here was soft and damp but no worse than anywhere else in the jungle and perhaps a little safer nearer the river. Kinimaka offered to take first watch and Yorgi went with him. Lauren sat down on the bank and Hayden radioed in their progress. Drake knew this wasn't the ideal scenario—preferably the tents would have been pitched before all light left the world, but the team were experts and he expected not a guy rope to be out of place. He moved off and kicked around for some dry tinder, then brought it back to camp.

"Figured we could afford a small fire," he said.

"I hope that's insect free." Alicia eyed the wood pile.

"I wouldn't worry. You're probably sitting on worse."

The blonde rose in a hurry, dusting herself off. "Right then, I'll help with the tents. At least that way we'll get a ground sheet between me and their tiny teeth."

"Don't forget the suckers . . ." Drake laughed as she moved off.

In less than twenty minutes the team were done with their chores and gathered for the night. They sat by the bank, in silence, watching the quiet waters flow by. Of course, there could never be silence in a place like this—the jungle was alive with sound from those that crept to those that climbed and prowled.

Drake leaned in close to Alicia. "So, how are you finding it?"

"The creepy-crawlies? I'll let you know when I see one of the little buggers."

"No. I meant the . . . new you. How are you finding it?"

Alicia inhaled. "Well, it's a battle if you must know, Drakey. Every minute. Like a bloody tug of war and no oily, hard bodied men on either side. And now I find myself stuck in the middle of a jungle with seven other rebels and not a minute of privacy."

Drake considered that. "Gives you more time to accept it."

"Oh, thanks, wise one. That really helps." Alicia drained her bottle of water. "You should go into religion."

"Nah. Couldn't do with all the fighting and feuding," he said a little ironically.

Alicia shook her head. "Says a man who's here now nursing bruises that haven't healed from the last battle."

"Bruises?" Drake winced. "More like raw scrapes from sliding down that friggin' cliff and onto the galleon. Dahl's bloody fault."

"Maybe. But you can't deny it was the best ride in North America."

"Steady on. You haven't ridden everything in North America. Have you?"

Alicia caught his eye. "Are we talking flumes, coasters, that sort of thing? Or things that wear Levis?" Her eyebrows rose suggestively.

Drake looked up in despair. "Part of you will never change, Alicia."

"Thank God for that."

"In any case," he went on. "Most of the bruises I have were inflicted by *you*."

Alicia smiled sweetly. "You're very welcome."

Drake nodded as if he'd been expecting the reaction. "Once we end this maybe . . . we could take a break." The pause and its significance was not lost on Alicia.

Her eyes bored into his. "Are you asking me to go away with you?"

"Well, Dahl keeps banging on about taking a family Caribbean vacation."

"And you want to go with him?"

"No! I'm saying we also deserve a break. Stop busting my balls."

Alicia didn't let up. "Let me get this straight. You, Drake, Matt Drake, want to take me—the Tasmanian Devil—on a short break." She shook her head. "Fuuuck."

Drake frowned. "What's wrong with that?"

"It's weird. That's all. Just weird."

And despite himself Drake knew exactly what she meant. Their life was not the life of people that zipped off for short breaks to European hotels. Dahl could get away with it because he had a family and a totally separate life with them. But Drake? Alicia?

"I do know what you mean," he said. "What the hell would we do with four days in Paris?"

"We wouldn't go to Paris," Alicia said. "Not us. If we went any-fucking-where it would involve a big room, a big bed and room service."

Drake understood of course, and looked down. His relationship with Mai was barely cool, but it was over. She had made that perfectly clear. And now, with Alicia turning over a new leaf she was also uncovering a new possibility.

The jungle teemed around them. As a contrast to the more recent missions this was about as far as they could get. The next few days weren't going to be easy. Drake took some time to acknowledge each member of the team, from those on watch to young Yorgi and Lauren Fox, the newest members who had earned their stripes. Dahl caught his gaze and smiled faintly as if accepting that the Yorkshireman was probably dreaming about being as good as the Swede, or maybe a step behind. Drake felt several moments of peace and happy acceptance. Even here, even tonight on the eve of what would surely be utter madness, his family were all around him, each man and woman content with their place in life. The watch changed and two more of the team headed into the darkness. A steady downpour then sent them all scurrying for manmade fabric cover, two to a tent and struggling to get comfortable. Rain drummed down for over an hour, drenching the forest and lending it life. Drake found it relatively easy to drift off, then woke himself up with a sudden feeling of satisfaction at that very thought. The years out of the service hadn't turned him soft.

With a smile on his face he fell asleep.

CHAPTER ELEVEN

Karin Blake had been battling inner demons her whole life. At a young age she had watched her best friend die because no one had bothered to listen to a young girl's screams. Upon leaving home and then gaining the very best grades she had rebelled against the system and her loving family, and hit some kind of rock-bottom. Later in life, still rebelling but in a more positive way, she had clawed her way back to where she really wanted to be—as a useful and productive part of a team that truly cared for her. She had learned to forgive and then to love. Having highly capable men and women relying on her told her just how positively she had been accepted.

And then, as her life tended to, everything fell apart. More death. First her parents and then her brother, and then her life's love, gunned down in an alley as he tried to protect their team. Karin Blake was stripped to the bone, exhausted with life and all its suffering, looking to find a quick way out.

To combat those thoughts she turned to the only people who she thought might be able to help—the Army. Though she had never told Matt Drake, those days of quiet she endured whilst they chased down the ghost ships had been made up of her trying to find an alternative to an easy, quick departure from life's chaotic terminal. In the end the answer was all around her—soldiers fighting for the best cause in the world whilst battling their own internal enemies. There was only one thing to do. Become a war machine.

Fort Bragg was, among many things, a training facility.

Inside its AOR—its Area of Responsibility—recruits were trained up to become some of America's finest soldiers. From the classroom to engagement training, vehicles to robotics, it had earned the enviable and apt reputation as one of the best in the world.

Karin had already been evaluated and thrust into lessons. Varied exercises existed that would reward her with engagement skills, egress skills, dismounted soldier training and "call for fire" expertise. There were virtual suites and good old fashioned obstacle courses and punishing down-in-the-mud days. But the rigors of any day were nothing when compared to the adversities she encountered when alone. They had already appointed her a psychological profiler who had the power to kick her out.

The men she had met—some of them practically boys—were supportive for the most part, only a select few following the old stereotype. The women were hard-faced and somehow looked a little lost, not in this place but with life, with day-to-day events in general. Karin remained aloof, friendly when required but almost unapproachable. She was not here to make friends. She was here to start afresh and, hopefully, become a valued field member of one of the best Special Forces teams on the planet. But she had already accepted that the key to her success was effort—determination, sweat and exertion throughout the day would pay off in the most positive way.

It had to.

This was Karin's last big push. Some people coasted through life but Karin fought her way through it—overcoming obstacles at every turn. But even a fighter sooner or later ran out of spirit. Karin had overcome her last obstacle.

The days dawned fresh and bright and all merged into one. Karin was the first at her post and the last to eat, the first awake and the last asleep. Nothing existed except this shiny nucleus of self-control, hour after hour, day after day. With the falling of night and the absence of urgency came the darkest of visions—so many graves she had not visited in months or years. Who visited the graves of those who died? Her friend, her parents, her brother, so alone out there and so isolated. It didn't take long to visit a cemetery and pay respects, and god knows her loved ones deserved it, but life . . . life always found a way to take those precious hours away.

Please, she thought nightly. *Please let the dawn rise. Let the day begin. So I can forget.*

CHAPTER TWELVE

The hardest thing Mai Kitano had to do in the days following Grace's shooting was tear herself away from the girl's bedside. The initial hours were the worst, the shock of that horrific twenty-second tragedy still finding no respite in her mind. Hibiki stayed with her, though he was barely able to string a sentence together so distraught was he at having to shoot Emiko. Chika told their story and the cops gave them a break, but they returned later.

Then Grace showed visible signs of improvement. Mai's fears eased but then her raging guilt took hold and she sought out Hibiki.

"Let's get out of here," she said, and they exited into fresh sunlight for the first time in days.

Hibiki told her he knew not of a cure, but of a way to take a breather, a pause from the rigors of real life. He led her to an underground parking garage where he kept a small open-top, two-seater sports car called Belle, and fired up the engine. Within fifteen minutes they were cruising outside Tokyo, along sweeping bends and long straights, greenery and stunning views catching their imaginations on all sides. The great vault of the sky stretched endlessly above them and the breeze in her hair made her wish for better days.

Mai realized not a word had passed between them since they left the hospital. She turned her face away from the sun and toward her old friend. "Dai, I just don't know what to say."

The cop's face remained stoic. "There's no coming back from this, Mai. It's one of those life-altering events you wish you never had to face. If it wasn't for Chika I'd be heading for a nut-house right now."

Mai gazed at the passing scenery. The panoramic blur reminded her of the flow of life—only certain images registered and stuck.

"We have to change this life."

Hibiki concentrated on a steady flow of rolling curves before letting out a long sigh. "And I guess that's as simple as it sounds?"

"Harder than that, Dai. It's impossible."

"That's what I thought."

A deep valley opened up below. Hibiki slowed the car and negotiated the road that tracked along the steep edge. Mai allowed her mind to clear as stunning images filled her brain. Hibiki was right, the trip was beyond therapeutic.

"Here," Hibiki handed her a packet of mints, "it'll help freshen your breath."

Mai blinked in surprise. It wasn't in her friend's nature to be so rude. Unless . . . she observed him for the first time and saw a tiny smile at the corner of his mouth. As much as it surprised her again it gave her hope too. It reminded her that Grace could live and grow up to be a wonderful, healthy girl.

And that led her onto another problem.

"We have to get Grace away from this life. As soon as possible."

Hibiki nodded and slipped a pair of sunglasses on. "Agreed. I think she should stay in Tokyo, either with or close to Chika and me."

"You're staying with the TMP?"

"I'm a cop. What else would I do? Do you know how hard it is to change lifestyles after a certain age?"

Mai did know what he meant, but said nothing. The fact remained that, although Grace would no doubt want to make her own mind up, Mai herself had life-altering decisions to make. Options did exist, she knew. The Tokyo Metropolitan could probably find her a position on the force which she could steer away from special or undercover ops. A consultancy business? Her own bodyguard company? None of it sounded particularly savory, but it beat getting shot at all day long.

But did it?

Mai reflected over the recent years. The adventures she had shared with Drake and the team stood out in her memory like shining beacons, like the Aurora Borealis of her life's events. Yes, they were tempered with loss but what kind of experience wasn't?

Hibiki glanced across. "Thinking about SPEAR?"

"How could you possibly know that?"

"Easy. That's the first flicker of a smile I've seen on your face in days."

"Am I that transparent? I thought my face was quite unreadable."

"Not to me."

"And you think I should return?"

"To SPEAR? I think it's the only thing that makes you happy. And bad things aren't going to stop happening, Mai, just because you chose to opt out. They happen every minute in every part of the world. All we can ever do is try to make things a little better."

Mai smiled wider for a moment as Hibiki threw the vehicle around another series of bends, the wind whipping at her hair.

The cop laughed. "You can hang your head out the window if you like."

Mai laughed too and saw a text message coming in to her friend's cellphone through the car's Bluetooth system. It appeared on the Sat-Nav screen as he pulled into a lay-by.

All well here. Enjoy yourselves! Chika xx

Mai settled back into the seat. "Thank you for falling for my sister."

"The pleasure was mine. We work well together."

Mai nodded. Of course she knew they worked even better together when they didn't have a crazy sister living with them. It was time to make that decision.

"Drive," she told Hibiki. "Just drive."

The road stretched far ahead, a ribbon of dreams, a snaking stretch of immersive inspiration, and Mai spoke no more but let her mind wander through a lifetime of experience and emotion. There was no pressure, no hassle, no reason to interrupt her train of thoughts. This was to all intents and purposes *tangible and true* Mai-time, and she reveled in it.

In the end, she picked her phone out of the glovebox and called a number.

"Hello, Hayden, it's me."

The voice at the other end sounded surprised. "Oh, hi, is everything okay?"

"Yes, yes. We're well and Grace is getting better by the hour. Something to do with a young person's fortitude, I believe."

"Sure, well, that's all five-by-five. Friggin' reception is bad here. You need anything else?"

"Yes actually, I do." Mai stared hard into the middle-distance. "Where are you?"

Hayden reeled off an explanation and a location, ending with the question that Mai most dreaded. "Why? Are you coming back?"

She answered as truthfully as she could. "I don't know. I'm going to try. But tell nobody, Hayden. Just in case I don't make it."

CHAPTER THIRTEEN

Drake awoke to the sound of a waterfall smashing onto the roof of his tent and washing down the sides. It took only a second to remember where he was and that the cascade came from the menacing clouds that no doubt hung low over the endless canopy of trees above. The hard rain practically surged against the flimsy material and, as he sat, up a disembodied voice drifted out of the near-dark.

"You snore like a moose in mating season."

Drake rolled over and drank from his bottle of water. "And I guess Johanna says you make little gurgly baby sounds, huh?"

"What my wife says to me in the morning is none of your business. And how did I end up next to you anyway?"

"I lost a bet. Now shut the hell up and find out the time."

Dahl lifted an arm out of his sleeping bag, squinting at his watch. "Dial says five-thirty. Shit, can we even make proper progress in this torrent?"

"Ordinarily, yes. But we're searching for a camp and need to be stealthy about it. Let's wait, it'll pass soon."

"Oh yeah? Expert on the Amazon now are we?"

"I read the crib sheet."

The two men lay in semi-dark for a while until the deluge eased. By the time they emerged into the drenched jungle the others were already breaking camp. The team worked quietly and efficiently, and soon were ready to set out. Hayden checked coordinates and pointed them in the right direction.

"Six miles," she said. "And then we really have to hit the stealth button. I reckon if the weather holds we'll make that in half a day."

"Longer," Dahl said. "We should be taking a break when the real heat hits after lunch time. I read the crib sheet too."

"We have to arrive before then." Hayden nodded. "We won't stop every transaction but we do have to halt the worst of them. Let's head out and see how far we get."

The team filed out, wet, disagreeable and sore from a night on the jungle floor. It took time to adapt to any new environment, and by the time they acclimated they all wanted to be long gone from the rainforest. The drizzle abated as they set off, and Drake took that as a good sign. Kinimaka took the lead, waving a machete like he didn't know how to use it, and even Hayden gave him a very wide berth.

"Watch out there, big guy," Smyth growled. "You're gonna have a tree down on us."

Kinimaka turned with a fierce frown. "You wanna take point, small fry?"

"Gladly."

Smyth relieved Kinimaka of the machete and forged a path. Rain dripped all around and on top of them. The light filtering through the trees was wan at first, but soon started to take on a brighter luster, each ray illuminating a new patch of unchartered territory. Drake hefted his pack and his weapons and followed Alicia, trudging through the undergrowth. The pace they set was necessarily steady because, even as the sun came out, conditions were always tough for hikers. It might have been easier if they could stop and stare, marvel at the crouching wildlife and the rising steam, the sopping underbrush and the living jungle, but everyone knew they were on a schedule and the last bazaar was about to begin. The whole team were on alert; this was not an uninhabited jungle any more. Drug lords and gun runners and all manner of law-breakers made this area home these days, and the SPEAR team were constantly ready with their weapons. The slow pace they adopted was partly to conceal their presence from them, as any sudden gunfire might warn Ramses and his security of their close proximity.

Drake slogged along at the center of the march, as wary as he was relaxed and focused on the sounds that surrounded them. Alicia turned, holding a branch aside for him.

"Who would *want* to live here? Yuk."

"Criminals." Drake shrugged. "No law exists in the Amazon rainforest, love."

"It's predator versus predator," Dahl said from behind. "But luckily, you have the top of the food chain right alongside you."

Drake allowed the branch to snap back against the Swede's forehead. "Whoops. Sorry, oh King of the Jungle."

"What?" Alicia looked aghast. "He didn't catch that vine in his teeth?"

Dahl wiped rain from his eyes. "Piss off, both of you."

They tramped on, the hours passing in soulless silence, their boots quietly absorbed by the mulch, moving from trail to trail if they could, but otherwise forging their own path. It was after eight before Hayden called a short break.

Smyth plonked himself down upon a fallen log, face dripping more with sweat than water. Kinimaka sat beside him and eyed what they could of the skies.

"Has it been raining again?"

"This is the face of a man working hard for a living," Smyth grated. "Not something you'd know about back on the pineapple plantation."

Kinimaka cleared his throat. "Seriously, I'll take over if you like."

"Nah. The rainforest's losing more than enough trees per hour as it is."

Drake made sure he checked on Yorgi and Lauren before they resumed. The Russian thief and the New Yorker were the least qualified of any of them to be carting weapons through a jungle, but both looked well hydrated and with an excess of energy. Hayden figured they had come three miles but then the going hadn't been as hard as they'd figured. At this rate, Drake thought, they'd come close to the site of the bazaar by late morning. He spoke quietly to Dahl and Alicia, careful not to let his voice carry too far into the surrounding vegetation. It was Smyth, sitting on his log, who clearly heard something ahead, for at that moment he signaled the group.

Get out of sight.

Drake rolled into the undergrowth, trying not to imagine what might already be housed there. Beneath the boughs and overgrown surrounds of an immense tree they crouched in silence.

Before long a group of men came by, clearly not natives. They wore dirty T-shirts and cut-off denims, carried Ak47s carelessly and stared only at each other. Drake was glad they had chopped at the trail so carefully, but at the same time believed these men wouldn't have spotted a man with scythes for arms standing in their way. At the same time, their confidence was discomforting. Drake knelt alongside his friends as the men filed by, speaking in Mexican and laughing among themselves. Ten minutes later the coast was clear and the group emerged, soaked, cramped, but still invisible to the world.

Another hour slipped by, broken only by bird calls, creaking boughs and the snapping of branches. Drake once thought he heard a low growl, but wasn't sure if it came from an indigenous cat or Smyth. It never came again so he assumed it had emerged from the latter. Hitching up their backpacks and readying their weapons they moved further and further southeast along a line that ran fairly parallel to the Jutai River, occasionally returning to its banks as the trail meandered to and fro.

It was after eleven when Hayden called another break.

With infinite care, the group came together.

Drake swigged more water greedily. "How close are we?"

"Very," Hayden whispered. "The dots are practically merging. From here on in you guys should use your GPS, scout the perimeter of the bazaar, and then rendezvous back here in an hour to compare notes. Let's say Yorgi, Lauren and Smyth wait here."

There were nods all round, and Smyth looked relieved to be taking a break. Hayden gave the trio a parting warning. "Stay alert for roving patrols."

Drake consulted his own GPS and moved in closer to their objective until a movement eight meters to his right made him freeze. With infinite caution he crept closer, sizing up the person who emerged out of the greenery. As he worked his way around he began to hear music in the distance, a dance tune, and considered the audacity of his prey. *That's good,* he thought. *A bold enemy is usually a dead enemy.*

The guard he evaluated seemed a little different from the usual type of mercenary. Drake studied him and saw a better edge to the vigilance, a certain skill to the way he handled his firearm and words passing between him and other watchers via some kind of headset. These men were real professionals, not just called so because they killed for a living.

Drake continued through his sector until he encountered two more guards. The third seemed to sense him, and that was fair praise, but Drake managed to slip away without detection. All the while the music pumped in the background and occasionally a gust of laughter rode the wind. Twice, Drake heard gunshots followed by either jeering or merriment and assumed some kind of game was underway. In any case, the bazaar was in full flow. Drake backed away and returned to the rendezvous, once more becoming accustomed to the rainforest's relative peacefulness. They had been lucky so far but now came another intense downpour. Drake found himself smiling.

That should dampen their masochistic amusements.

Back at the rendezvous the team were already assembled. Dahl looked ready to poke fun for his lateness—and for that matter so did Alicia—but their need to keep to murmurs robbed them of their fun. Within minutes the various reports came in.

"Guard every fifty, sixty feet," the Swede said under the punch of the rainstorm. "Capable looking. Probably hand-picked. Some kind of group communication so no chance of picking 'em off one at a time. A solid cordon, I'd say."

Drake affirmed with a nod. "Agreed. If we're trying to get in there unnoticed we'll have to come up with another way."

Hayden pursed her lips. "I'm of the same mind. Distraction is a possibility to draw some of them away, but that would only draw attention, and these guys don't seem particularly dumb. I think we need a way of blending in."

"Count me the fuck out," Smyth griped.

Alicia tapped the watery jungle floor. "I came across a tributary of the Jutai that seemed to run close by the main camp. Couldn't get too far along to get a better look, but a small barge did pass by with guards stood around the top deck."

Kinimaka crossed his large arms. "So where does all that leave us? We might as well have HALO'd in. Saved us all this hoofing about."

Hayden shook her head. "The camp, the main bazaar, is

huge. No way will we get away with storming it. And even if we did get lucky with the guards we'd lose three quarters of the people we came here to get. And don't forget Webb, the CIA and Big Dog. No, this one's gonna take a little finesse."

Dahl looked blank. Drake coughed. Kinimaka narrowed his eyes. *"Say what?"*

"Finesse. Skill. Flair. Elegance. You know."

Dahl continued to stare. "I'm not following."

Alicia scratched her head. "What the hell is she talking about?"

Hayden threw up her hands in despair, but refrained from shouting. "All right, boys, less of the wise guy routine. Let's use that incredible wit to come up with a solution, eh?"

"At some point we need to gauge the conviction of Ramses' soldiers," Smyth said. "If they're fanatics this thing could be a whole lot harder."

"It also means Ramses is good," Drake said gloomily. "Probably better than all the Pythians put together."

"We have to assume they have contingencies in place to guard against a full-scale invasion," Dahl said. "And covert infiltration."

At that moment the downpour began to lessen. The team took a moment to adjust to the softer noise levels and mopped water from their clothes. Within moments they were sweltering from the new, humid heat.

"Anyone get look at actual bazaar?" Yorgi asked.

Blank looks were returned, so the Russian thief whispered again. "So far, there is only one way in. Yes?"

Dahl thought about it. "I'm assuming you mean the river?"

"Dah. The river."

Alicia quickly shook her head. "Full of parasites. Piranhas. Maybe even a caiman or two. We ain't swimming in there, Tarzan."

"Speaking of Tarzan, you could probably branch-creep your way in from tree to tree." Drake pointed up at the densely packed, incredibly thick branches. "But I don't think even we are that good."

"Too noisy," Yorgi agreed. "And slippery, but one man could. *I* could."

Hayden thought about it for a while before pulling a face. "It's not enough. One man inside is not enough. I'm liking the sound of the river more and more."

"I forgot my cossie," Alicia said without humor, further hammering home her point of a few moments before.

"There's always skinny dipping," Smyth said with a rare grin. "I'm game if you are."

"In your dreams . . ." Alicia paused, then said, "What the hell is your first name anyway?"

"Look," Yorgi interjected quickly. "When I mention river I do not mean we swim. I mean we take boat. One of *their* boats." He made a snaking gesture. "Cruise in."

Drake knitted his brows together as the idea suddenly flourished. "Pretend we're one of them? A guest? Yorgi, that's brilliant!"

Hayden shushed him. "Keep it down. It's risky. I can think of three big obstacles without breaking sweat."

"Shit, Hay, look around. What *isn't* risky?"

"So you're thinking: Board a boat, seize it, hold its occupants hostage and take their places at the bazaar? Assuming they're guests."

Alicia grinned. "Fuck yeah."

Dahl clenched a fist. "I'm liking the sound of that."

Hayden looked to the skies. "I was going for sarcastic, guys. But, hell . . . do you think we can do it?"

"It's a long river," Drake pointed out. "Nothing says we have to nick the boat this close in."

"IDs may be a problem," Lauren said.

"Doubtful," Hayden said. "It's a terrorist arms bazaar, not a United Nations charity ball. Of course, there will be an entrance tag of some sort, which we will have to extract from whomever we grab."

"Let's hope it's not fingerprints, facial recognition, retina scan . . ." Smyth started.

"Again, doubtful," Kinimaka spoke up. "For similar reasons."

"But we can still take the boat without assuming that risk," Drake pointed out. "If we decide it's impossible to gain entrance after that, then we can find another way."

"Time is against us." Hayden tapped her watch. "So, if we're all agreed, let's get going."

"This is good," Dahl said as they walked. "From inside we can identify weak spots. People we should acquire. The expendables. The VIPs. Booby traps. Weapons caches, that sort of thing."

"And just as important," Hayden said. "We could identify items that need safeguarding. Items that should never fall into a terrorist's hands."

"So plan is . . . a go?" Yorgi asked in a faltering attempt at American slang.

"Aye lad," Drake gripped his shoulder. "It'll be a scorching hot day in Hell when all these nasty bastards get their just desserts. We're about to start fanning the flames. Stoking the fire. Lighting the—"

"Look," Alicia interrupted, pointing ahead. "The river."

CHAPTER FOURTEEN

Drake followed Alicia as the team wound their way downriver, searching for the best spot from which to ambush a passing boat. As they walked, Hayden held up a clenched fist, her entire body freezing. Drake saw it immediately.

There, to the left, twisted around a moss-infested tangle of tree branches, dead undergrowth, and lumps of soil and vegetation, sat the biggest snake any of them had ever seen. Mottled browns and blacks and even a little yellow shone in the direct sunlight as a body the size of a man's thigh coiled lazily. The entire group took a big step to the right.

Hayden went first, followed by Kinimaka and Lauren. Drake took his time, aware that they were pretty much safe but suddenly even more conscious of the dangers that lay all around and even underfoot beneath the carpet of mulchy leaves.

What we can't see could kill us even faster than what we can.

He filed that thought away. Ahead, the river narrowed on both sides and where it was most slender the ground rose a little. Hayden motioned for a halt.

Alicia cast a glance backward. "A little close to our big friend."

Drake sighed. "Anacondas are pretty slow. Even on your worst day I bet you could outrun one."

"My worst day? Shit, Drakey, you don't know me at all."

He acknowledged that with a nod. Hayden beckoned them closer. "Let's get into position and form a plan."

And then they waited. The bazaar no doubt was in full

swing by now as midday passed. The scorching heat blasted at them like a brazier. Drake took the time to apply even more insect spray and drain his canteen. It took an hour but at last Smyth signaled that a vessel was approaching the choke point.

"We're on, guys."

Drake ignored the muddy bank to eye the incoming vessel. The boat did resemble a barge, but with a long, smoked-glass cabin, a figurehead in bronze and various roof-antennae that screamed out the presence of a wealthy individual. He checked his weapons and his safely holstered machete and then took stock of his teammates.

"Let's keep the noise down, folks," he said.

They rose as the boat reached its closest point, then ran up and leapt from the raised bank and landed on the deck of the ship, boots striking the planking as lightly as possible. Of course, the three guards spotted them quickly and turned, rifles swinging from around their necks into their hands.

Dahl barreled into the first, smashing his body into the cabin bulkhead, the sound of breaking bones probably loud enough to make even the anaconda take note. Drake rolled into the second, taking his legs, and the two men went down in a tangle. Smyth landed carefully and threw his knife at the third—who was the furthest away—making him duck to the side and lose precious seconds. The knife stuck hard into a wooden upright, quivering. Smyth bounded across the space between them, catching hold of the guard as his weapon came up. The barrel pointed to the skies, but the man's finger tightened on the trigger. Smyth wrenched at the man, throwing him bodily to the floor, the movement sending him sprawling. Then Smyth jumped on top, pinned his arms away from his body and reached up for the knife.

Drake pummeled his opponent's kidneys from on top,

ensuring the rifle was crushed to the deck and essentially unusable. When he sat up his enemy groaned. Drake clasped his knife and ran it through the back of the man's neck, then glanced around.

Alicia and Hayden were by the cabin's side door, pushing it open and slipping inside. Dahl confirmed his own foe wouldn't revive later to give them away and then followed. Drake ran quickly after them, signaling to Kinimaka and the rest of the team that they should wait a while longer.

Inside the smoked-glass cabin the boat lived up to its opulent promise. Luxurious seats stood all around and the control panel flashed with hundreds of lights. Alicia stood beside the padded steering wheel with her hands around a man's neck, while Hayden paused at the top of a set of stairs.

She put her fingers to her lips. Drake nodded and signaled that he would back her up. Dahl joined them too. Quietly, their team leader descended the wooden risers and gradually they began to make out the sound of a television. Raucous, bottled laughter boomed out intermittently amid cheers from what sounded like a well-sozzled audience. Drake felt the boat shifting and wondered briefly if Alicia had stopped its forward momentum or was guiding it.

God help us.

A narrow passageway led to three open doors; each room had to be relatively small. Hayden signaled that they should take one each, but then a bare-chested figure appeared at the far end.

"What the . . . who the hell are you?"

Drake reacted first, sprinting down the passage as he recognized that this man was their quarry, listening to him yell out a warning and knowing that down here it wouldn't carry, understanding that they needed him alive, but already eyeing him for hidden weapons and other devices. The yell caused a scuffle behind and he guessed Dahl had attracted a guard; then Drake was at the man's throat, forcing him back into the far room.

"Shut up," he said. "Sit down. And you might live through this."

The complication sat rigid, her eyes wide as side-plates, a handful of buttery popcorn halfway to her mouth. The TV no longer engaged her attention—rather it was the black-clad soldier holding her husband by the throat.

Drake sensed the scream coming, threw the man over the back of the couch and flew over to the woman. Quickly he held a finger to her lips. Hayden took control of the struggling man. Drake grunted as the woman struck out, catching him a glancing blow to the chin.

Hayden met his eyes. "Where's Dahl?"

Drake frowned. The Swede should have dispatched his enemy and be here by now. With a nod of warning at the woman, the Yorkshireman slipped quickly back into the passageway, concern written all across his face. The scene wasn't good. Dahl lay on his side in the middle of the corridor, unmoving.

"Mate." Drake felt his heart sink through the bottom of the boat. "Torsten?"

CHAPTER FIFTEEN

The problem wasn't with Dahl's health or lack of it—it was with the big bruisers he'd head-locked under each arm. Two strapping guards were almost too much even for the Swede and he was having trouble keeping them subdued. Lying on his back, he looked down the corridor at Drake.

"A . . . little . . . help . . ."

Drake nodded at the upside-down face. He removed his knife from its sheath and moved in close. The guard on Dahl's right struck up at him but Drake ducked to the side. Dahl could now concentrate on the one man and grappled alongside, the silent battle taking place on the floor with all four men crammed up against the passageway's wooden walls. Drake struck fast and hard, but his blows were deflected by his opponent's raised arms. When the guy found a way to strike back, Drake let it fly past and punched at the kidneys. The man's yell of pain was a double moan, one for hitting the wall and another for the punishment to his side.

Dahl was slowly overpowering his own opponent, bringing strength and weight to bear until he gained an advantage. All four men dripped sweat like rain and grunted like rutting pigs—the air down here was stifling. Drake saw the glint of a knife in the other's hand and caught the wrist, snapping it. A yelp ensued, but by then the Yorkshireman had his own knife unsheathed and to hand. One thrust was deflected, another pushed aside desperately by flesh that began to bleed. The eyes that stared into Drake's own were merciless.

He plunged the blade to its hilt and watched the life

extinguish, then rose. Dahl rose too, retrieving his own blade and wiping it off. Together, they trudged back into the room where Hayden held their hostages.

Dahl grunted under his breath. "Thanks . . . mate."

Drake struggled to shrug off the terrible dread that seized him when the Swede failed to appear. "Next time, don't hug them, put them down."

"I'll try to remember that."

Then Hayden fell against the door frame, arms flailing. Drake caught her and moved her aside, spotting the rising welt along the side of her face. A moment later the bare-chested man appeared, clutching an empty beer bottle to his chest as if it were a lifeline.

"Save yourself some pain, knobhead," Drake growled. "Put it down."

"I no understand." The man rubbed day old stubble in agitation, hopping from foot to foot.

"We don't have the time." Dahl pushed past, gripped the man by the scruff of the neck and threw him against the far wall before the bottle even moved. A wall-light smashed and a narrow bookcase fell over, scattering paperback tomes everywhere. Drake prevented the Swede from causing further damage by holding him back.

"We need him alive and kicking."

Hayden rubbed her face and walked over to the woman. Drake guessed from rings on the left fingers and even a framed picture on the wall that this was the man's wife. Other tell-tale objects revealed that they were wealthy, well-traveled, and possibly hailed from the country of Albania. Tattoos on the man's hairy arms appeared to be of Mafia origin, but Drake was no expert. Safe to say though, this man was about to be a guest at Ramses' last bazaar.

"I no understand," the man said again with a heavy accent.

Drake smiled softly, catching his eyes. "I'll say this once and then we're gonna resort to pain." He allowed the blade of his knife to glint in the remaining light and watched the Albanian's eyes widen. "Yeah, you understand all right. It's very simple. Tell us about this bazaar, about Ramses, and why you're here."

The man's face ran through a myriad of emotions, as if contending with an inner struggle. Drake would not hurt the man's wife but *he* didn't know that. With a flick of his head he indicated that Hayden should round the woman up. Popcorn fell to the floor. The woman's long dark hair fell free as she began to sob.

"Start talking." Drake raised the knife, keeping it neutral but projecting threat.

"I know nothing of Ramses. This is—how you say? A . . . third party made invite. Through my third party. You see?"

Drake actually did "see". These parasites were too clever to get personally involved in such communications. "Go on."

"Bazaar is—" the Albanian spread his hands, still clutching the bottle "—a way to make money. Buy and sell. Or buy something . . . want."

Drake accepted by now that the man's English was somewhat lacking in depth. These were only trial questions anyway—gauging the man's honesty.

"We here . . . vacation." The man shrugged. "It is different, yes? Just a few days away."

Drake tried to ignore that statement, not wanting to become submerged in the innumerable questions it raised. "We want the passes," he said. "All of them. And we want the protocols, the etiquette. Everything. Do you understand?"

The Albanian nodded. "You want in?"

"Exactly."

Hayden added another question. “And these boats? Are they private? Your own?” She pointed to the man and then the room. “Or can Ramses’ men board when they like?”

“Mine.” The Albanian nodded again. “My boat. They not come here. Bazaar very private and . . .” he paused. “Anon . . . anony . . .”

“Anonymous,” Drake helped out. “Okay, okay. So they give you your own space. That’s good. What about entry?”

The Albanian indicated a low coffee table that sat in the center of the room, in front of the television. Upon its smoked-glass surface lay a number of glossy black plastic cards, oblong in shape and about the length of a letterbox. Dahl moved over to them, scooped them up and examined both sides.

“No ID pictures,” he said. “Just a chip embedded in one side. What information did you have to give?”

“Name. Country. Time of arrival. Any special needs.” A shrug. “No more.”

“And why are there five?” the Swede asked.

“Us, plus bodyguards. Protection is . . . must.”

Drake caught the man’s attention. “Did you have . . . shall we say an inventory? Or an index of items.” He searched for an easier description. “A wish list.”

“No. Ramses’ reputation is enough for me.”

“What were you hoping to buy?” Hayden asked suddenly, changing the flow of questioning.

The Albanian’s eyes fell. “I not know. Browse, you say? Yes . . . browse.”

Drake gulped down a rush of bile born of pure hatred for such creatures as this who murdered and destroyed lives because they thought they had a right to. He signaled and Dahl went off quickly to tell Alicia to shut the boat down. They didn’t want to be drifting too close to the bazaar just yet.

"So that's it?" he said. "The bazaar is a basic market place with stalls and entertainment. Ramses is in it to make a few quick bucks and seal a few deals. Will it really be so easy to get in?"

The Albanian understood the last sentence. "All hard work done," he said. "To get passes. They know you don't keep . . . people waiting."

Drake met Hayden's eyes. "Five passes," he speculated. "I wonder . . ."

With shocking swiftness the Albanian's wife struck out, battering Hayden's already bruised face with a mug and then kicking her in the chest. Hayden tripped over the coffee table and went sprawling. Drake ignored the shock and leapt at her. The Albanian man struck too. Drake reached the wife first, but she danced away, kicks and blows well aimed enough to make him slow down. The Albanian hit him from behind, the bottle coming down against his neck, but over the thick jacket he wore so the pain was dulled. Drake flicked his shoulders, throwing the man off. The wife came in again. Drake batted her foot away, grabbed her ankle and pulled, overbalancing her so that she smashed through the table. Hayden rose once more, face now bruised in two places, and shouted a warning.

"Quit!" she cried. "As of now, you guys live. Any more of this shit and I'll personally gut the both of you!"

Drake spun to face the Albanian, hands ready, but the man backed off, holding his arms high but still clinging to the heavy bottle.

"Had to try," he said, fingers grasping around the neck.

The wife picked herself up off the floor, brushing glass from her clothes and wincing from the dozen or so cuts she'd received. Drake noted that she still did not stop even as the blood flowed and caught Hayden's attention.

"I think the two Albanian Kruegers really need to be restrained and guarded. No slacking. These two are bloody dangerous."

"I agree."

There was the clatter of footsteps and then the rest of the team joined them. Drake regarded Alicia.

"How close are we?"

"No sign of the bazaar's guards. We're okay for now."

"Good. Because we have decisions to make before we go in."

"I'm all ears."

"Five passes," he said. "Eight of us. Who stays?"

"Soldiers should go," Yorgi said immediately. "More training if something go wrong. If I am needed I can help better alone."

"Then that rules me out," Lauren said. "But I agree. I'd be no good in there."

Smyth watched her. "I'll stay with them," he muttered. "That makes it easy and they're gonna need a guard."

Drake agreed with him. His eyes took in Alicia and Dahl, Hayden and Kinimaka. "Then it's all up to us. Are you ready to crash the last bazaar?"

"Are you kidding?" Alicia grinned. "Crashing parties is my thing."

"I don't doubt it," Drake said automatically, then added, "In fact, I remember it."

Dahl stayed serious. "We should conduct a little extra interrogation first. Get them to tell us about what we're allowed to take in—weapons and the like."

Kinimaka couldn't take his eyes away from Hayden's bruised face. "Shit."

Hayden ignored him. "All right, let's do this. And *in there* we're in hell. Murder central. Surrounded by the worst of the worst. This is gonna be like nothing we've experienced before, boys, so be careful. Danger, literally, will be all around."

"Better than that other fucker that they reckon is all around," Alicia murmured. "Love."

Dahl rubbed his hands together a little too gleefully for Drake's liking. "So come on," he said. "What are we waiting for? Ramses' bazaar isn't going to obliterate itself."

CHAPTER SIXTEEN

Tyler Webb rather enjoyed wandering anonymously from tent to tent, pavilion to pavilion by way of several cut-back jungle trails. Yes, the persistent showers were annoying and, in truth, they were a little more than that but Webb began to welcome the heavy downpours because they actually brought a little relief from the incessant heat. Of course, their aftermath brought even more humidity as the jungle dried out, but most of these tents were air-conditioned anyway. How else could you attract so many wealthy people to Purgatory?

Webb sensed Beauregard at his side the entire time, except for twice when the lithe Frenchman was forced into action. The conflict didn't last long, though the one time Webb noticed his adversary was a woman several words were passed along with wry smiles. As darkness fell on that first day, Webb found himself enjoying the diversities. Wealthy, privileged men like himself craved uniqueness and Ramses' bazaar was as unusual as it got.

Guards moved aside, their weapons pointed upward, as Webb ambled by. This pavilion extended up to a point, white fabric stretched and adorned with lights, bathing the key area in a golden glow. Webb's interest centered on a long, low sturdy table where sat three familiar items.

Julian Marsh's plan of using a so-called suitcase nuke to force the US to capitulate to the Pythians' demands—as China previously had over the Z-Boxes—had forced both Webb and Marsh to become doyens of what was once simply Cold War tech. The only nations with enough expertise and money to successfully develop a tactical nuclear weapon small enough to fit into a backpack or large suitcase were the US, the Russians, and the Israelis. None of these three had acknowledged the existence of a weapon compact enough to be able to fit into a small suitcase, but the original technology was now at least thirty years old. It was also claimed—but never proven—that a dummy suitcase nuke was regularly carried on internal airline flights in the 1980s. For training purposes naturally. Webb allowed a little smile of disdain to creep across his features. How many times per day did a government lie to its people? And how many of those lies were for the people's own good, rather than the politicians'?

He moved closer to the table in question, studying the item it held. The backpack was large and shapely enough so that it would stand out in a crowd, even scream for a closer inspection. The coloring was distinctly military, the strapping old and worn. It actually looked to Webb like half an oil drum wrapped in canvas.

The surprise must have registered on his face, for a man stepped forward out of a discreet shadow. "Is this not to your liking, sir?"

Webb scowled. "When I heard the term 'suitcase nuke' I imagined something smaller."

"These three items are overlarge for your purposes?"

"They were overlarge for Hussein. How the hell am I supposed to utilize them?"

"Might I point you this way then, sir?"

The salesman, a young African who sported a name badge with the code word: Clay, which Webb really didn't understand, waved him toward a set of curtains on the far side of the tent. Though the screen was merely fabric, the way it was hung and with two more beyond, it formed the perfect barrier. Webb passed through all three to find himself in a much smaller area bordered by two exterior sides of the tent. Clay left him and Beauregard to face a man whose face and demeanor was much more in keeping with the nature of the bazaar.

"You want buy? Buy these?"

Webb looked away from the pockmarked, scarred face, the dead eyes, the lank hair and filthy clothing, to the merchandise on the table. Surprisingly, it was the opposite of the man—clean, new, advanced.

The man coughed harshly. "It cream of crop, yes? Those others they too big. Old. Dangerous. This new and only one left. Yes?"

Webb tried to keep his face blank. What the hell was he looking at? Assuming the nuke was already inside then the delivery system was everything he'd dreamed about. "How did you get it so small? If an employee presented me with a suitcase nuke the size of those I've just seen I'd terminate his contract with excessive prejudice."

Rat Breath, as Webb now designated him, just shrugged. "New," he said. "Best."

Webb nodded. What he found of most interest about suitcase nukes was that, according to several high-ranking Russian defectors, since the Cold War many of these devices had gone missing. It turned out that the number of "missing" nukes was almost identical to the number of targets on which they might be deployed. Might it be possible then, that they may already be deployed on US soil? Wired to batteries with several redundant backups. Just waiting . . .

They claimed to have hidden untold caches of weapons, sleeper agents and bomb-making materials. Of course, these days it was getting harder to smuggle anything into the States, but most of the stuff was already there. Webb snapped his thoughts back to the present, focusing on the wheeled suitcase that lay on the table.

"Is it wired to the case?" he asked, then sighed. "Remove?" he asked. "Can weapon be removed?"

"Oh, no." Rat Breath looked terrified. "All one. Only detonate."

"Nobody ever admitted to building one smaller than a foot-locker," Webb breathed to Beauregard. "And yet here we are. Imagine if governments, for the last thirty years, had poured as many resources into disease control, famine prevention and catastrophe awareness as they have weapons. The world would be a far different place, my friend."

Beauregard inclined his head. "Shocked to hear you say it but also pleased."

Webb shrugged. "Hey, not that I give a fuck, right? They make their own beds, these war mongers. Tie them to what they reap. Let them burn."

"Is that really you, sir?"

Webb laughed. "Oh, perhaps the wine has gone to my head. Or whatever that concoction was. Rice vodka? Who cares, right? Anyway, back to work. Julian should have arrived about an hour ago and will be fretting. How much for this new weapon, Mr. Rat—" Webb coughed to cover his error, then finished lamely. "Mr. Man?"

"One million dollars. The larger ones are half that." Rat Breath shrugged.

Webb threw his arms in the air. "Then we celebrate!" He reeled off an account number and then privately entered a pin that allowed these dealers to extricate funds the potential buyers had deposited earlier.

"Transaction good." Ratty showed his rodent-like teeth at Webb. "You take."

"That I will," Webb smiled. "That I will. Oh, and what guarantee do I have that this thing actually works?"

Rat Breath looked understandably nonplussed. "Can't

test," he said with a verminous smile. "That would be problem. Have clever man check wiring."

Webb leaned forward, grinning too. "But carefully, eh? Super careful?"

"Oh, very careful!" Rat Breath cried.

"It will be checked," Webb said seriously. "And any problems will be taken up by my associate here."

Beauregard hefted the suitcase at arm's length.

Rat Breath said nothing, but grinned.

Webb exited the tent, still smiling and feeling good about himself. With all prospects of even the lightest, mildest forms of stalking currently on hold he had expected this trip to be more than depressing. But on the contrary, it had injected a feisty little spirit into him that he quite liked. The path outside twisted among dark boughs and Webb took a moment to lean against one as he checked his cell. To hell with the creepy-crawlies. To hell with anything else. Tonight was for living . . .

Marsh was here. Webb felt instant depression. Marsh was a frigging oddball, one part of him normal the other part, well, *odd*. The man's message said to meet near the caiman pit so Webb took some bearings, headed off, and then switched to the opposite direction at Beauregard's wry insistence. He'd never been particularly good at finding his way around.

Not exactly right, he thought. *I've always been good at finding my way around people's homes. And lives.*

Water dripped without end, a constant accompaniment to whatever revelries were happening tonight. Webb trudged through wet leaves and piles of mud, passing the slave tent once again and the sports pavilion. Many were inside catching up on live matches and results they were missing, but Webb had never cared for games of any kind. Beyond the pavilion lay the caiman pit, bordered by a high fence and still well-lit, but now patronized only by one man—Julian Marsh.

Webb blinked twice as he saw Marsh climbing the fence to peer over the top, face pressed firmly between wrought-iron barbs, as if he couldn't see straight through the gaps between the uprights. This was not a good man to send out into the world with a nuclear weapon. Not a good man at all.

Webb coughed loudly. "Julian?"

"Yessss?" Marsh turned, still clinging to the uprights.

"Come down from there. I have our merchandise."

Marsh leapt from the railings, arms and legs out in a star-shape, landing awkwardly but without injury. Webb stared openly at the contrast of sheepskin jacket and tailored pants, the luminous green gloves and purple rain boots. The doubts in his mind suddenly gelled.

"Julian," he said carefully. "Are you okay?"

"Never been better!" the last of the Pythian generals squeaked. "And you and the French condom? Okay?"

Webb gave in. The end-game here was actually the scroll, not the damn nuke. "Well, here we are. As agreed. Smuggle this into the US and then New York City. Once you're there, let me know and we will start the show."

Marsh reached out both hands for the suitcase. "Looks a little small, boss. Some FBI agent gets a look at this he'll pee himself laughing."

Webb hadn't had time to formulate a believable story. "It's real, I'm sure. Get it checked before you reach the United States though. And be careful, Marsh. This is the Pythian swan song."

"Cool, cool. So . . . what do I do with it when we're done? Throw it in the Hudson?"

Webb winced. "Umm, no. Let me get back to you on that. Use the burner phone method. No dead drops anymore. They got that covered these days. Code words as we agreed. This is it now, Julian. You are a Pythian carrying out his duty. Possibly the last. Do not stray from the road, my friend."

Webb needed the distraction. Ramses' new ultimatum may have painted this picture with a wholly different brush, but Webb needed it to happen one way or another. Once the Saint Germain angle was in play Webb would be free, whole, able to live and stalk and destroy without restraint or restriction. Quickly, he sent Marsh on his way, marveled at how the man stayed upright in those rain boots, and then used a two-way radio to contact Ramses.

"The matter we spoke of? It is in play right now. My man is on his way to the final destination, but carefully. It will take some time."

Ramses voice was deep and sonorous. "Not too long I hope."

"Next week perhaps."

"That is acceptable. So now I assume you require this scroll?"

Webb allowed the excited tingle to spread from his skull to his feet. "I do."

"Tomorrow," Ramses breathed. "Seven p.m. At the slavers' tent."

Webb barely refrained from letting out a frustrated sigh. "Seven p.m.? No sooner?"

"It is what it is, friend."

"Very well." Webb tried in vain to hang on to his feeling of wellbeing. "I will see you then."

He glanced around at Beauregard. "Find my tent. I've had enough of this shit. I want a bottle of rice vodka, Cinnamon Buns ice cream and a DVD player with *Once Upon A Time* already loaded. Can you do that?"

"I'll do my best, sir."

"Make sure you do. Oh, and Beauregard?"

"Yes, sir."

"Next week, tell any friends you have in New York to take a vacation. But for now, keep the rest of these murderers, betrayers and savages away from me. Okay?"

"Got it."

"We have two days left to make this bazaar work for us," Webb said. "Tomorrow, we'll shop like we're on Rodeo."

CHAPTER SEVENTEEN

In the heat of battle and the intense pressure of a soon-anticipated conflict the wisest person will always grab a little respite when he or she can, and Matt Drake's came in the form of watching Alicia Myles play dress-up. It had now been decided that Yorgi would play the Albanian mafia boss and Alicia his wife, as they were the closest physical match team SPEAR could find at short notice.

Out in the Amazon, Drake had said. *It's you, Alicia, or a cougar.*

That one earned him a bruise.

But there were more, so many more potential wisecracks, as Alicia and Yorgi donned the bespoke clothes of the wealthy terrorist couple and figured out a way to conceal their new, slimmer body armor and several weapons. Alicia in particular looked uncomfortable wearing civilian clothes, not to mention customized fabrics, and took some time to tug at the neckline, hemline and sides of her black dress.

"Is it me?" she asked. "Or is this a little inappropriate for the fucking Amazon?"

The Albanian terrorist's wife shrugged, her blond locks bobbing. "I just dress nice. All places we go are same."

Alicia stared. "Do you even know what the Amazon is?"

The wife shrugged again. "It is the next place we go. After that it is Cairo. Then the Atlantis Dubai. Then—"

Her husband cut her off with a hiss. Drake grunted. "Don't count on it, love."

Alicia gestured feverishly at the window. "Don't you ever look out the window? There's a jungle out there not a fucking shopping mall!"

Drake burst out laughing as Dahl grinned. The Yorkshireman said, "You're perfect for the part, Alicia. A proper terrorist princess."

"One more crack out of either of you and we'll be a guard short. Believe *that.*"

Yorgi stepped up, adjusting a tie and shrugging into a dinner jacket. The young thief also looked out of place, but Drake thought he carried it off quite well. Maybe it was the criminal in him—his life of wearing a disguise. Of course, Lauren would have been better for the job Alicia had been lumbered with but the team would not take her quite literally into the dragon's den unless there was no other option.

Drake, Dahl and Kinimaka donned new jackets taken from the now trussed-up guards, the Hawaiian having most trouble and having to tear several ambiguous holes to get the right fit. "Next time," he told the Albanian, "get some guards with a proper set of muscles on 'em. Not toothpicks."

"Be careful you don't rip that jacket in half," Hayden fretted a little. "Just . . . be careful in there, okay? All of you."

The five-person team nodded, ready to go. Smyth managed a grimace, still with his weapons trained on the Albanians, and Lauren manned the helm to guide them closer to the site of the bazaar. Very soon, Drake saw guards appear dotted at the top of the riverbank, all with weapons pointed at the skies but on full alert. Again he was reminded that these men weren't the complacent mercs they had grown used to. Some stood in full view whilst others lurked in the dark, covering their colleagues. Dahl pointed out what appeared to be an anti-aircraft set-up and inhaled loudly without speaking. What was there to say?

Soon, a makeshift dock appeared ahead and Lauren

guided the craft slowly in. Once they were docked and tied, the five-person team climbed up on deck, attitude and pass-keys at the ready. Drake stayed close to Alicia and Dahl to Yorgi whilst Kinimaka hung back a little to gauge reactions and study the area.

Drake took in as much as he could without appearing suspicious. The rickety dock led to a flat, muddy area that had clearly been cut out of the jungle and leveled off. He was lucky to be wearing boots but didn't hold out much hope for the Albanian couple's shoes. More fortunately it appeared Ramses had thought of everything—including his special guests underestimating the jungle's hostility—and pairs of rain boots were provided as they came ashore. Drake glared at the bright lights that emanated through the densely packed trees and caught the sounds of laughter, shouting and music, but for now they were stopped at a polite but necessarily suspicious guard station. Here, Drake noticed, the gun barrels were much lower.

Without a word or barely a glance Yorgi handed five pass keys over. The inspector, suitably attired in a penguin suit and white gloves, plucked the pass keys from the Russian's hand and placed them all, golden micro-chip up, on his table. With an emotionless smile he glanced past them toward the boat, then surveyed the rolling waters and silent banks. Drake said nothing, but prayed there wouldn't be a series of questions.

Moments dragged on for hours. Drake eyed the guards and they eyed him back. His weapon was holstered but close at hand. The white-gloved concierge waved the first black plastic key onto a portable scanner and waited for a beep. Information must have flashed up on a hidden screen for the man then asked for names and nationality.

Yorgi spoke for the both of them, as haltingly as the Albanian, and trying to keep any Russian inflection from his voice. Drake saw the concierge's eyes flick and a flex in his fingers, but the look was only a surreptitious one to take in Alicia's form and soon passed. Drake however noticed Alicia's sudden tension and prayed that she wouldn't decide to teach him a lesson. Not here. Not now.

"All keys are good." The man smiled. "As expected, of course. Please," he stood aside and indicated a path of stones that had been inlaid into the jungle floor, "follow the . . . yellow brick road." His polite laugh at the end was well rehearsed and clearly performed hundreds of times. Yorgi ignored him and pushed past, waving at Alicia to follow but not watching to see if she did. Drake thought the Russian had the terrorist's mannerisms down to a T and followed Alicia across the unstable stones.

The noise and light drew nearer. Drake saw more guards, their eyes roving the group and nearby shadows. Then they rounded a huddle of trees and entered the bazaar and paused for a moment, looks of shock on their faces. What could only be described as state-of-the-art market stalls lined a wide pathway, their supports and coverings wound among upstanding trees and foliage. Floodlights illuminated all, and helped keep unwanted insects at bay. Vendors hawked their wares, but their offerings were not ordinary merchandise. Drake saw compact sub-machine guns, boxes of grenades, rocket launchers and a missile battery at just a glance. Guards were stationed everywhere, and groups wandered the winding pathway, stopping to peruse stalls at their leisure. Rising at the end of the path Drake saw a pavilion, its opening framed by lights. An odor of cooked meats drifted on the wind. A mini-explosion in the jungle testified to the presence of interested predators.

"They don't care," Dahl said, nodding at the buyers. "It's just another day on the road to them."

Drake also whispered. "They buy and they buy and it

funds more terror," he said. "Many of them don't see what they reap. These people are the money, not the zeal."

Yorgi pretended some interest in a crate of missiles, pointing out the fact that they did possess the Albanian's pre-paid credit card. More stalls offered knives, swords and military gear. More pavilions appeared ahead and, on quick inspection, presented every sort of deadly paraphernalia Drake could think of, and more besides. All in all, the bazaar was an extreme show of incredible excess, tailored toward the more mature lunatic and his doting wife.

Alicia spoke little as they walked, so far out of her comfort zone even she couldn't poke fun at it. Banquets lay spread alfresco on tables covered in satin. Auctioneers sold men and women to left and right, so blatantly that the entire five-person team were forced to employ all of their self-restraint not to step in. By contrast the next cleared area along had been overlaid in some kind of thick fabric to allow men and women an area to dance slowly to quiet tunes.

The owner of a shooting range encouraged them to take a try, whispering that he would take any currency that they had. A quiet, domed tent required inspection by Yorgi and turned out to be a drugs boutique. Drake was surprised to see Italian and French designer stalls too, though who could say if the goods were genuine or fake? Certainly not him. None of this interested him too much, but what he did find noteworthy was that none of the guests spoke to or barely glanced at each other. He wasn't sure if this was sheer snobbery or precautionary but, if pushed, would have bet on the former.

A small array of private tents passed and then they were nearing the end of the bazaar, a railed hole ahead. Drake briefly wondered what might lay inside when Dahl leaned in to Yorgi.

"Think we should buy something? For appearances sake?"

Drake took that one. "Let's leave it tonight, it's getting late. We've done the groundwork. Tomorrow the real work begins. We find Webb, Beau, and the bloody CIA. And whomever this main man may be."

"And then Ramses," Alicia breathed. "After all I've been through, I am so looking forward to putting that guy in his rightful place."

"All you've been through?" Yorgi echoed, looking a little hurt. "Playing at being my wife, you mean?"

Alicia scowled. "You're too young for me, Yogi. And too dainty."

The thief's expression was a study in hurt.

"Look, I'm sorry, okay? I like my men with a bit more meat on them. And more definition. Experience. Weathered. Been around the block a few times . . ."

Yorgi held up a hand. "Please don't go on. I understand you."

Drake still stared at the railing. "Not sure where you're gonna find one of those around here, Princess."

"Are you sure?"

Drake turned around to find Alicia considering him. Quickly, he coughed and gave Kinimaka a push. "C'mon, pal, let's find our tents."

"Maybe I don't want to go to bed." Alicia pouted. "The night is yet young."

"Big day tomorrow. Huge day. This isn't going to be easy."

"Nothing worth doing ever is," Dahl said.

The group took a last look around the meandering throng, the sparkling tables with their gritty, dirty commodities and the attentive, well-spaced guards. The main players, it seemed, had all retired for the night.

Tomorrow would be madness, Drake thought. Without a plan, backup, or up-to-the-minute intel they somehow had to take down and capture what amounted to a village full of high-class terrorists, a splinter of the CIA and the Pythian leader, not to mention the revolutionary myth himself—Ramses.

Dahl caught his eye, clearly thinking the same thing. "Let the games begin."

CHAPTER EIGHTEEN

The night was not yet over, Alicia saw to that. An intercom system linked to Wi-Fi had been installed inside their sumptuous tents and the Englishwoman made full use of the amenities. "After all," she said. "You don't stay in a five-star, all-inclusive hotel and not make use of the friggn' facilities, do ya?"

So, Drake stood guard and watched as she snuggled in next to Yorgi and waited for the bottles to arrive. In keeping with the superior service of the place two waiters appeared within five minutes, immaculately tailored even down to their black Gucci rain boots, holding silver platters in white-gloved hands. The first knelt beside Alicia and poured red wine, the second set out a table full of cold cuts. Almost before they were gone Kinimaka was falling upon the food.

"Ah, ah," Alicia clucked. "Prince and princesses only. You peasants can go catch a wild boar or something."

The Hawaiian glanced at her, a slice of ham dangling from his mouth. "You're kidding, right?"

Dahl grinned. "If I don't get my steak I'm going to punch somebody in the face."

Drake laughed and grabbed a handful for himself. Alicia toasted the team and then went down to a little more snuggling. "So, Yorki, how do you like being married to a treasure hunting, ball-busting chickadee?"

Yorgi, never totally comfortable in Alicia's presence, inched away. The glass of wine in his hand was already half empty. "Umm, fine. I am good."

"Good?" Alicia snorted. "I'll show you good. We just

need to ask the guards to leave," she hesitated. "Unless . . . unless you'd preferred they stayed?"

Yorgi spluttered some more as Drake turned away, hiding a smile. One thing you could say for the inimitable Alicia Myles—she always livened up a room. Or a *tent*, to be more precise. With Kinimaka still filling up it had left Dahl to quickly check the perimeter and the Swede now returned.

"Quite a community," he said. "I counted over thirty tents like this before I gave up and half a dozen more in a clearing fit for a king. Probably Ramses and his finer guests. Now what is Alicia doing to Yorgi?"

Drake walked to the tent flap. "Any guards around?"

"Bloody hundreds. Add all of these people's personal minders to Ramses' own security force and you have a genuine army."

"So we stay covert."

"Absolutely. Though with Mano's appetite and Alicia's antics I'd say we're already on somebody's radar."

Drake perched on a footstool. "What are they gonna do? Call the front desk?"

"Out here," Dahl said. "Nothing would surprise me."

"Point taken." Drake cleared his throat. "Umm, Alicia, be a good girl now and put Yorgi down."

The blonde rounded on him. "Careful, Drakey."

"You're making too much noise."

"Never been accused of that before. Okay, okay, whatever. Hey, I have an idea!" Alicia drained her glass and reached for a walkie-talkie. Drake rose to stop her but paused as she held up a hand.

"Hey," she said when a voice answered. "Do you guys do dancers? Y'know, male dancers?" Her sly glance at Drake ensured he knew she was trying to provoke a reaction.

Drake nevertheless ended the communication for her,

urging her to keep a little restraint. "It's not *One Night in Bangkok*," he reminded her. "It's a terrorist arms exchange. And all the staff are slaves who either work or die, I'm betting. So stay focused."

Alicia sobered at his words, finally relaxing her grip on Yorgi's neck. The Russian headed over to the other side of the tent.

"So where are we supposed to sleep?" Kinimaka asked. "Us guards, I mean."

"I guess we don't," Drake said. "We guard."

"There's always the jungle," Alicia said a little petulantly.

"Oh yeah. I'd just love to get snuggled down with a bird-eating spider for the night."

Alicia eyed the sides of the tent as if expecting a visitor. "They have those here?"

"Oh aye," Drake drawled. "Bigger than a kitten, hairier than a gorilla. They have a sound like a horse's hooves chasing you through the trees. Great bedfellows, I hear."

Alicia sniffed. "No doubt I've had worse."

"Classy." Drake looked away. "So, how about we try to get some rest and wake up refreshed for the morning? I get the feeling tomorrow's gonna be a blast."

Dahl eyed him. "Are you being ironic?"

"Sure, mate, sure. Aren't I always?"

CHAPTER NINETEEN

The morning welcomed them in spectacular and now sadly familiar fashion. The heavens spared no quarter as they opened up a deluge of gargantuan proportions, the rain slamming against the tent with a fury none of them could have imagined. Dahl thrust his head into the downpour to get a look at the morning's proceedings but soon reported that the bazaar seemed to be taking a break.

"Funny that," Drake said.

An hour later the torrent subsided and the group made their way out of the small tent village. A huge snake lay across their trail but even as they all paused, startled, it slithered away, its lazy undulations almost mesmerizing. Alicia took a deep breath as if she'd just faced down the worst horror of her life and then moved off. Drake grinned at her back. Dahl warned him with a finger to his lips.

"I'd stay quiet, mate, if you fancy keeping your wedding tackle."

Drake nodded. The bazaar was back in full flow, gaudy market stalls open, tents with openings flung wide and pop music drifting in the background. Groups and couples were already wandering the byways, stopping to browse at various stalls. A group of tired-looking men dressed in white thawbs and keffiyehs emerged from one of the privately marked tents, moving as if they'd been involved in negotiations all night. Drake would have given a year of his life to know what they'd been plotting. If only the CIA had been concentrating more on surveilling this event rather than attending they might have made the world a safer place for decades to come.

As they paused near the end of a trail, dripping trees all around, a chopper rose into the air carrying some unnamable extremist back to his homeland. This was the bazaar's middle day and some deals had already been struck. The team made a point of heading back toward the river and watched their boat for a while. Smyth made an obvious figurehead, standing atop the deck, looking fresh and staring at the skies as if daring them to drench him again. Nothing passed between the team but judging by the sight of him, Drake had to assume all was well. The nearby guards eyed them carefully, and soon Yorgi signaled that they should return to the bazaar. As they walked away one of the river boats started up and also left the bazaar, its owner's deals all done.

They made a point of attending the slave market, having agreed the previous night that this was one place they would ensure was liquidated of scum before they left. Crowds of buyers and their entourages were now walking outside and gathering in the tents, the bazaar at its busiest. Drake saw how the deals were made, where the slaves came from and then were stored for later collection, and which guards were the most vicious. The auctioneer in particular warranted something special, maybe a visit from one of Kinimaka's spiders. The evil, vile glint in his eyes and his actions were not those of a man whose humanity might be salvaged.

Half an hour later, sick to their stomachs, the team exited the slavers' tent and huddled for a brief confab.

"It's time to find Ramses," Kinimaka said. "Vulnerabilities. Targets. Weapons of major interest . . ."

"Dude," Alicia breathed. "What the hell do you think we've been doing? Ramses' tent is a two minute stroll that way, and his neighbors are probably worth a prod or two." She indicated a game trail made larger by the men. "Guards are either facing in or out, not both. Also they don't appear to call in at all, for some reason, so if one disappears the rest don't know. No communications center, either. We haven't identified who's in charge yet. As for weapons—didn't you see the suitcase nukes, the PU94 plutonium inside their radioactive carrying cases, the stock of prototype RPGs and fluid body armor? Man, we can't let a single terrorist get away with a single item of that lot. And as for targets, well why the hell do ya think we're doing all this strolling? For our good health?"

Drake grinned. Alicia was clearly on her game, making up for last night, and the Hawaiian scratched his head as he absorbed all she had just said. "The CIA don't work that way," he said. "When we're gonna do something we say so. At least, we do to the one percent we trust."

"Not in the CIA—" Alicia tapped his shoulder "—any more."

"Yup, I got that."

Again they emerged from the enlarged trail close to the fenced off pit, and now saw several men and women peering down through the bars. With a horde of people between they walked soundlessly toward it, peering at every face and inwardly bemused by the absolute lack of eye contact.

It was then that Drake saw familiar faces. One that caused even him a moment's panic. Quickly, he caught everyone's attention and pulled them aside to stare with interest into the forest as two men walked by.

Tyler Webb and Beauregard Alain.

Drake allowed his head to hang, his shoulders to slump. Anything to appear different. Alicia struggled not to send a quick glance at Beauregard. Not one of the team could safely stare at the passersby because they knew of Webb's stalking abilities and that he would no doubt know them all by sight, but they did manage to piece together the scenario between them.

"Webb's here to buy," Drake said as they turned to watch the men's backs move away. "And Beau's here as his bodyguard. Shit, Beau might have purposely let this thing slip but I didn't realize they would be *attending*."

"Nor me," Alicia muttered. "Whoa, that man looked good."

"If Webb's here to purchase," Dahl said, "then it can't be good. We have to mark them down as a definite target."

"The leader of the Pythians? Most wanted man in the world?" Drake said. "Oh yeah, he's on the list."

As the group watched, Webb and Beauregard abruptly stopped, confronted by a small entourage of bearded men. All wore the traditional Arab dress except two, and it was these two who looked to be the most interesting. Drake studied a huge man, up to seven feet tall, and the other who appeared to be his bodyguard. It was a giveaway how both he and Beauregard squared up to each other, equals, and stopped studying their surroundings for danger. It was enough that they watched each other. Drake saw Webb engage in conversation with the lofty individual—whom, he noted, was also quite muscular and probably capable—and tried to read lips.

"Now there's a shocker," Dahl said. "You see the big guy? How he holds himself? How the others all defer to his gestures and looks? He's royalty, I'm sure. That's our man."

Kinimaka tried his best not to stare. "Ramses himself? Are you sure?"

"Who else could it be? Expert bodyguard. You can tell by the way Beauregard is so hyper-alert. Entourage of normal guards. His comportment. And the other giveaway—Webb, the so-called Pythian king—has actually been stopped by him and is holding a conversation."

The group stood carefully, stealing glances, but careful of the vigilant guards both beside Ramses and close by in the jungle. Danger lurked everywhere. As if to corroborate this a thin, bright snake slithered past their feet with no real interest, one of the deadliest creatures on the planet. Drake found himself suddenly unsure which predator to look at next.

"Shit, we're in trouble here."

"Don't worry," Dahl said, "I'll look after you."

"Thanks, Dad. Now, what the hell do we do next? We can't just follow 'em around."

"I'm thinking—" Kinimaka began, but then just stopped. The expression on his face put Drake in mind of a coronary and he moved closer to his friend.

"Mano? You okay, pal?"

The Hawaiian's mouth moved but nothing came out. Shock and quite possibly terror controlled his every decision.

Drake noted the man wasn't looking in the direction of Ramses but to his left. To another group of men. To . . .

Drake gaped.

"But that's . . . that's impossible."

"It is." Even Alicia sounded shaken. "But he's standing right there. Large as life. Attending a fucking repulsive terrorist bazaar with the scum of the earth. Oh shit, guys, what the hell do we do now?"

CHAPTER TWENTY

Drake tried to calm his pounding heart, tried to reel his eyes back in from the stalks on which they currently perched. Three men wearing Armani suits was bad enough; three men wearing *Men In Black* sunglasses was a tad worse . . .

But three men who were clearly agents of the American government, strolling along with smiles and handshakes and knowing glances, already holding wrapped purchases and designer carrier bags, one of them having inserted a red tag inside his breast pocket—which signified that he'd ordered a slave to be collected later—was mind blowing to say the least.

And that wasn't the most shocking thing about the scenario.

Kinimaka still struggled to draw breath. Drake saw the world spinning inside his own head as everything he knew became unbalanced. Dahl grunted and grunted, trying to come up with a suitable remark and failing. In the end it was Alicia who finally put a voice to their utterly terrifying vision.

"I'm not mad am I? That is who I think it is?"

Drake nodded, mouth dry.

"It's Robert Price." Kinimaka's knees were actually shaking. "The fucking US Secretary of Defense. I . . . I . . ."

Drake swallowed hard, caught in a gamut of emotions. It wasn't simply a horrendous shock, a terrible betrayal, an unthinkable scenario; not only did it pull the carpet from underneath every hardworking, patriotic agent and solider on the planet, but it also besmirched the memory of

Jonathan Gates. The old Secretary had been a good man, loyal to the core, a champion of his country and his friends, but his successor was now proving to be the complete opposite.

"We need to move," Dahl finally blustered. "They're heading over here."

The team suppressed their shock and got to work. The actual act of concealment wasn't hard—this was the jungle after all—it was the performance they required not to draw attention to themselves. Yorgi ended up facing Price as he strolled by, grinning everywhere as if he owned the place—and the rest stood around in a half-circle as if being berated. Price nodded to Yorgi as he sauntered past.

"Take no shit, lad. Take no shit."

Drake stiffened and felt Kinimaka do the same. Robert Price was drawling it up, no doubt enjoying his dangerous freedom, acting a mean part. The man should be as far out of his comfort zone as Colin Firth playing one of the world's most bad-ass assassins, but hey, he pulled it off.

Drake waited as the footsteps went away, loud on the mulch. At Yorgi's signal the entire group headed back to the bazaar's main street, quietly reeling from what they had seen. *Webb, Beau and now Robert Price!* Drake allowed the information to assimilate. This coupled with the appearance of the great and mysterious Ramses started to give him pause for thought.

Have we taken on more than we can chew this time?

"Yorgi," he said. "The tent. Now."

"I figure so."

They took a meandering route past the river, wanting to hop over there and confer with Hayden but unsure as to what protocols might be in play. Smyth still stood atop the deck though, a dependable sentry. Kinimaka walked slap-bang into a tree, so disturbed was he, and failed to notice the flailing arachnid that came crashing down and bounced off his broad back. Alicia let out a stifled gasp as the monster scrambled away.

"Shit, let's get this mission finished so I can get out of this place. My skin is crawling, my body itching. Even my toes are starting to curl."

They continued in silence, finally reaching the tent and stationing both Dahl and Alicia outside. Kinimaka found his phone and dialed Hayden.

"Hope to fuck you're sitting down," he breathed when she answered.

CHAPTER TWENTY ONE

Torsten Dahl listened in silence to the exchanges between Hayden Jaye and the rest of the ground team. SPEAR's leader was understandably upset and shocked to hear of the US Secretary of Defense so blatantly attending a terrorist arms bazaar but reminded the team that his bodyguards weren't CIA, and that they had yet to spot that element of the game. She told them they had to be on Price closer than the paparazzi at a Miley Cyrus photo-shoot. Dahl understood that the presence of Price trumped all else for now, but that still left several angles uncovered.

Webb. Beauregard. Ramses. Dahl wasn't exactly sure Robert Price was a bigger threat to the world than Ramses right now. But he knew where the heated conversation was going. There really was no alternative. As he listened he sat down, relaxing for a moment. For several months now he'd been feeling a little frazzled. Family time was not extensive enough and taking out one enemy was always going to lead to the emergence of another. It was a defeatist attitude, he knew, but it was more than time to take a short break.

A family holiday.

He dreamed a little now, taking himself away from the debate, cutting himself a small slice of heaven. Maybe the Caribbean, no pirates, no bloody terrorists. Just Johanna and the kids, the sapphire seas and a cool breeze.

Soon, he promised himself. *Very soon.*

The Swede shut away the guilt and the hurt, saving it for another hour, another day. It would still be there lingering like a knowing predator, waiting to strike. Johanna had removed herself from home once for him, uprooted the kids, and now they lived in Washington DC, still as lonely and even more isolated. The world would continue without Torsten Dahl fighting evil, but his marriage wouldn't survive much more.

Forcing it down, burying it deep, he shrugged on the armor required for the work day and faced Matt Drake.

"We ready?"

"Aye, lad. That we are."

"You do know they hate Yorkshiremen out here in the Amazon basin, don't you? They think you're all just a bunch of pie eaters."

"And I guess they love super-smooth Swedes, eh? The baby-soft bone structure don't get caught in a cannibal's teeth."

"Stereotypical ass."

"Local pub lunch."

Then Hayden's voice became louder. "Please tell those two asses to tone it down, will ya? This is one of the biggest threats to national security in recent years and has to be taken seriously. We need photographic, video, recorded evidence. Something. We have to know why he's there."

"Remember General Stone?" Kinimaka put in at that point. "Back in the Pandora event. He warned us about Price even then."

"I remember. " Hayden said. "And I took him seriously despite his many catastrophic failings. But Price has been clean and surprisingly helpful the last few months."

"Do we have a plan?" Kinimaka looked around.

Drake smiled. "Do you have to ask?"

Alicia raised a hand. "So long as it doesn't involve the woman seducing the hired help then I'm in."

"You've seen too many movies," Drake said. "Besides, isn't that your forte?"

"I've changed. No more free shags, eh?"

"What? You're gonna start charging?"

Alicia struck out, maddened by the Yorkshireman's persistence. Hayden again brought them under control.

"I feel like a friggin' teacher supervising a kindergarten. Now guys, get it done. You've already wasted enough time talking to me. Price is here for something and he could be doing that something even now. Find him, get close, and report back. That's all."

Dahl rose. "You heard her. Let's move."

The team rose, hard-faced and no doubt still reeling from shock. Dahl could only imagine what a US official might be here to accomplish and the reverberations made his blood run cold. They left Yorgi and Kinimaka inside the tent—Yorgi because he was the recognized leader of their infiltration team and might be conducting business and the Hawaiian because he was simply too big and detectible. Not to mention ex-CIA.

Dahl followed Drake and Alicia out into the jungle. The air was humid, steam rising toward the canopy and the blue skies. Men and women walked around in full attire, some dressed for the conditions, others choosing to suffer them. To be fair, Dahl knew, most of the tents offered air conditioning so it wasn't exactly challenging to the bazaar's clientele. The first area Drake led them to was the row of designer boutiques, where they all purchased sunglasses and hats. The adage "even a little helps" was not lost on Dahl. He donned a pair of Oakleys and crammed down a ridiculously priced Armani beanie before taking a quick glance at the others.

"Do I look as daft as you lot?" Drake asked first.

Dahl nodded. "Much worse."

"For once, I think you may be right."

Dahl had been in odd situations before, many of them, from his early army days to undercover ops, weeks of slow infiltration, to the time he commanded a Special Forces team of his own. Those days had been dangerous, wild and oddly simple. The complications and unease had set in not when he married Johanna, but when the children came.

Everything changed. He had been told as much, warned about it, but failed to fully understand the significance of being responsible for someone who couldn't take care of themselves until the whole thing landed on his lap. Literally. Since that moment, he'd struggled, developing a second persona to fight through the tough times. He followed Drake along the trail and then Alicia stopped, surreptitiously pointing to the right. There, at the side of a white pavilion, stood an entire gaggle of men, some suited, some dressed in the Arab garb, others clad in jeans and T-shirts and leather jackets, engaged in a very animated conversation. Alicia had spotted Price because of his two sunglasses-wearing bodyguards. He basked at the center of the group, loving the attention. Alicia drifted toward them and stayed around the fringes.

Dahl strained to hear anything. With everyone chatting, one man's words were lost beneath another's. Drake infiltrated the group from one side, patting shoulders, whilst Alicia hung back, sensing some kind of male gathering and not wanting to draw even a moment's attention. *That woman,* Dahl couldn't help but think. *Has really grown.*

He eased several bodies out of the way, slipping through purposefully but carefully. When he was six feet from the Secretary's side he dared go no further. The bodyguards were annoyingly vigilant. Instead, he turned to the nearest individual—a black T-shirt wearing twenty-something who looked like someone's son.

"Enjoying it?"

"Oh yeah!" the youth bellowed. "Did you get a look at the

bulletproof G? Whackadonk, man. Fucking whackadonk."

Dahl hadn't, but filed the consideration away for later perusal. What he really needed was for this kid to speak a little lower.

"So," he whispered. "Buy anything?"

The kid grinned and dropped his voice too. "Oh yeah, a fuckin' bevy. The first . . ."

Dahl tuned him out, nodding along, but listening in a completely different direction. There was an art to eavesdropping. It involved picking up on your target's tones, their timbre of voice, and focusing only on those qualities and pitches. It took a moment but he soon placed Robert Price's tenor on his radar.

"They're here." Price's words clicked into place.

Dahl immediately regretted not having eyes in the back of his head. *Who's here?*

Price again. "Stay as sharp as a bath of acid, boys. These assholes are the dregs of the world."

Dahl doubted the veracity of that statement, considering who spoke it, but stayed on point, hoping Drake and Alicia had spotted the arrivals.

"Where we going?" Price asked.

One of the bodyguards answered. "Gazebo number 8, sir. To your left."

"Gazebo? Is that a fancy word for a tent?"

"Yes, sir."

Dahl chanced a glimpse. Price was heading away, flanked by his men, brushing shoulders with a disguised Drake even as Dahl started to move. He made a show of staring at the skies and adjusting his glasses, then scanning the surroundings.

More black-suited men made a beeline for Price. *Ah,* Dahl thought. *The CIA have arrived.* Or a nasty little tributary at least.

What interested Dahl mostly was why Price would choose to meet with members of his own government here. Surely there were easier places? But a quick analysis of that thought offered several answers almost immediately—perhaps these guys were stationed here, or close by. The location was above top secret, offering absolute anonymity. Ramses' reputation was solid. And who knew what goodies they might have dropped in to buy?

Dahl drifted in as they passed a sign that read *Gazebo #7*, and then walked on as the guards arranged themselves around the next tent and Price walked inside. Drake was at Dahl's shoulder.

"You catch any of that?"

"Yeah. Nothing clear, but they're here to make a deal."

Alicia popped up beside Drake. "We have to hear that conversation. You know what Hayden would say—'ain't nothin' more important'. 'Safety of the nation', and all that." Alicia's American accent left much to be desired but this wasn't the time to comment. Dahl agreed with her.

"I can sneak around the back, through the jungle. You two should distract the guards."

Drake halted. "How the hell are we gonna do that? Those boys're ex-military for sure, not morris dancers."

"Talk to them." Dahl was already walking away.

"Yeah," he heard Alicia say. "Talk to them about boy stuff, y'know? That silly AC Cobra car thing, like the one I torched. Remember?"

"Remember? It haunts my bloody dreams."

"Well, there you go . . ."

Dahl moved out of earshot, ensuring his instinct was correct about being in a blind spot before creeping soundlessly among the trees. If his calculations were correct—and they were—then only one of Ramses' guards was placed between him and Price's tent, and he could skirt that obstacle with a three minute journey deeper into the jungle.

Silence surrounded him very quickly as he walked, the rainforest enforcing its will. Dahl watched for predators in all directions, the four points of the compass as well as straight down and straight up. The trees were quite dense at this point, making a soundless skulk almost impossible. He paused on seeing Ramses' guard, then inched by a small step at a time. It took ten minutes of hard, wet slog to reach the back of Price's tent and then another two to steal in close. Now was the significant moment, but he saw no reason why these tents, built purposely up against the dense forestry and marked private, would be singled out as special inside this nest of murderers, thieves and leaders.

Dahl crept low on his belly right up to the leading fabric at the back of the tent. It had been fastened to the earthy ground using pins at varying points and, as hoped, the material between the pins was loose. Dahl shuffled relentlessly closer and gently lifted a piece of fabric.

Again the voices were distorted. He couldn't make one from the other. Surveying the area one more time, ensuring there were no footprints anywhere close that might attest to a guard patrol, he rearranged his body so that it lay lengthways to the tent and scooped up even more material, a half inch at a time. Eventually, he could lie with one ear flat to the wet floor, eyes peering into the tent to establish some bearings.

Robert Price traipsed up and down the side of the tent whilst the three CIA agents lounged on comfy chairs facing him. Of course, the agents still wore sunglasses and Price was puffing on a cigar. Probably Cuban. Dahl waited for somebody to speak.

"This is the last bazaar," Price said finally. "You people need to get your heads around that. Unlimited offshore funds. Goodies that can't possibly be traced back to the United States or even the CIA. We're looking at an immense opportunity."

"I think most people wandering around here have unlimited funds. Sir." The agent deliberately paused before adding the title. "It's being selective that counts. We know the jobs we have planned and the items we will need."

"A little short-sighted don't you think?"

"Black bag is by its very nature fast, fluid, and impossible to predict," another agent said carefully. "Primary at the moment is the African deal."

"Yes, yes, destabilize the Congo and some other third-world cesspit, I know, I know. Who cares really? Nothing changes, eh? We fight and fight, we plot and plot, we work with them, we kill them, we help them, we destroy them, and it's all the same. Nobody wins except those who make the money. Well, it's our time to be winners. Do you agree?"

"Off the books?" an agent asked.

Price snorted. "Did you just fall off a banana boat, son? Black bag means 'off the books' as far as I'm concerned."

"There are always books," someone said. "Always."

"Not on my watch," Price said a little theatrically. "Not on *this* watch. Am I understood?"

"Sir," the most vocal of the three spoke up. "Considering where we are and what we're doing I think we should be perfectly frank here. Are we talking treason?"

Price didn't answer directly. "We will buy arms for our allies in Africa," he said. "And we will cause chaos there. And we will become rich. I don't see any government *not* currently employing that tactic in the third world, do you?"

"The chaos helps to fuel drug wars, inflates prices, causes wars and makes us money," another said. "Same as it always is."

"And stay out of the hot zone." Price let out a laugh. "I hear Ebola's bigger than Britney out there."

Guffaws ensued. Dahl clenched both fists until the knuckles hurt. It took all his training and composure to remain aloof. Price and the CIA splinter team were planning the worst kind of genocide and all for their own gain. He listened closely for a few moments more but then it started to shower and the sound of raindrops overpowered all other sound. Dahl crept away into the jungle and made his way carefully back to the bazaar.

Turmoil raged through his thoughts, tearing them apart.

By the time he met up with Drake and Alicia he was fuming. "One more snake in this nest of vipers." He spat. "One more poisonous mouth that needs closing forever."

Drake frowned. "Mate, I'm all for the reptilian metaphors, especially out here, but what exactly did you hear?"

"I'll explain. But now, it's even more essential we act fast. We can't let any of these power-mongers escape. Not one."

Drake blinked. "That's easier said than done."

"But it's the right thing to do," Dahl said. "And believe me, we're going to do it."

CHAPTER TWENTY TWO

They returned to their tent, and explained all that had happened to the entire team with help of the sat-phone. It was getting on for lunchtime now on the middle day of the last bazaar, and the morning's shower was descending in full force. Still, the security that surrounded them was first class and the attendance was high, which in itself provided many more capable enemies. Drake listened to the chatter, then nodded in approval as Kinimaka proposed a quick trip to buy some food.

"I'll go with you," Alicia said. "Get my shower for the day."

Drake attacked what they brought back with gusto. Sausages, bacon and beans went down well at any time of the day and in any corner of the world. He listened to Kinimaka rave for a while about the choices on offer before being brought back to reality by Hayden's tone.

"And where did Webb go?"

Drake ate slowly. "Haven't caught up with him again yet."

"Ramses?"

"Ditto."

"There are too many players," Dahl said. "What we need is to herd them all into one area."

"Ain't the bazaar an area?" Hayden drawled.

"Shit, not exactly. And it's crawling with hostiles. You should see this place, Hay." Kinimaka nibbled at a slice of bacon as he talked.

"Well, I see you guys're running out of time. People are already leaving. We can't follow all of them once they float or fly away so make a plan. And let's do this."

"She's right," Drake said. "Time is running out. We don't want to be choosing between the Crown Prince of Terror, the leader of the Pythians and the treacherous American official now, do we? We want all of them, trussed, boxed, bagged and tagged. It's time to make a play."

"All right," Alicia mumbled, her mouth full. "Soon as I've finished this bloody lovely bacon and brie sandwich I'll go save the world, but not a moment before."

The scene rasped on Drake as roughly as if a cheese-grater had been dragged down his skin. A diverse group of guests were gathered at the clearing where the caiman pit lay, and at their head, raised on a podium though he barely needed it, was Ramses. To Ramses' right was the man who appeared to be his bodyguard and to his left stood a prisoner.

Restrained by two burly men, the prisoner stared, terrified, in all directions. His eyes were wide, his nostrils flaring. Panic etched his face, carved into every furrow. Ramses—or more likely his slaves—had dressed the man in beachwear: brand new Speedos, sandals and a classic vest, all in bright pastel colors. His hair was brushed, his skin glowing. Among the crowd were those who watched in silence, those who laughed out loud and those who shuffled eagerly from foot to foot.

Drake looked across at Dahl. "This isn't gonna happen."

The Swede nodded, grim-faced. "The fight starts with this man. Right now."

Ramses' voice boomed over the heads of the crowd. "And here we are, my good friends! As promised, one of the highlights of the weekend—a live hunt! The prey shall be loosed in one minute, and then yourselves in five. The person who brings me his head wins a free toaster!"

Laughter broke out in the face of the prisoner's terror, but Ramses' voice cut through it all. "No, no." He turned and smiled at the prisoner. "Just a joke at your expense, I'm afraid. I think it would be fairer to offer a tank for your head. Yes, an Abrams tank, delivered anywhere, for this beach-bum's head. Oh, and remember, both Akatash and I will be joining the hunt."

Yorgi pulled himself upright as if in anticipation. The other four fixed their game faces. Drake counted eighteen other people in the huddle. This hunt was going to get intense, violent and bloody.

"Don't worry," Alicia whispered. "We ain't scrapped in the jungle for a while. This should be interesting."

"We still have to keep it low profile," Kinimaka said with worry in his face. "The three main targets are well divided."

Before anyone could answer, the individual dressed as a beach boy was let loose, kicked in the back and shown a game trail to escape on. The young man bolted like a rabbit, glad to be free and making the most of his four minutes head start. His sandals slipped on the mulch, but he caught the fall and plunged into the jungle.

Ramses smiled magnanimously as his audience chuckled. Akatash flexed his muscles. Dahl eyed the bodyguard dubiously. Men and women all around tightened clothing, cracked knuckles and readied weapons. The frantic sounds of the man fleeing soon died away and all that was left were the seeping trees, the sparkling midday sun and the almost tangible, rising humidity. Drake inched his way around the group and considered breaking away among the trees but guards watched over them all as if expecting such trouble. Even making their way carefully to the front of the pack put them under scrutiny.

Ramses held up one huge arm, showing off a rose gold Rolex. "Get ready."

The hunt was on.

CHAPTER TWENTY THREE

Drake charged into the rainforest with the pack, just to keep up appearances. As expected, most of the crowd rushed on, their bodyguards resigned to following when they most likely should have lead, but a half dozen held back, inspecting the trail. It wasn't hard to find footprints, but it was hard following the crowd and finding where the imprint of sandals veered away from the trail. Drake saw the distinction first and tried to hide it by muddying the impressions as he went, but it soon became clear that at least Akatash was following closely. The group fell silent as they went, partly to conserve energy and partly to help conceal their path. As the minutes passed all around became silent and they could have been the only people on the face of the world.

Drake found another imprint, this one so fresh it might only have just been made. Dahl's job was to scan the trees and look for any telltale signs; Kinimaka's job was to keep an eye on the pursuit. The path veered again and again, the prisoner perhaps trying to throw them off but more likely scared out of his wits. Drake saw movement ahead and crouched low, expecting the others to do the same.

Three Asians crossed their path; the primary guest and two bodyguards. This man was using his hired help, and they were tracking well. As Drake watched he saw a flash of pastel green ahead, the color though widespread, not natural in this place, and saw how close the Asians were.

"You see that?" he murmured.

Alicia placed a hand on his shoulder. "Yes."

Drake crept toward the three Asians, who were making

very little noise. As the moment neared when he could go no closer without alerting them to his presence he rose and laughed aloud, giving their leader a shock that registered clearly on his face. Both minders turned, weapons raised. Drake saw military knives in their hands and remembered this was a hunt, not a war.

Alicia walked right up to one of the guards. "How's it going? Find anything?"

Drake skirted her and neared the other. "Bloody hot day, what?" He affected the poshest accent he could manage, and not well. "The sodding mozzies are knackering my A-negative count, eh, eh?" He snorted out laughter.

The knives lowered and the SPEAR team launched their attack. Alicia struck at her opponent's throat and slammed his wrist. The knife fell and the man choked, but he remained in her face. He blocked her next attack, moving aside. His eyes watered. He brought a knee up to fend off her kick, found a tree and slipped around its wide trunk. Alicia followed, to be met with a swift kick to the face. Her nose bore the brunt, making her own eyes water and blood to start dripping down her face. Kinimaka then appeared on the Asian's other side, forcing him into a swift decision. Of course, Alicia anticipated the decision correctly. He came at her, fast and deadly, striking like a true denizen of the jungle.

Drake grappled with his opponent, bearing him to the forest floor. They fell as one, landing softly amid the forest floor's organic matter. The smaller Asian was fast and sprightly, squirming snake-like in Drake's grip and trying to shift his blade around. Drake gripped the wrist hard, but as the men rolled, their flesh and clothes became slippery and he found it increasingly hard to hold on.

Dahl approached the main guest and told the well-dressed man to fall to his knees. When a confused expression lit his features the Swede moved in closer, and that's when the Asian struck. Three blows, fast, hard and debilitating, connected with Dahl's head, chest and groin and sent him falling to his knees. The next was a knee to the side of the head, but Dahl resisted the temptation to collapse.

Tricky little . . .

He bore another breath-taking blow to the vest and grabbed the leg that apportioned it. Pulling hard he sent the man toppling backwards. When he hit the floor, head-first, the Swede scrambled atop him dispensing hammer blow after hammer blow. The first responses were strong, skillful, but Dahl would have none of it. His fists rained down like the deluges they had endured in this very forest, but bloodying and bruising and bordering on terminal.

Yorgi motioned at Kinimaka as the pastel green shirt broke cover. The Russian thief was off like a gazelle, fast on his feet, and the big Hawaiian plunged right after. Yorgi called to the man to slow down, but the line between too much shouting and not enough was ambiguous enough to be non-existent. Yorgi closed the gap, but not nearly fast enough.

Alicia backed away from her own dazzling opponent, barely seeing some of the strikes but far enough away so that they glanced off. The jungle slowed him down. Seeing his ankle snag between branches the Englishwoman plucked out a knife and stabbed. Her attack was deflected, blades clanging. Alicia thrust it harder on the backstroke, nicking her assailant's neck.

"Good to see you can bleed too," she muttered.

He launched himself at her. They fell back among the fallen branches, foliage surrounding them. She grabbed his arms and felt the muscles tense. He drove the blade at her. She deflected it so that its point sank into the ground, then used her legs to scramble onto his back. Bringing everything she had to bear she put pressure onto the back of his skull, forcing his face into the same earth and readying her own blade once more. The final thrust went between his ribs and through his heart and the struggle was abruptly over.

Twice now, Drake found his textbook grip spoiled by slippery skin. Luckily, it was the same for both men, and the Asian had lost his knife among the trees. As they parted once more Drake saw a new party following a trail to their right. Alerting them to the struggle could end everything. He punched his opponent in the teeth, receiving split knuckles for his trouble, and then fell upon him. Yorgi and Kinimaka were long gone. Drake rolled as his opponent grabbed hold of his thick vest and pulled. The fist that then came at him missed as he turned his head, instead striking a tree. Drake slammed the palm of his hand into the man's mouth to stifle the scream. Stunned, the Asian blinked twice.

And that ended it all. Drake finished it quick and then rolled off.

Dahl trotted to his side. "Took your time. Playing doctors were you?"

"Make sure you tie them up, and gag them."

"No need." Dahl shrugged.

Alicia crouched beside them. "Same here. My guy's already spider food."

"Give me a sec." Drake used nearby twine to secure his unconscious opponent and then fashioned a gag. "If the animals don't get him," he said, "we'll send someone when this is over."

They bounded away, following the path taken by Yorgi through impossibly overhanging trees and a huddle of jagged rocks down which a waterfall rushed. The stream at its base gurgled happily. Another few meandering jungle bends and they saw the pastel green easily through the vegetation. Then they saw Yorgi and Kinimaka.

Half a dozen men stood facing them in a semi-circle with guns drawn and faces inwardly lit at the prospect of committing murder.

"Last chance," one of them shouted. "Give us the prey or you die too."

"Look guys," Kinimaka rumbled. "It's a fair hunt. We found him first. Come on."

"So give us his head." One of the men laughed. "You keep the rest."

Yorgi stood in front of the prisoner. "He is ours."

"Have it your way."

Drake gasped as the six men opened fire.

CHAPTER TWENTY FOUR

Bullets ripped into the ground at Kinimaka's feet as Drake leapt forward. Yorgi danced away, his own shoes also being used as target practice. Dahl and Alicia circled the six men, weapons leveled. The prisoner in the pastel colored T-shirt quivered in fear, pressed up against a withered tree.

"Cool it," Drake said. "Or you all die."

Three gun barrels rotated in different directions, giving Kinimaka chance to draw his own gun. Drake breathed almost silently as a sudden tension fell over the clearing, each man eyeing his enemy in the Amazon-Mexican standoff. Even the breeze dropped and the only sound was the quiet ooze of the forest.

Ramses stepped into view. "Well!" His voice boomed so loud every eye swiveled except those of the SPEAR team.

"It seems we have a problem." The prince chuckled. "I see no winner here and I really don't want to see guests shedding each other's blood. Put your weapons down, my friends, the prey is going nowhere."

Drake saw Akatash sidling up behind the prisoner. *Never even saw the asshole coming.*

Weapons were lowered; Ramses was respected in the wild as much as in his element, even outgunned. The Crown Prince of Terror nodded with satisfaction.

"Good. Good. So what say we let the quarry loose again? After all, the game is unfinished, yes?"

A flick of his head and Akatash jabbed at the prisoner's spine. When he flinched, rooted to the spot, Akatash persuaded him some more, then drew a wicked, blood-encrusted machete. Even Dahl's eyes widened slightly at the size of the thing, which had to be three feet long. Ramses smiled as his future victim departed.

"The hunt resumes. Shall we give him, oh, sixty seconds? And dear guests, please know that committing murder at my last bazaar comes with the punishment of death by machete."

Alicia motioned at the still-twitching underbrush. "Then why are we chasing this guy?"

"Of course, I should have specified Ramses' law only protects human beings. Animals, they're fair game."

The countdown commenced and Drake made a point of moving away from the six-man pack. Ramses and Akatash watched, easy in their surroundings and confident with their expertise. Drake rendezvoused with his team and leaned in for a quick confab.

"Any ideas?"

"Distraction," Dahl said. "Melee. You guys cause it and I'll grab the kid."

"And where will you stash him?" Alicia scowled.

"There is only one place," the Swede said. "Back at the boat."

Drake exhaled. "You might be mad, mate, but even I don't think you're crazy. You'd never make it."

Dahl tightened his grip on his rifle. "As a team we wouldn't make it, but two men might."

"Ready?" Ramses called out.

The team straightened and rolled out stiffening muscles.

"Go!" Ramses and Akatash turned and sprinted. Drake raced after them, leading his team down a parallel game trail. The track was narrow, the ruts and channels perilous, winding to and fro, but Ramses had the same problem. Drake assumed Akatash, ranging a dozen steps ahead, was tracking the boy.

He nudged Alicia as she panted behind his right shoulder. "You're the distraction."

A shake of the tied blond locks. "And nothing really changes."

She sped up, taking the lead, and employed skill and risk to close the gap between herself and Ramses' bodyguard. It took a moment for the man to notice her, so intent was he on following their quarry's trail, but when he did she immediately saw the deep light of cunning in his eyes.

" 'ow's it hanging?" she asked as she ran. "The machete, I mean."

Akatash ignored her. Alicia took in his frame, his physique and posture. "Work out, do we?"

The trails parted for a moment, looping apart before coming back together. Alicia heard footsteps at her back and knew the team were close.

"Seriously though. If you get a few spare minutes later I could teach you how to put that body to much better use."

Akatash swung his head around, slowing. Alicia knew this approach could have gone one of two ways—and still might. But all was well as her team and Ramses crashed past.

"I do not have time for games," Akatash said in a thin voice, an accent she couldn't place. "This is your warning. Do not push me, married woman."

Alicia held out both hands as she slowed even more, making Akatash slow right along with her. "Hey, people have fought over this body."

"But I am a man of the strangest tastes and, I fear, not even a whore like yourself could survive my attentions."

Akatash ran off as Alicia sputtered and searched for a reply. A small part of her held back though. She had seen that feral light, the presence of something broken and vicious, an inner fury that could never be sated. She had seen it and wanted no part of it.

Allowing the bodyguard to leap away she followed carefully, hoping she had gained the team enough of a lead.

*

Drake recognized Alicia's ploy and led the entire team, barring Dahl, slightly away from the trail their prey was leaving. His plan was based on Ramses' inability to track, his reliance on Akatash, and it bore fruit. Ramses joined them on their trail, smiling broadly, an inharmonious giant in the rainforest.

Drake ducked a low bough, skirted a fallen tree and then leaned over as he sprinted around a long bend; water, mulch and tree sap dogging his every step. Twice, his boots slipped but he caught the slide. Once, he heard a booming gunshot echo through the jungle. Another half minute and he caught sight of the six-man team crossing their path, arrow-straight and unfortunately heading in the right direction. He made a show of pointing out their "mistake", and received more than a few puzzled looks and comments for his troubles.

"Guy's lost it. Trail's clearly this way."

"Idiot's lost it. Ignore them."

"Hey, what if they know something we don't? Ramses is with them."

Drake was passed by that time and still following the rough track. Outwardly he had shown no signs of concern for Dahl's plan, but inwardly something acidic burned his stomach.

Dahl bounded after the man dressed in pastel, knowing that the hounds of hell would soon be snapping at his heels. Before long he was reminded that the combatants they had thus far seen weren't the only ones vested in this chase as he came alongside two Americans arguing about which way to go. Both sported double-barrel shotguns bored out for the sport of it all. When Dahl passed they followed and he let out a silent curse.

No helping it. I'm too close to the victim to lead them astray.

He slowed, whirled and threw a hammer blow into the face of the first. The man fell, poleaxed, as if he'd sprinted headlong into a stationary elephant. The second slowed more quickly, brought his double-barrels down and fired without thought.

Dahl was already moving, anticipating it. The heavy shot slammed into the fork of a tree, sending twigs, branches and foliage scattering in all directions. Dahl bent low and came up like a charging beast, ramming the American at mid-chest level and lifting him off his feet. There was a gasp of pain, a painful smashing together of teeth and the shotgun arced away. Dahl plowed on, keeping the advantage and driving his opponent into the nearest tree. Staggered, smashed from two sides, the hunter wavered in place for a moment. Dahl finished the job with a pounding to the ears.

Without pause he raced off again, picking up the quarry's trail and closing the gap. Quiet as a snake gliding on ice he approached the man's blind side and then stopped him by scooping him up in a bear hug.

Screams ensued. Dahl clamped a large hand over the man's mouth and met his eyes. "Quiet," he breathed. "I'm here to save you not hurt you."

Confusion and disbelief followed, but Dahl let go, holstered his gun and took a breath. "Come with me," he said. "I'll take you to safety."

More crashing resounded from the undergrowth and Dahl saw the six-man team approaching through a nebulous pattern of trees. His face urged Ramses' prey to action.

"Okay, help me. Please."

Dahl herded him into dense jungle, squeezing through

branches for almost a minute before finding another trail and pausing to reset his bearings. He remembered the small stream from earlier and, for the first time, wished for a heavy downpour. Of course, when required nothing happened so the Swede set to a more reliable means of escape. Treading lightly they both crept among towering trees, avoiding all paths until the Swede's sense of direction brought them back to the stream. Stepping straight up to their knees in it they increased the pace, now following the rushing water toward the big river.

Dahl stopped as the high banks came into view.

"Now we swim," he said. "And hope anything with teeth, suckers or abilities to swim up a urethra are fast asleep. You ready?"

"To be honest I'm ready to drop."

"Never give in," Dahl said. "Or admit defeat. Hold out, my friend. Hold out until your very last breath."

Drake stumbled at the head of the pack, seeing the sloping banks of the river ahead and hoping to gain the Swede a few more precious moment of time. They were downriver from where he would be, but still dangerously close. Alicia and Akatash had caught up to them a moment ago and they had also managed to incorporate the six-man team. One look back at Ramses' dour face and Drake knew the Arab was starting to regret this imperfectly organized hunt.

He caught himself by placing a hand to the ground, ran up the slight incline and then came to a sudden, abrupt halt at a gap in the overgrowth that bedecked the muddy bank.

"Oh shit. No!"

He turned fast but Alicia, in her eagerness, was trying to catch up with him and couldn't stop herself. Next came Kinimaka, never one to avoid a mishap; his solid impact sent the three of them tumbling down the slope, right into a writhing mass of black caimans.

Drake heard shouts from above, saw two members of the following six-man team also rolling down the bank and Ramses standing watching with interest, and then his world was a splashing, seething mass of scales and teeth. He needed purchase, and to help save both Alicia and Kinimaka. His fingers scraped across hard scales. Water splashed into his eyes as his sunglasses dislodged, dark and fetid, and he spat leaves from his mouth. The river's sloping side gave purchase to his feet and he rolled. A dragon-like tail flashed across his vision. A caiman lay immediately to his left, terrible eyes unblinking, making no movement as limbs flailed all around it. Maybe it was wondering who the hell ordered such noisy takeout, but its brethren were another matter. Drake's vision filled with teeth as a caiman squirmed up the bank toward him, teeth bared and already mere inches from his feet. Again he rolled, slamming into one of the strangers, grabbing his vest and using sheer adrenalin to hurl him in the direction of the approaching beast.

"Oh, ha, ha, ha!" boomed Ramses' voice. "Look at it chasing down that bone!"

Drake felt revulsion at himself and at the terrorist, but that feeling soon passed as the second of the strangers confronted him. An elbow, its impact lessened by a heavy jacket, smashed into his cheek, sending him onto his back.

Alicia scrambled across them both, the encrusted nose of a predator at her heels, its mouth closing fast close enough to make her squeal. The caiman turned its attention to an easier prey—Drake and his opponent. Drake saw it first and struggled up the bank using his elbows to get purchase. The caiman brushed up against the other man with its heavy snout, sending droplets of water flying. If that wasn't enough, Mano Kinimaka then came into view, standing upright, bellowing and holding a caiman close to his chest, its belly exposed and its vicious mouth snapping at the Hawaiian's face.

"Now *this* is what I call a little friend!" he roared.

Drake focused on his own caiman, but then saw yet another sliding over this one's body as the two marauders battled for the right to kill. This new threat clamped down viciously onto the stranger's exposed leg, inducing a terrifying, bloodcurdling scream.

A gunshot rang out. Yorgi stood halfway down the bank, Glock clutched unsteadily in one hand. The slug came closer to Drake than his attackers and sent Ramses into almost uncontrollable guffaws. Drake gasped then as Kinimaka body-slammed his own caiman right down on top of the other two, shocking all three beasts who had never known such impudence.

As one, they writhed. Drake saw a chance.

Kicking the stranger in the face he crawled backwards and then twisted around as he managed to grab a thick branch. Alicia slogged beside him, and Kinimaka leapt over the mass of bodies. Drake never took his eyes from the scene below so wasn't entirely surprised to see the stranger they'd left draw a pistol of his own.

What did surprise him was that it was deliberately pointed straight at him.

"Are you joking? Your friends aren't about to save you, asshole."

The gun wavered. The caiman bit deeper and started to move, trying to drag its victim into the water. One of the other nightmarish monsters clambered across the man in an effort to latch onto his upper torso. Drake's gaze never wavered.

Sharing in the terror of the man with the gun. *That bullet is your only escape.*

Drake gained the top of the bank, helping Alicia with one

hand. Kinimaka stumbled past them, dripping and covered in rotted vegetation. Now, the lowest of their number was Yorgi, who still held the Glock sighted below.

"Sir," Drake had no clue how Kinimaka managed to stay in character but was glad he managed it. "He's not worth saving. He tried to kill us."

"They're *all* worth—" Yorgi began, and then stopped and turned his head, staring with dread at Ramses. The stare then turned to cold stone and a shrug as he reverted to character. "Maybe you're right. Really, I don't care."

Ramses eyed him closely. "And that's the first time I've seen the superior risking himself to save the subordinates," he said. "Why would you do that?"

The Russian shrugged indifferently. "They are my guard," he said shortly. "And for my wife. The answer is obvious."

"Maybe," Ramses mused aloud. "Maybe."

A gunshot interrupted them. Drake winced as the man caught below chose to blow his own head off. The caimans squirmed and twisted, smelling blood and tearing at flesh. Drake winced again and turned away.

"Shall we go?"

"In a moment," Ramses insisted. "I want to see this."

"Your beachcomber will escape. Don't you want to . . . catch him?"

"I think he is gone and the jungle will take care of him. Or maybe one of the others had better luck? Your missing friend perhaps?"

Drake screened his reaction. He was hoping they wouldn't notice the missing Swede. Yorgi shrugged and said nothing.

Finally Ramses turned away from the grisly scene. "Well, what a pleasant diversion. Shall we return to the bazaar and the delights I have planned for this evening?"

CHAPTER TWENTY FIVE

A half hour later and they were free of Ramses, alone in their tent and fishing around hastily for replacement clothes. It took them a while to remember where they were and what type of stalls were scattered all around.

"We're dumbasses." Kinimaka hung his head.

"Not really," Alicia said. "We're just not used to shopping at designer boutiques inside a war zone."

At that moment the tent flap opened and Dahl stepped through. He took one look at the state of their clothes and then shook his head.

"Couldn't manage without me, huh?"

Drake apprised him of all the details, bemused at the Swede's reaction and knowing he shouldn't be.

"Caimans!" Dahl shouted. "You fought caimans and I missed it?" He sounded truly crushed. "Hell, Mano and I could have started a new sport. Caiman tossing."

Alicia looked up. "Any way you view that comment—it's dangerous."

Dahl scowled. "Best part of the bloody mission, and I'm babysitting a surfer."

Drake then mentioned how their chase had finally ended. Dahl winced and quickly sobered. "This Ramses then, and Akatash—they're the real deal? Cunning as car salesmen, crooked as Wall Street and crazier than your resident Swedish pin-up boy?"

"Not that I'd agree with some of that," Drake said. "But yes."

"Then who's the priority?"

"What did Hayden say?"

"Shit, I barely spoke to them. I wanted to get back. Hayden's chomping at the bit, wants in on the fight. Lauren's tired of guarding our tame terrorists and Smyth's, well . . . grumpy."

"Can we pause this?" Alicia complained. "We really need to change these underclothes. I'm heading to the shops."

Drake hung his head. "I really don't like this new you."

"Just sit on yer damn man bench and complain. I'll grab you a nice tight pair of undies."

In the end they all shopped and were back at the tent within ten minutes, stripping down and changing with professionalism and maturity, all of them knowing there was a time for ribaldry and a time for gravity.

"Plan?" Kinimaka said when they were finished.

"Pinpoint the main players," Drake said. "Follow them and keep tabs. When we have all three in our sights we end this corrupt jumble sale."

Outside, the post-lunch shower had just arrived, mercifully light and brief this time. Still, the humidity rose fast and the ground steamed in protest as Drake and his colleagues set forth with their eyes peeled and intentions clear-cut. Past the boutiques and the slavers' tent, the private viewing areas and the caiman pit they walked. Groups wandered to and fro, some silent, others laughing or joking drunkenly. Sellers hawked their wares. Drake scanned every nook and cranny. At his side, Alicia pretended tiredness as she peered intently into all the bazaar's darker places. The leafy canopy waved overhead, spangled with sunlight. Drake was momentarily distracted as a woman dressed like a princess walked by, head and shoulders held regally and gown wrapped around her svelte body in such a complex fashion she might never escape its many folds. The Yorkshireman shook his head sadly. These people were about as out of touch as a London-based politician. The incredulity level rose even more when another princess strode by, her three-foot train held aloft by two servant girls. Drake looked at Alicia and found her, for once, at a loss for words.

"Amazing," he said. "Even my favorite gobshite is dumbstruck."

But Alicia hadn't even seen the princesses. "As endearing as that statement is—alluding to my penchant for adverse commentary—I have to say that I am truly flabbergasted and don't know what the hell to do."

Drake followed her gaze. "What is it? Who's that?"

"Oh fuck. What is *she* doing here? Guys, stop. This is big trouble. See that woman over there? Her name is Kenzie and she's an artifact and arms smuggler. I came up against her recently during the crusader gold jaunt, and she almost killed us all."

Drake stared. Dahl stared. Nobody had heard such respect in Alicia's voice before.

"When you talk about me," the Swede said, "to others. Do you feel a similar reverence?"

"Shut yer mouth, bitch boy. Listen, Kenzie is an extremist. Lost her family to government mismanagement and went rogue. Turned on them. Now she's as hard and ruthless as they come."

"Looks can be mightily deceiving then." Dahl measured her.

"She wields a katana."

"Fuuuuuuck." If the men's tongues could have bounced off the forest floor that was the moment. Drake tried to reel his back in. "So . . . um, I mean what's your plan? Mark her as another target when we have three already? Is she that dangerous?"

"I wouldn't know whether to kiss her or kill her," Alicia said. "Maybe I'd do both."

"Just to distract her, right?" Drake wondered.

"Decision is out of our hands now," Alicia breathed. "She just saw me."

Drake reached for his guns.

CHAPTER TWENTY SIX

Birdcall echoed across the clearing. Groups of men huddled and emitted a muted chorus of whispering. Heavy animal movements crashed through the rainforest.

Drake scrutinized Kenzie and her seven bodyguards, wondering who was the most lethal. For their part the other team appeared just as surprised to hear what Kenzie had to say. The artifact smuggler turned a frosty glare on Alicia to convey what was about to happen.

"Move!" Dahl snapped. "We don't yet have eyes on our three principals. The bazaar must stay in play, for now."

Knowing he was right, Drake made a run straight at Kenzie as the others fanned out around him. They gambled that Kenzie would choose not to draw attention and might yet have business to finalize. The woman tested them, waiting as long as she dared before whirling and melting into the compact jungle. Alicia crashed in seconds later, as headlong as a deer running for its life. Drake had no time to check who noticed their aggressive departure, but hoped everyone would remain as aloof as they had been to proceedings all along. The chase was on; Kenzie's men didn't defend their rear this close to the bazaar which told Drake all he needed to know. The woman was here on business and couldn't risk shutting this thing down.

The mass of the jungle enveloped them almost immediately as they plowed deeper in. Dahl and Alicia ran alongside as best they could with Kinimaka and Yorgi bringing up the rear, the Russian thief hampered by his fancy clothes. Drake tried to recall the last time he'd seen Alicia spooked, and couldn't. Maybe it had something to do with this change she was undergoing.

Maybe not. Just trust her.

Of course he did. Drake shook the misgivings from his mind. His closest quarry was only two or three meters away but might as well have been a hundred due to the thick undergrowth and necessity to not use a gun. Kenzie blazed a new trail somewhere ahead, following a route only she knew.

Drake thrust branches aside and leapt across clusters of fallen branches, vaulted ankle-hungry ditches and squeezed between boughs. The trailing mercenary then turned and risked a glance, saw Dahl only a meter from his heels and withdrew a knife. Drawing a hand back to throw he stumbled into an unseen channel and crashed among the fallen vegetation. A scream was muffled by the jungle. Dahl fell on him with gusto, pent up from all the sneaking around and necessities to make nice to evil men. Drake forged further ahead, closing in on the next merc.

The man sensed him, withdrew a gun whilst facing the front and then whirled quickly with it clasped in one hand. The shot blasted past Drake's shoulder, thudding into a tree branch. Drake jumped onto a tangle of brush and used its spring to launch himself at the other man. The impact sent the gun flying and another shot zinging upward at the canopy. Drake throat-punched his man and took an elbow to the eye. Grunting, he flinched away but still managed to throw an extra-debilitating set of knuckles to his opponent's own eye socket. With the man clutching at his head, Drake finished him off.

"Hurry up, for fuck's sake," Alicia growled from up ahead. "Bitch is getting away."

Drake chased her further into the thick mass just as it began to thin out. Ahead he spied a clearing, a stream running through the middle and a set of dark huddled shapes. Alicia quickly flung herself headlong as Kenzie and her boys whirled and unleashed lead.

Drake hugged a tree. Dahl crouched at its base, prepping his handgun as splinters whizzed by his head. After a moment he glanced up at Drake. "Ready?"

"Just waiting for you."

Dahl returned fire, sending the mercs scrambling for cover. Drake took a moment to survey the clearing, seeing now that the set of dark shapes were long thatched huts with ragged holes for doors and no windows. Drab gray in color they appeared run down, overgrown and abandoned. Kenzie, it seemed, had known about them.

Drake called loud enough for his team to hear. "Move in carefully. She may have some kind of a stash here."

Dahl and Alicia laid a little covering fire as the team maneuvered to a more advantageous position. As he moved to the far side of the huts, Drake began to see a much larger picture. What had appeared to be a small clearing was actually a larger encampment. Two separate rutted tracks led away into the jungle with two old Jeeps and a rusted, multi-colored bus to one side. A more modern, timber-built building stood with its back to the high trees. Drake even saw a bright yellow prop plane at the far side of the clearing, though how it had arrived was a mystery. The trail was just too narrow. As they watched, Kenzie and her men broke across the large encampment, skirted a small lake and made for the building. Drake and Alicia picked off one man between them and the others scattered.

"Move!"

Dahl and Kinimaka crab-walked to the side of the hut, flattening their bodies to the leafy wall. The team closed in fast before their enemies could establish valuable positions, harassing them all the way. Drake ducked two bullets, realized his luck wouldn't last much longer, and jumped headlong into one of the Jeeps. More bullets clanged off the hood and one ricocheted around the interior. Alicia was crouched at the rear and now crawled into the open bed.

"Let's go!"

"I can't . . ." Drake clammed up as he raised his head and spied the keys dangling in the ignition. So this had been Kenzie's way in and way out—an old meth station probably that she'd commandeered for the day. He turned the key, cranking the engine as Dahl and Kinimaka ducked around the back. The windshield exploded in a hail of glass. Drake squirmed into the footwell, depressed the gas pedal and aimed the Jeep in as straight a direction as he could manage without lifting his head above the steering wheel. Lead zipped and popped off the paintwork as the vehicle closed in on the mercs. Alicia groaned as she unbalanced in the back, slamming her shoulders against the rear window which exploded into jagged splinters.

A moment later Drake saw the edge of a roof block out the green leafery.

"Brace!"

The Jeep smashed into the wooden structure, luck sending it against a load-bearing support. When the thick member splintered, the entire construction creaked and the guns suddenly went quiet.

Drake slipped backwards out of the car. The vision ahead was utter chaos. The roof came down fast, the walls buckling as three men disseminated as fast as their legs could go. A jagged portion of roof sliced down on top of one, the blood fountain causing Drake to avert his eyes. The other two stumbled into the roadway, one tripping over the deep ruts. Then, the edge of the roof smashed onto the Jeep and Drake was struck. Throwing up a hand he warded off the lighter chunks but a heavier piece sent him to his knees.

Alicia pulled him aside. "Legs," she said. "Put there for a reason."

Drake wrenched his body upright. Ahead, Dahl and Kinimaka were already pursuing the two fleeing mercs. Beyond that, Kenzie and one other man were attempting to climb aboard the second Jeep. Drake stopped, raised his gun and sighted on the tires.

One burst should do it . . .

The fourth or fifth bullet destroyed one of the tires and then Drake was changing mags.

Kenzie shouted out, enraged. Drake saw a glimpse of her character as she lashed out at the man at her side, sending him out of the Jeep and backwards into the dirt. Then the woman was jumping out herself, and Drake saw the gun held at her side and the sword strapped to her back. Dahl pounded one escaping merc as Kinimaka dealt with another, then both men ran hard at Kenzie. Drake followed, eyes wary and Alicia approached from the far side. Kenzie didn't wait around to chat, running for the broken-down bus. Drake adjusted his course and then paused as Dahl took his breath away.

What the . . .

One minute the Swede was loping after the last remaining merc, the next his body was flailing in the air with a rope looped around his ankle. Dahl swung head-down in a wide arc, shouting and cursing his bad luck.

Drake followed the rope to its source, an overhanging tree branch. In many ways he wished he could leave his friend swinging there . . . dangling . . . at least for twenty minutes or so, but the Swede would make easy target practice for their enemies.

Kinimaka lifted Dahl as Alicia unlooped the rope. Kenzie jumped into the bus. The last merc took aim but Drake was faster, knocking him off his feet with three to the chest and one to the middle of the forehead.

To his credit, Dahl hit the ground running, having kept a

bead on Kenzie the whole time. Drake struggled to catch up to him, an entire book of wisecracks desperately hovering on the tip of his tongue.

"Hold up, Kenzie," Alicia called out. "You're on your own."

"Yeah," came a reply. "Just how I like it, bitch."

Drake reflected that these two were probably not compatible as they all neared the bus. It took him a second to realize something else.

"Back!" he cried. "Get back now!"

No way would this woman, whom Alicia respected, corner herself this way. And if there was one trap . . .

The team reacted to his instruction, stopping and then diving for nearby trees. Drake hauled at Alicia's jacket and thrust her down as she chanced one last glance toward their prey.

The bus shuddered and jigged in a set of mini-explosions, nothing major. More like a string of small charges, timed to burst as Kenzie's pursuers ran down the length of the bus. *Shit, this woman's deadly.*

Alicia took off immediately, snubbing the explosions and flying glass and metal in her attempt to chase Kenzie down. Drake saw a figure leap from the front of the bus followed by legs pumping into the undergrowth, Alicia in hot pursuit.

The bus split in half, both sides sliding away from each other with tortured shrieks of metal. One of the halves smashed to the thick earth with a massive soil and leaf displacement, filling the air with a cloud of vegetation.

Another minute of running and a mound of huge, black round edged rocks formed the start of a steep hillside. Kenzie was already two levels up and now turned, rifle in hand. Everyone dove left and right, rolling for cover.

"Not alive," Drake heard the woman's words forced out

through intense stress. "Never alive."

He understood a moment later it wasn't true. Bullets slammed all around. If Kenzie really wanted to die she could take her own life. The Amazon offered many ways. He peered around a green cluster to see Alicia making her way up the side of the boulder mass, unseen by Kenzie.

One chance.

He fired, keeping Kenzie's attention riveted firmly below.

Alicia slipped between rocks, fleet of foot and as fast as a cat. Soon, she had reached a higher elevation than Kenzie and signaled to the rest of the team.

Drake took point. "Give up now!" he shouted. "And we'll take you back alive."

Kenzie emptied a mag in answer.

Dahl fired back, then shouted. "Look above. You're covered. You're finished."

Kenzie growled, locking eyes with Alicia, then appearing to quickly decide that the rest of the team at least wouldn't fire on her. She leapt off the rock, hit the jungle floor and rolled, coming up several feet from Dahl's position and snarling.

"You want me? Take me down, if you can."

Dahl deflected blows as he retreated. Kenzie kicked at his midriff, sending him over a log. Drake leapt in from one side, and Kinimaka from another. Suddenly Kenzie was reaching to her back and then the katana was in her hands, swinging left to right and glinting like the murderous eyes of a madman. All eyes swiveled as Alicia skidded to a stop only yards away.

"Don't . . ." she began.

Then Kenzie whirled the blade left and right, her movements an orchestrated dance as her arms swayed and her body rolled. Drake evaded fast but still saw a rip appear in his sleeve and a line of blood open up across the top of his arm. Kinimaka saw his Glock whirl through the air, knocked form his hand. Terrified, the Hawaiian wasted a valuable moment checking that his hand was still attached to his wrist, and then Kenzie's blade pushed at his throat.

"Walk away," she hissed. "Or he dies."

Alicia pressed the barrel of her gun against the back of Kenzie's neck. "Drop the sword," she said. "Or lose the head."

Drake rose slowly. Dahl emerged from the undergrowth, covered in mulch. The Yorkshireman unleashed the first of many. "Not having your best day, are you pal?"

Dahl merely growled and then brushed himself down. "She's not going to kill anyone. She wants to live."

Kenzie's mouth became a thin, hard line. Kinimaka's eyes betrayed just how close to puncturing his neck she was.

Drake didn't move. "If you shoot her right in the head she should be brain dead before she could force the point of that blade home."

Alicia sidestepped so that Kinimaka was out of her line of fire. "Close your eyes, Mano. Oh, and your mouth. Don't wanna be swallowing anything too nasty."

Kenzie tensed. "You are really calling my bluff? Damn."

The katana swung away from the Hawaiian, arcing around as Kenzie spun and aimed at Alicia's midriff. It flashed by with a millimeter of clearance as Alicia, alert and wily as ever, stepped beyond range. Drake watched in frustration as the point returned to Mano's throat.

"Mate," he said. "That was your chance to move."

"I realize that now." Kinimaka nodded then winced as the steel cut a little deeper.

Dahl stepped forward and tried his luck. "Can we talk about this?"

"Yeah," Drake said. "He'd like to see your swing again. For that matter I'd like to see it again too. Maybe take a few photos."

Kenzie blinked a little despairingly. "Shit, if you were both my men I'd have shot you by now."

Alicia couldn't hide a grin. "The gun is pointed at your head. Otherwise . . ."

Now the woman dropped her eyes. "They work for you?"

"They do as they're told," Alicia said with a straight face. "When they're told to."

Kenzie eyed Dahl. "I bet."

"We can talk more about that," Alicia said. "When you put the bloody katana down."

"And my terms of surrender?"

Dahl took that one. "You live. You stick with us until we can safely remove you from the bazaar. You play along."

Drake didn't like it, but saw the Swede's reasoning. The bazaar was entering its final stages. They couldn't risk not capturing their primary targets by hauling Kenzie to the boat. Like it or not this was their very last chance.

Kenzie appeared to weigh her options. "I choose to fight then. I have nothing to lose."

"You're looking to die?" Alicia snarled. "Then put the blade down and let me shoot you in the head."

A heavy stillness descended, a blanket that spread the entire scale of the human conscience. Alicia looked ready to commit murder whereas Dahl held both hands out in a placating manner. Kenzie simply walked her body around whilst holding the blade tip in place to stare Alicia right in the eyes.

"You're gonna shoot me right here? Then do it. Leave no enemies at your back, eh?"

Alicia stared. "You said it."

She fired.

CHAPTER TWENTY SEVEN

Kenzie, battle-hardened, jaded, cynical and dangerous as she was, flinched when the gun went off. She recoiled even further when the bullet, traveling at 2500 feet per second, flashed across the side of her skull, leaving a blood trail in its wake. Kinimaka turned as Kenzie dropped the sword in shock and then stared, open-mouthed, at Alicia, nothing but a mixture of hatred and respect in her eyes.

"Fucking bitch. I'll pay you back for that one day."

Alicia shrugged. "But not today. Makes you look more appealing anyway."

"It does?"

"A bit of character does a lot for a stupid face."

Dahl moved in, but this time Kinimaka retained his wits and was already scooping up the long, single-edged sword. The Swede's eyes were a little crazy as he took the shoulder-holster from Kenzie and then motioned toward Kinimaka.

"I'll take the sword."

Drake sighed. "Shit, you're crazier than she is."

Kenzie flicked a glance at them. "He is? I knew we shared something. Or perhaps we will do later."

Drake laughed. "Now, don't hurt my feelings, love. I guess you like 'em dumb, huh?"

Alicia glowered.

Kenzie almost smiled. "As a matter of fact, I do."

Of course, Dahl hadn't heard the conversation, so enamored was he of his new weapon. He made a show of sheathing the sword and then re-joined planet earth. "So? What's next?"

"Back to camp." Kinimaka rubbed his throat a little

daintily. "It's getting dark and the revels will have started already. Hayden will be hopping up and down."

Drake eyed the jungle. "Let's make it quick and cautious. I don't think Ramses' guards will venture so far away from camp, but they just might."

"Unlikely," Kenzie put in. "This area of the Amazon is a hive for the drug and gun running cartels. That's why I chose the abandoned base. Honestly, it's almost expected that there will be trouble around here."

Alicia prodded her with the gun. "Honestly? From you? I think you need to take the soap outta your dirty mouth and start again."

"Like I said—you'll get yours."

"Oh, I hope so."

Drake made a point of taking charge of Kenzie, separating the two women. They vacated the boulder mound area and made their way back to Kenzie's camp, where the bus still shouldered and tearing metal emitted screeching sounds. Past that, they returned to the vicinity of the bazaar and the place they had first entered the jungle.

Drake whispered in Kenzie's ear. "Just so you know—we'd rather not do it right now but we intend to raze this place to the ground. Respect us and you live. Reveal us, and you'll be the first to die. Are we clear?"

"As moonshine," Kenzie muttered.

Drake thought that was probably an affirmative and pushed her forward. Together, the team emerged from the foliage, glancing surreptitiously at the guards who picked up on them. Yorgi, remaining in the background until now, immediately emerged at the head of the group and brushed himself down.

"Spot of fun," he said, his accent seeming strange when forced, but receiving little attention from the guards. Drake reasoned their directive was no doubt to stop and prevent any trouble inside the bazaar. What happened beyond its confines was up to the guests themselves.

"Go," he muttered to the Russian. "Back to the tent. A little regroup first and a chat to Hayden. Make sure nothing's happened and then back to it."

As if with perfect timing, the rain began to fall.

If Drake had thought the tent a little cramped before, the addition of Kenzie and her ego practically filled it. Though a prisoner, the woman acted as if in charge. Drake listened to Kinimaka making his quick call to Hayden, heard the expected insistences, and then watched darkness fall through a slit in the front of the tent. It took a long time for the rain to stop, and when it did the bazaar's entertainments had become muted. Dahl and Alicia took a walk and returned fifteen minutes later with glum looks on their faces.

"No go," Alicia said. "Everyone's hunkered down for the night. Guess even hardened terrorists don't like to get wet."

Dahl nodded along. "The few specimens who are out barely warrant a second glance. I remember one of them from my days with the Swedish Special Forces. Elusive old boy; looks a thousand years old now."

"I had to drag ole Torsty away," Alicia said with a frown. "Almost blew our cover."

Kenzie eyed the Swede. "Now I am jealous."

Drake ignored the antiquities smuggler though watched carefully as she began to pace. "We stay on mission," he said. "No exceptions."

Alicia glared at Kenzie. "Can I gag her?"

"Not without a hell of a fight," Kenzie shot back. "But Torsty can, just for fun."

Drake rose, hands out, feeling a little like a parent trying to calm squabbling kids. “Tomorrow is our last day. Let’s grab a little rest. Doing this thing in daylight will only make it more dangerous, but we can’t go creeping around every single tent at night. One way or another, tomorrow, there’ll be a hell of a fight.”

The mood turned somber, the pitch of conversation quieter. Drake plonked himself down beside Alicia and Dahl at the front of the tent, peeling back one half of the flap and staring into the black, seeping jungle, counting down the hours. They talked quietly, murmuring of their exploits, their past and their better times together. After a while, as moonshine appeared over the heights of the trees, Kenzie crawled over to join them.

“I’ve been listening to you guys,” she said quietly. “You’re real heroes, huh?”

“Nope,” Drake said shortly. “Just soldiers doing our jobs.”

“Speak for yourself,” Dahl said. “I’ve been more than heroic on several occasions.”

“I was heroic once,” Kenzie said unexpectedly, staring straight ahead. “An agent with Mossad. We took people like this—” she waved a hand outside. “Down every day. And every day more rose. What is it they say? Kill one of us and a thousand more shall arise? I don’t know . . . but it is true.”

“So you became dispirited?” Dahl asked.

“No,” Kenzie said quietly. “I became a victim.”

They fell silent for a time, and then Kenzie shuffled a few inches closer. “One time I stopped a firebomb attack from two thousand meters.” She clicked her tongue. “Two shots. Two kills.”

Drake wanted to believe her. “I killed Dmitry Kovalenko, the Blood King, up close. Put an end to his savagery.”

“I think you’ll find that was me,” Alicia said.

“Nah, you put down the guy in the bullet-proof kill-suit. With a knife.”

"True. I did both."

"Another time," Kenzie said. "During a stakeout, the cell we had under surveillance received a tip-off. They torched the entire floor of the apartment block to escape, but we caught them and pulled everyone to safety. No casualties that night."

Dahl sighed. "Well, where do I start? Odin? North Korea? Earlier—"

"You defeated Odin?" Drake blustered. "Wow."

Kenzie allowed a small smile. "I never had what you have. The companionship. My *team* was never that. We were always for ourselves and so were our superiors." She shook her head sadly.

"Truth be told," Drake said, also despondently. "It's much the same everywhere. Our team? It's different, but it works."

"But you have lost people along the way?"

Drake nodded but said nothing.

Kenzie massaged her forehead as if to wipe away memories. "I lost everything. We were in the field, isolated, dependent upon our satellite office. Our superiors were sat on their fat behinds in Tel Aviv, feeding the bullshit that they wanted us to believe. My team were caught without hope; we were exposed, identified, our families laid bare." Kenzie paused, swallowed and then went on. "They were slaughtered as our superiors rubbed their hands and accepted bribes. And then we were allowed to live as punishment, as warnings to others that law enforcement didn't work."

"You took your revenge?" Dahl asked, his eyes far away.

"Of course. Every one of them saw my face covered in *their* jetting blood before they died. And now I am a fugitive, a criminal, a terrorist," she spat.

Alicia cleared her throat. "All that withstanding, you do

smuggle artifacts, guns and drugs."

"It is safer than being a Mossad agent."

"So you are a criminal."

"A girl's gotta eat." Kenzie jerked her head up, as if shaking off a terrible, old nightmare and fixed on Dahl. "Speaking of which . . ."

"He's married," Drake said.

"Oh. How about you?"

"I'm . . . umm . . . I'm—"

Alicia laid a hand on his arm. "He's under offer, and you can't match the highest bid, bitch."

"Uww, snappy, snappy. And you said I had a dirty mouth."

"I could match you for insults any day."

"Really? Then let's—"

"All right." Dahl stepped in quickly. "Playtime's over. We all need a little rest before it starts to get light."

Kenzie looked away. "The last time I slept properly I was in my twenties."

Drake made a motion to include the entire tent. "You won't need to keep one eye open here, I guarantee it."

"That's not really the problem."

"Yeah," Drake agreed quietly. "I know."

CHAPTER TWENTY EIGHT

In the blackest, darkest watches of the night a great evil stirred. It stalked the narrow paths, watchful as it progressed, mindful to sneak a glance inside every open tent. It saw things it enjoyed and others it simply dismissed. It catalogued each spectacle and stored them for later. Perhaps it could make use of the pick of the bunch in its own delicious endeavors. But this night was not for distractions; this night was the culmination of a lifetime of investigation.

Beauregard went ahead, vetting the way. Tyler Webb paced in his wake, basking in his preeminent status, his untouchable prestige as the leader of an organization that had brought America to its knees, and knowing that its success had been dependent entirely upon him. This trip, this little journey, sealed his legend.

Webb was in such high spirits that he knew the trees would not drip on him; the rain would make way. The ground, though slippery, would not make him fall and the face of the moon had emerged primarily to light his way. Such were the perks and expectations of greatness. All he needed now were half a dozen men and women to lie along his path to stop his boots from getting muddy.

Something to work on.

Webb couldn't remember a happier time. This was the allotted hour when Ramses had promised to offer up the scroll—the very document Webb had been working toward for over thirty years. The Pythians might have been formed to further his quest for Saint Germain, but the scroll was the answer to every riddle, the gate to eternity.

Goodbye Pythians, Julian Marsh and New York. Hello Tyler Webb and the entire meaning of my life.

Beauregard stopped and peeled apart two tent flaps, shaking the material first so that it wouldn't drip on Webb's bent head as he entered. Webb found himself inside a small place, lined and floored with padded quilting the color of blood, stitched with gold. A man dressed in a loin cloth sat cross-legged opposite him, arms covered with bracelets and wristlets, and ears pierced, his lobes pulled taut by tear-shaped weights. The man was dirty looking, and greasy as if smeared with oils. His lips were almost black and his eyes were pits where poisonous snakes and spiders fought for supremacy.

Webb halted, surprised. "Where is Ramses?"

"He is . . . engaged." The despicable individual's voice was deceptively smooth, vowels rolling like well-lubricated cogs. "I am . . . the man whom you seek."

"This is not what I was promised."

"Is it not? How do you know? You have not yet seen what I offer."

Webb remained tight-lipped. He wasn't about to blurt out his life's greatest secret to a stranger. To the man's right, he now saw, lay a large, haphazard mound of Egyptian rugs and discarded furs, beneath which something moved very slowly. A human shaped mass if ever he'd seen one, and no doubt one of this man's bought slaves.

Webb's euphoria got the better of him. "All right, do you have it? The scroll? I mean—how could you? I can verify its authenticity so do not try to dupe me."

The unusual figure studied him for such a long time Webb almost called on Beauregard's assistance. Finally though, he began to speak. "Ramses did indeed tell me about what you seek. You know there is a prosperous trade in everything illicit—from scrolls and parchments to enormous bronzed statues, from Akkadian to Mongol and from the bones of gods to the skeletons of Alexander and Genghis Khan themselves. They are the prized possessions of the filthy rich, trophies with which to impress and control your peers, currency in which to trade. How many thousands, or hundreds of thousands, of scrolls are out there, my friend?"

"I only want one," Webb snapped.

"And that is why you are still searching. It would have been easier to find an honest man on Wall Street."

"Don't be ridiculous." Webb decided he'd gone off topic and a prompt might be in order. "Have you done it?"

"Wall Street? No. But I *do* have your scroll."

"Prove it to me."

Shifting a little, the peculiar man drew a long, deep breath. He took a moment to rearrange the rugs at his side, affording Webb the view of a pale, naked flank, before completely covering the slave, and then clucked what Webb could only assume was a black forked tongue.

"Well . . . well. To business. The German, Leopold—I am sure you know his name—was an addict. A man much like yourself—obsessed with this legendary figure they called Le Comte de Saint Germain. A wealthy explorer, he spent most of his life searching for clues. He was considered the world's foremost authority on the Count."

Webb knew everything there was to know about Leopold, but it helped to hear this man speak of him. He had been trying for decades to gain access to the man's archives, his vaults, even his home, but had always failed to find a single shred regarding Saint Germain. Leopold's craftiness was just too sharp even for Webb, it had seemed.

"This scroll fell into the wrong hands following Leopold's death. As you know it forms part of the journal he took around the world, cataloguing every find, every quest, every single strand of evidence. From Stonehenge to Paris and Milan, it is a scruffy, well-used tome. Inside Leopold has used many pens, always hurriedly, a moment stolen in time as he continued his endless quest. It will need collating, but it is the real deal and it is worth more than the life of any normal man. What would you offer?"

Webb would offer the world, but kept his face neutral. He knew that with his additional knowledge and familiarity with Saint Germain, with his wealth of contacts and data, he stood the best chance of cracking history's greatest secret . . .

Who—or what—was Saint Germain and where are his greatest treasures?

To believe in one acknowledged belief in the other.

"I offer . . ." he paused, mindful of the fact that the expected monetary accoutrements arising from Marsh's New York escapade would now never materialize. However . . .

"Everything I have," he said seriously, holding up his black pre-paid credit card. Material possessions did not matter anymore. He could find the man and the treasure on his own and with what little he had frittered away elsewhere.

"Then we have a deal," the man said, taking the card and swiping it through some kind of reader. The numbers must have pleased him, for Webb saw his eyes widen. Quietly, he then issued an order.

The rugs and furs slithered away from a rising shape. Webb averted his eyes from the man a moment too late, leaving a lingering scar across his memory.

"Take it."

Webb reached out and took a proffered pouch about the size of a small backpack, feeling the supple brown leather between his fingers and then turned to leave. It took a moment to remember to check the disorganized contents, but he did so briefly for he wanted to save the luscious pleasure of full revelation for a most intimate moment.

CHAPTER TWENTY NINE

Hayden Jaye stayed low and well away from the barge's round windows as she spoke on the sat-phone. The interior was in semi-darkness, illuminated only by one dim lantern, but that was good. Several times these last few days she had seen guards venturing close, as if trying to see inside. Smyth had positioned himself on deck, the eternal guardian and soldier, and Lauren had busied herself by helping out with the "guests" and their food. The news coming back from the bazaar was hardly reassuring; the revelations surrounding Secretary Robert Price and the CIA particularly damning. Trouble was, Hayden wasn't entirely sure what their next move should be.

I don't like this one little bit.

Part of the reason a leader became a leader was that they acted well under pressure, made the right decisions and brought their people home. During this mission Hayden had acted more than a little impetuously, reacting immediately upon Beauregard's tip and dragging the entire team into the jungle. She wondered what Price would have said about it if she'd had chance to consult him.

None of this matters. Yes, she was crowding her brain with unnecessary evils. What mattered was Price, the CIA, Tyler Webb and Ramses.

And now Kenzie.

Dahl spoke rapidly on the sat-phone, explaining the latest developments. Hayden listened with amazement, surprised that Alicia had come across her latest nemesis in the midst of the Amazon, then accepting as she heard what the ex-Mossad did for a living. Dahl's description of her was somewhat colorful—at first tempered with dislike and wariness but later also with a little pity and maybe even some respect. He didn't explain why, but she sensed a kinship somewhere.

Hayden checked her watch. Coming up for 8:00 a.m. now on the last day of the last bazaar. No matter what happened, this was the end. The variables though—they were endless.

"We know where Ramses' tent is," Dahl was saying. "But not Webb's or Price's. We're still outgunned and outmanned, though several players have already left. The worst of the bunch though—they're still here, cavorting until the very end."

"Distraction?" Hayden sipped from a bottle of water.

"Hard to pull off. The guards are well laid out and unlikely to bunch."

"Shock and awe?"

"If we had reinforcements."

Hayden wondered about that. Time was fast running out, and they were eight against hundreds. Their direct boss couldn't exactly help them. She saw only one course of action.

"Dahl," she said. "Give me an hour. I have to call someone."

The connection was verified, passed through countless channels and then verified again. One more time, one more connection, and she addressed the most powerful man in the world.

"Sir?" she said.

President Coburn's voice held tones of stress but came across as warm as summer DC sunshine. "Hayden Jaye. What can I do for you?"

Hayden took a huge breath and then gave him the bare

facts, straight up. This was no time for embellishments, and Coburn listened without interrupting. When she had finished he stayed silent for about a minute.

"Sir?"

"Yes, Jaye, I'm here. Just picking myself up off the floor. And there's no chance Price might be there undercover, like yourselves? No chance he's playing this Ramses character?"

"From what my team saw and heard," she said. "No chance at all."

Coburn fell silent again. Hayden could imagine the thoughts running through his head—of black bag and need-to-know, of rendition and dark sites, of intelligence gathering and the lives of ordinary Americans.

"The logistics are . . . thorny," Coburn said. "Brazil's Department of State are working well with us at the moment but assets in the region are too minimal to make a difference. Unless . . ." he paused, and Hayden could almost see him smile. "Unless there's something I don't know, of course. Which is perfectly possible. An additional problem is the region you're in—it is teeming with criminals, desperadoes, gangsters, you name it."

"It's okay, sir." Hayden heard the regret in his voice quite clearly. "We can still do this. I only want . . . clarification . . . on Price."

"Ah, well, that's not such a gray area. Resolve that situation, Jaye. In any way necessary."

The comment surprised her a little. She had fully expected Coburn to insist that Robert Price be allowed to return to the States to stand trial, or face interrogation, but instead he'd given her carte blanche. As a soldier in the field, she couldn't ask for more.

"Understood, sir, and thank you."

"What's the time scale on this?"

"Eighteen hours, maximum," she said. "We're counting down, sir."

"I want to know the moment you settle this," Coburn said. "Good luck to you and your team, Jaye. And please, be careful."

"We always are, sir," Hayden said, her head filled with images of Torsten Dahl grinning like crazy and Matt Drake leaping after him into battle. "Our team is as sane as they come."

Coburn hesitated. "All right, then."

The call died. Hayden put her face to the window and viewed what she could of the bazaar and the lightening skies. The conversation had turned out better than she had hoped in one way, but worse in another. Price was expendable, but they were on their own.

Again.

She called Dahl back and told him the news. "I did tell the President that we would be careful," she said. "And that we're all well-balanced, rational human beings able to make sound decisions in the heat of battle."

"Fuck, yeah," Dahl growled.

Hayden closed her eyes. "Have at it then."

CHAPTER THIRTY

Drake listened as Dahl picked up the bazaar's laminated agenda and read out a relevant part.

"On the last day at 10:00 a.m.," he read. "Morning speech, thank yous and final acquisitions," he said. "Wind up. It's the best news we've had since we arrived. Everyone should be there."

The Yorkshireman nodded. "And if we plan it right, we can use it to pick up on all our targets. Let's assign villains."

"I'll take Webb alone," Alicia said. "Beau will help."

"Are you sure?" Drake met her eyes.

"Jealous much?"

"Who? *Me?* Stop blethering, y' daft apath."

"Shit, is that some kind of Martian tongue?" Dahl looked over.

Drake realized he'd reverted to type in his non-jealousy. "Anyway. Price is mine, Dahl's and Mano's. Yorgi, you can watch Ramses and wait for everyone to regroup before we move on him."

"It makes sense," the Russian said. "Ramses will be one of the last to leave."

The foot traffic passing outside the tent began to rise and grow more vocal. A sound echoed through the bazaar, deep and booming, the reverberation of a huge gong.

The team rose at once, Drake eyeing Kenzie one more time. "Remember what we said."

"I'll do my best, lover."

Outside, the crowd strolled noisily toward the large clearing that also held the caiman pit. Drake kept his eyes on the jungle at first, ensuring the guards were positioned as before, then turned his attention to the crowd and scanned for targets. A flash of red caught his eye as he turned from the jungle, just a flicker, but the location and quickness told him one clear and obvious thing.

Somebody else is out there, watching. His heart sank. *Not another enemy, I hope.*

No time to worry about that now. It could even be one of the local drug gangs or a native. Drake blended with the crowd, following Yorgi and Alicia with Dahl and Kinimaka at his side. Conversation pummeled him from all sides. The ground squelched with every step and sunlight filtered intermittently from above. Drake was so sick of the thick, fetid rainforest stench by now that he considered holding his nose. Soon though they were streaming out of the narrow trail and grouping around a podium—the same one from which Ramses had issued his welcome speech. Drake joined his friends in scrutinizing the bobbing, talking heads of the crowd.

"This is more like it," Alicia said. "I see Webb already."

"Oh, and who's the tight hunk next to him?" Kenzie craned her neck, a crafty glint in her eye, proving that she'd read the situation between Drake and Alicia correctly.

"The French Condom," Drake said. "At least, that's what his friends call him."

"And his enemies?"

Dahl nudged Drake. "Look."

"Thanks for the bruise. Where?"

"Bruise? All I did was give you a prod. Two o'clock, front row."

Drake saw the suits, the mostly shaven heads, the gray hairs of Robert Price. "Gang's all here," he said.

"It is now." Kinimaka wiped sweat from his forehead as the terrorist prince appeared.

Ramses took the stage, closely followed by his

bodyguard, Akatash. The bazaar's patron stood bigger than Drake remembered, as tall as a garage door and unbearably bulked out, as if he'd had basketballs implanted alongside his normal muscles. His face broke into a smile as he took the podium and stared out across a sea of faces.

"My friends, my friends! What an occasion, what a magnificent affair. Am I right?"

Cheers erupted, a wall of sound flooding toward and swallowed whole by the all-encompassing rainforest. Ramses basked in its wash, a happy man.

"Make no mistake," he said, his voice amplified by unseen speakers. "This mission of ours will not see an end in our lifetime. It will take time. But we are already the aggressors, not the pacifists, and they will lose. We are stronger together. Stronger by far. These deals we make in places like this, they will have far, far reaching successes. Look to New York for some solace—" he smiled malevolently "—next week. But do stay away."

Drake turned wide eyes toward Kinimaka and Dahl and then did his best to hide them. *What could this Prince of Terrorists mean?*

"Coalition airstrikes?" Ramses laughed. "They will soon learn the futility of their actions. We have no timetable, no clear path to resolution or retribution. We will never die. We will never stop. And our gods will make an eternity of shining days for us all!"

In closing, Ramses held both hands aloft, face turned toward the skies, and waited once more for the overwhelming wave of applause and approval to pass. Drake watched Dahl's face, and reached out a steadying hand to stop the man exploding right there and then.

"For New York!" Ramses called out.

Another swell of applause.

Drake was watching Tyler Webb, and saw the terrible

smile as the man turned knowingly to gauge the crowd's reaction. A female hand on his arm made him glance to the right.

"I'll be back soon." Alicia, her blond hair caught by the sun, gave him a grave smile.

"What?"

"I have to go see Beau. This is about to go down and it's gonna be the hardest thing we've ever tried to do. He has to know."

"But . . . Beau?"

"Don't worry. Been there, done that. Won't try it again."

Drake grimaced. "Oh, thanks for sharing. And, in any case, that's not what I . . ."

"Sure it isn't. Bye lover."

Kenzie's face suddenly blocked his eye line. "Hey, hey. You crying?"

CHAPTER THRTY ONE

As Ramses rambled on a little more, Alicia threaded her way through the crowd. Though this mission necessarily entailed a constant level of watchfulness, a level that soon became stressful to a point where she couldn't even wisecrack properly, the blonde was actually reveling in it. *Different, yes, but then so am I.*

For the first time she could remember she was totally focused, able to push all other considerations to the back of her mind and work on a new future. *With Drake?* The thought came fast and unbidden, and with surprise. She'd been trying to suppress that profound nugget until she could figure out a way to understand her own feelings.

The two of them had been burned enough in this lifetime. Neither of them needed a new heartache.

Alicia stopped close to Beau, but the bodyguard was focused entirely on his charge and the areas around him. Also the jungle, where Alicia fancied she saw a flash of something or someone on their way to the bazaar. It was gone before her mind could form an opinion, fleet and fast like smoke and rain, but maybe Beau had noticed the same thing. Alicia found her mind wandering, and for a moment old fears started to fight their way back to the surface, claws flashing above the still waters, but then she thought back to Arizona and their quest for the ghost ships, and remembered her own storm amidst the mega-storm. Decisions had been made that day, a willingness to try, and try she bloody well would.

Beau was staring at her, face betraying his surprise.

Alicia inclined her head. Beau would understand. He

immediately nodded at Webb though, indicating that he would only draw attention by leaving the madman's side. Alicia wondered what expression Webb's face would snap into if he saw Kinimaka approaching and desperately wanted to see that darkly comedic scene, but understood it couldn't happen.

Not yet.

Just then, Ramses finished his ridiculous tirade and several people rose quickly and moved toward him, needing perhaps some clarification or just trying to bask in his wicked magnificence. Webb was one of them. Alicia followed Beau, grabbing his shoulder and moving him a few feet away from Webb as the Pythian king stared up at Ramses, his lips working quickly as he tried to grab some attention.

"What do you know?" she asked. "Webb. The Pythians. New York. All of it."

Beau glared. "And nice to see you too. Do you know how many nights we have been here? I have been," he rolled his hips suggestively, "saving it all for you."

Alicia coughed. "Well, that's very nice of you, Beau, but you're gonna have to tie it off around your waist for now because we're in the middle of a crisis. Too many targets and no time. We're struggling. Your input and help is required."

The Frenchman checked his ward, who had sidled right up to Ramses by now, and turned back. "It is very bad." His manner changed on a dime. "For New York, it is very bad. The last Pythian, Julian Marsh, is smuggling a suitcase nuke into the country, into the city, with an intention to prove its authenticity and then extract many dollars from the American government. What he doesn't know is that Ramses' men intend to hijack the bomb once it's in the city and set it off."

Alicia took a moment to digest that. "*What?* And you haven't communicated that to anyone *sane* yet? Fuck!"

Both looked to the ground as heads turned their way. Then Beau said, "I didn't know where you were sleeping. There are many men's tents."

"What the hell is that supposed to mean?"

"Nothing. But you obviously did not know where I was sleeping, since you have not come to visit."

Alicia breathed deeply, annoyed and confused that Beau was making this about their relationship. It was pure jadedness, she knew, from a man who had seen it all and lived it all almost every day. Familiarity bred contempt, yes, and also complacency. Cynicism. She resisted the urge to shake the Frenchman.

"Marsh doesn't know Ramses' intent," Beau clarified.

Alicia thought about their very immediate future. "Tell me where your tent is."

Beauregard began to smile and then realized her mind was working in an entirely different way to his. Quickly, he explained, then sighed loudly.

"I also think you should know Webb's true intent for being here. It wasn't the nuke. Nothing like that. He's bought some kind of scroll that was part of a journal compiled by Leopold—a German who spent his whole life researching Saint Germain."

"Fuck, that wanker again. What is it with old bell ends and their bloody secret lives? I'm pretty sure that in fifty or a hundred years, someone will be studying the secrets of people we see as famous now."

Beau blinked. "Really? Who?"

"Dunno. Terry Wogan? Jay Leno? Jennifer Lawrence?"

Beau grimaced. "Now who is kidding around?"

Alicia tended to agree. "All right, but New York has just taken priority."

"Of course. That was always Webb's plan. Distraction so he can focus entirely on the journal, working out its secrets."

"That man is a devil with a demon's heart and mind," Alicia said. "I'm really gonna quarter the bastard and bury the parts at separate ends of the earth."

"I will help you."

"We'll see. Now, is there—"

Alicia stopped abruptly as she saw Beau check on the whereabouts of Tyler Webb—now physically talking to Ramses—and then lean in, put an arm on her shoulder and his lips to her own. Alicia immediately felt a rush of heat and an urge to drag her own personal python off into the jungle, but then stood stock still and forced it all down. Gently, she pushed Beauregard away.

"Not now."

"Not now?" He watched her. "Or not ever?"

"I don't know. Damn, being normal is so complicated. I'm trying to be different, a new person, and I won't lose my way in that stuff anymore. Does that make any sense to you?"

"I am not sure. All I offer is hot, sweaty sex."

Alicia gulped. "Stop it. I need more than that. Longer lasting emotions and some kind of commitment. Is that what you're offering too?"

Beau turned away, torn, as Webb wound his conversation up with Ramses. Or had he averted his eyes because of Alicia's question? His next words illuminated her. "I can't offer that. I don't think so anyway."

"Well, make your mind up fast. Because one day, I'll be gone."

The Englishwoman slipped away, already thinking about their targets and New York and how to get a message to Hayden on the boat. People had to be made aware. How long had Marsh been on the road anyway?

He might already be there.

Drake stared at her when she returned, reminding her of Beau's own expression as she left. Mixed feelings plagued every nerve in her body.

"What happened?" Drake asked.

"Yes, he tried to kiss me," Alicia blurted. "Yes, he succeeded. No, we didn't slip off for a short interlude. Not that anything's ever short where Beau's concerned, if you get my meaning. Yes, he wants me and yes, I have no idea what to do about it."

Dahl touched her. "We meant—what does Beau know?"

Alicia patted the gun holstered at her waist, and then explained everything she knew. "All I know," she finished, "is that we need to roll the credits on this shameful bazaar and get our beautiful butts en route to New York."

Her comrades were still reeling from the shock. Alicia held her hand sup. "Don't worry, we have time. Ramses is still here, yes? And he wants to be the orchestrator of New York's final symphony."

The team gathered a little closer, sensing a new and terrible severity to their already challenging mission.

"We're on the edge," Drake said. "If that bomb goes off . . ." He shook his head. "We're on the edge of Armageddon."

A shout brought their heads up fast. Ramses had taken to the podium again and was calling for attention. Guards moved up behind the small structure, partially hidden, and Alicia strained to see why. They had caught some prisoners, it seemed. Maybe they had captured drug runners in the surrounding jungle and were about to execute them as a final gesture.

Ramses' eyes swept the crowd. "Some of our guests, it seems, are imposters."

The crowd went deadly silent. Alicia felt Drake stiffen and saw Dahl's face turn to white granite.

"But how do we find out who they are?" Ramses made a show of clicking his tongue in thought.

Alicia saw Beau turn, his face appalled. Then she watched in horror as the prisoners were dragged into view—Smyth, Lauren and Hayden were escorted around the side of the podium, hands tied and pushed along by a dozen men.

"If you want my input," Ramses grinned, "I say we feed their friends to the caimans and see what shakes out."

He laughed uproariously.

"To the pit!"

CHAPTER THIRTY TWO

Drake forced his limbs to stop working, wanting to charge forward with all guns blazing. He reached out to both Kinimaka and Dahl too, steadying them.

"Timing," he said.

Hayden, Smyth and Lauren looked a little beat up. Bruises stood out on their foreheads and blood trickled from their lips. Their bonds were tight, painfully so, causing them to grimace in pain with every movement. But thank God they were still alive and Ramses enjoyed his awful spectacles. This entire situation was about to explode big time. Drake checked his guns, his knives, his spare ammo. He checked the positions of Ramses, of Webb and of Robert Price. He fixed Kenzie with a momentary stare, wondering how she might take advantage of such an unforeseen dilemma.

All the while, their three teammates were herded amid a gaggle of squawking guards ever closer to the stinking caiman pit. One ran ahead and started working on the padlock that allowed entry. Ramses walked behind them, an extremely attentive Akatash at his side. The two men now sported AK47s, borrowed from guards. All of a sudden the strangely cheery atmosphere of the bazaar had turned very deadly indeed.

Drake and his colleagues drifted ever closer, using the crowd for cover and remaining as placid as they could. This outcome was all about surprise, made harder by the clear fact that everyone was expecting something to happen.

Hayden stumbled. Smyth bent down to steady her and received a rifle-butt to the back of the neck. He didn't go sprawling, but took it with a glare of anger, making sure Hayden was stable before staggering to his own feet. Drake dogged the guards now, still amid the crowd, and was surprised when Kenzie put an arm around him.

"You might be surprised, soldier boy, but this shocks even me. What they're about to do."

"They're terrorists," he mumbled. "What did you expect?"

"Professionalism. Restraint. This is a public forum despite its secrecy."

"These are the people you chose to run with."

"I take my own path. I am not like them. I can't help what they do in private or among themselves but this, feeding humans to animals . . . this is beyond reprehensible."

Drake nodded. Maybe this woman did have some heart after all, buried beneath all those layers of hardiness, hatred and dreams of vengeance.

"I will help you," Kenzie said. "Until they are free or we're dead."

"And then?"

"Don't get in my way."

Drake grimaced inside. Somehow, he believed she might help them and then try to kill them. With this woman it made sense, and at least she was open about it. The guards reached the edge of the pit and halted, waiting patiently for Ramses to pick his way through them as their captives continued to struggle. At length, the Prince of Terrorists stared down into the hidden depths of the deep hole.

"Ahh, my friends, you do look hungry down there!"

Spontaneous laughter broke out. Hayden stood upright, no fear on her face as she eyeballed Ramses. Smyth moved next to Lauren as if his body might shield hers from harm. Drake wondered briefly how the angry soldier might have been surprised, then decided it didn't matter. Tension settled over the crowd as most of them watched each other, waiting for some kind of reaction. Hands hovered over weapons. Hammers clicked back on dozens of guns as the tension rose high enough to trigger lightning.

Ramses was ready.

"Throw them into hell!"

CHAPTER THIRTY THREE

Drake stood as close as he dared without arousing suspicions. It was whilst he scanned a dozen different positions and possibilities, the guards' faces and stances, that he noticed the red flash among the nearby trees.

For the second time.

One moment it was there, the next it was gone. The distraction cost him though—as the guards pushed their bound prisoners to the edge of the pit and only then slit their bonds. Smyth immediately lashed out, as did Lauren and Hayden, but their feet were already slipping over the edge, dirt and vegetation crumbling beneath them, the hands of the guards driving them, the unstoppable force of sheer momentum thwarting them.

Time slowed, stretching out like elastic. Everyone moved. Everything changed. Drake raised a rifle in one hand, a Glock in the other and charged the guards. Dahl battered men aside and raced headlong toward his falling friends.

Caimans writhed and churned, their mouths agape, slashing.

Alicia helped Dahl's charge by encumbering the enemy. Ramses looked surprised, recognizing them from the jungle, then began to grin. All distances were halved even as Hayden, Smyth and Lauren scrambled to stay at the rim of the pit, and as the guards kicked at their chests, sending them tumbling helplessly head-over-heels straight down.

Drake fired, the bullets hitting their marks. Kenzie picked up a dropped Uzi and sent three guards flying into the pit, their chests pumping blood. Dahl hit men so hard they were lifted off their feet. The crowd parted all around them, terrorist leaders and decadent procurers unused to putting themselves in the line of fire, now showing fear. Drake finally approached the edge of the pit edge and found his way blocked by eight guards, Ramses and Akatash.

Shit, we've left it too late. God help them down there . . .

Despite their desperate efforts they would not make it in time.

Then, like a streak of lightning, like the Ninja she truly was, Mai Kitano came speeding out of the jungle. Leaping from a standing start she jumped up to the top of the railings that surrounded the pit, balancing on a pinhead for a second, and then launched herself through the air, over the top of the pit, and into the backs of the guards, scattering them like bowling pins.

Alicia gawped for many reasons. "Fuck. Me." She used two sentences.

Drake leapt high, then was among the enemy punching and kicking, firing a shot. Dahl plowed through. Alicia elbowed one and kneed another in the crotch. Kinimaka bellowed with rage. Without a moment's hesitation those four leapt over the edge of the caiman pit and followed their downed colleagues into its lethal depths.

Drake slipped feet-first down a hard-packed slope, hindered by tree roots and exposed boulders. The pit was wide even at its narrowest point and God only knew what incredible skills Mai had employed to leap clear across it. Dahl careened down only a foot to Drake's left, unable to keep a wide grin off his face, and Drake remembered his intense disappointment at missing the caiman fight of earlier.

"You are fucking crazy!" he yelled.

Dahl only grinned even wider.

Down they went, bouncing, scraping, jolting bruises

already raw from the ghost ships sliding escapade. Drake remembered what Dahl had then said: *Drake made me do it*, a new and not entirely adored team catchphrase.

Well, Hayden might feel bloody different about it now.

Below, huge black caimans writhed and splashed, rippling under water or breaking through the waves. Tails lashed at the sides of the pit. Some tried to crawl out whilst others simply waited with jaws apart. Smyth hit the water first, unable to control his fall, going straight under without a word. Lauren tumbled in next, across the back of a caiman. Hayden flailed last, almost halting her descent by grabbing hold of a jutting branch but screaming when it snapped clean off. The caiman she landed on broke her fall, its jaws snapping shut as if in pain.

Suddenly, the bottom of the pit became a churning, screaming mass.

Drake took a final glance upward before joining the incredible fray—above, guns were being trained down upon them and spectators lined the rim of the pit, Ramses among them. Then he flew off an outcropping, sailed through mid-air, and splashed down into the very center of the roiling waters. Underneath, it was a barely penetrable gloom. Snapping jaws passed an inch from his nose, their fury felt even in this subaquatic murk. Drake powered upward, breaking the surface and blowing water from his mouth and nose. The visage that faced him was harsh, unforgiving, and very hungry.

"Alicia," he spluttered at her. "Move!"

A caiman darted in from the left, cutting a swathe between them. Drake had valiantly kept hold of his Glock and now fired two shots into the beast's flank. It rolled, blood leaking out, and ducked away. Ahead, Dahl had already gained a foothold, standing upon two stones jutting out of the bank, a wriggling predator held in each hand. He struggled to hold the beast's scaly tails, jaws gnashing close to his nose.

Drake fired at a second beast as it set upon Lauren. Smyth rolled with another. Hayden went under as a black shape landed on her shoulders, its tail whipping the waves. Dahl somehow managed to punch one adversary right in the face, then sniffed as it exhibited no reaction other than to somehow get even angrier.

Alicia swam in circles, unable to locate a foe or rescue anyone. Finally, her attention was grabbed by a set of eyes floating toward her—a caiman waiting to pounce. She reeled back as it struck, slamming Kinimaka in the process. Her pistol went off, thudding into the animal's flesh. Drake hit the bank and pushed upward, gaining a little traction. To one side Dahl still stood, and now to the other Kinimaka climbed hard out of the water, twin waterfalls dripping from his shoulders, a huge black caiman held in his hands.

Incensed, he stared it right in the eyes.

"Try to bite me would you? Try to bite my girl? Not today, bud."

He held its powerful jaws away and wide open. After a moment his eyes met Dahl's. The Swede was already on the same wavelength, eager to proceed. At the same time they swung their captives. The sound of them meeting in mid-air made even Drake cringe. The twin beasts dropped back into the deluge and didn't twitch again.

Drake fired at another caiman. Hayden fought one off with her bare hands, but would only survive moments longer without help. Kinimaka launched himself high off the ledge, a human cannonball, and came down on top of the caiman with the most enormous splash. Water exploded everywhere. Kinimaka, the caiman, and Hayden all vanished. Dahl spotted another hunting marauder and hammered down onto its flank. Alicia fired a bullet into another.

Drake eyed the steep banks of the pit. For the first time since they jumped in, it was time to look for a way out.

But high above, gun barrels bristled, lining the pit. And Ramses stood up there with one arm raised.

The single word sent chills shooting toward Drake's heart.

"Fire!"

CHAPTER THIRTY FOUR

Like death's shadow she slipped among the guards, a knife in each hand, corpses left lying in her wake, but the simple crush of bodies between her and the edge of the pit prevented her from reaching her friends. The journey to this part of the world had been a long one for Mai Kitano, made possible by Hayden's provision of coordinates, but the last thing she expected when she arrived was to have to pull her teammates from deadly danger. Now, she jabbed, she thrust, she darted to and fro like smoke and magic woven together; she ignored the pain of not-so-old knife and bullet wounds, the throbbing scar across her face, putting her friends first and the rest of her life on hold. As she stalled, as she despaired of ever seeing them alive again, a stranger appeared at her side.

"Mine's bigger than yours."

The woman wielded a katana, given back to her by Yorgi who had been concealing the Samurai sword beneath his robes. She started to forge a path through the throng.

Guns appeared in several hands but Mai made quick work of their owners, flitting among them. As even Kenzie started to stall they neared the edge of the pit. Ramses stood only two figures removed, a crowd around him. Mai saw other guards rushing toward them and, again, felt her heart sink down toward the caiman pit itself.

"Still too many," she muttered.

Gunfire erupted. Yorgi, standing alone, made himself a target to draw some of the killers away. Several guards fell, bleeding. Mai and Kenzie forged a few steps closer. Then Kenzie's katana was bludgeoned out of her hands and Mai received a debilitating blow to the back of the neck. For the last time, their progress faltered.

Stopped.

Screams echoed up from the bottom of the pit. Laughter spread along the top. Ramses was holding up one huge arm, a bear's paw it seemed, and chatting to those around him about what would happen when they unleashed two hundred rounds of lead. Some were taking bets, others craning their necks for a better view. Mai ignored the agony, met Kenzie's eyes and nodded.

"For our friends."

Kenzie gave her a tight-lipped smile. "If you say so."

Then, from out of nowhere, shot a lithe, black streak, a living blade that chopped, tore and slashed through their opponents as if they weren't even there. Mai stared open-mouthed as Beauregard Alain squeezed among guards and other fighters, beyond her own capabilities, incapacitating them faster than they could blink and sending them to their knees.

A gap opened up.

Mai shot through it, flanked by Kenzie and Beauregard, heroes shouting and screaming and coming to the rescue. Guards found their flesh turning red, appendages severed, and then turned to run without even knowing the cause. Guns clattered to the floor. Ramses turned and saw the danger, his bodyguard Akatash wrenching him away at the very last moment. Mai kicked three people over the edge of the pit. Kenzie buried her retrieved katana into a shoulder and then a skull. Beauregard broke limbs and spleens and throats and ribs. His opponents died before their brains registered the fact, expressions of shock engraved forever on their faces.

Mai reached the edge of the pit and stared down. Drake was already halfway up, the others following. Alicia was shouting at Dahl, trying to encourage the Swede to leave behind the caiman that he was dragging along with him. Nothing had changed there then. Yorgi's machine gun rang out again, further scattering the guards, organizers and attendees of the last bazaar.

Everything had been blown to hell and now time was the vital factor.

"Hurry!" she screamed into Drake's face.

"Sprite!" Alicia cried back. "Where the fuck . . . ?"

"Tell you later, Taz. Just move your knobblies, fast as you can."

Alicia moved fast enough, her eyes riveted on the scene at the top of the pit. "Is that Kenzie? And . . . and Beau? Fuck me. What is this—an alternate reality?"

"Your *desired* reality," Kenzie said with a mischievous smile, reaching out a hand to help the Englishwoman over the top.

Alicia beamed at Mai, then at Kenzie and Beau. "Damn, I do like the sound of that."

Then Drake put himself into her line of sight. "Really?"

The team struggled out of the caiman pit, dripping, bruised and tired but all in one piece. Dahl hauled his prize up and then watched it slink off into the jungle. "Guys, when we get home we should get one of those for the gym. What a workout!"

Drake paused for breath and a moment to take in the scene. Shocked, humbled, overawed, he saw the entire SPEAR team gathered around him, together at last and again, united in battle.

Family. It had been such a long time.

"You guys," he said. "Thanks for being here."

Beauregard and Kenzie offered tight-lipped smiles. "Seriously." He offered a hand out to each of them. "You helped save our lives. The SPEAR team owes you one."

Then Hayden stepped to the fore. Dahl immediately gave her a fast update on events. Her face blanched terribly when she heard about the bomb and that they had no way of communicating the information.

"Time to get paid," she said, indicating the uproar that had become of the bazaar. "Targets first. Let's move out."

Drake scanned the heads for those they needed. "Webb." He pointed. "And there, Price. C'mon."

Alicia jogged alongside Beau. "So Webb's aware you're a plant?"

"A what?"

"Undercover. An agent."

"Yes, but it will not bother him. This is what he wanted. The madman has everything he needs to slink away and locate these ancient treasures."

With weapons out and eyes glued to their surrounds the SPEAR team plunged into the running throng. Dilemmas prodded at Drake from every angle—terrorists ran alongside him clutching their new purchases and staying close to their personal bodyguards, but Drake's quarry was far, far more important. Kenzie didn't seem to share that value, swinging her katana at almost everybody, most likely seeing it as a new way of extracting an old vengeance. Drake turned a blind eye, not wanting to test that morality for himself.

The jungle practically shook as hundreds of feet pounded its verdant byways. Soaked leaves dripped with water and slime. Vegetation, churned up by the runners, floated in the air. Sunlight dappled the clearings. Boutiques and stalls flashed by to either side, some destroyed and one being ransacked, its owners killed. Drake tried to keep tabs on their objectives, but the crush of bodies made it increasingly hard. Twice he had to fend off attackers, finishing them with bullets. Smyth followed suit, snarling into their faces.

"No," Hayden shouted at his side. "They've split apart . . . look! We'll take Price."

With that the team split in two, together for so short a time, and Drake concentrated his efforts on chasing down Tyler Webb. His hopes were raised when he saw that Webb was chasing Ramses, the terrorist prince surrounded by guards. *Two pricks, one stone.* He flexed his fingers and checked to see who was with him.

Dahl. Alicia. Mai and Beau.

Not a bad set.

They ran hard through the streets of the bazaar, Drake noticing that several of the attendees were now fighting each other. *Rival factions?* Who cared? You didn't get this kind of action at Comic Con. He elbowed another attacker in the face and threw a second against a tree. Dahl performed a two-leg flying kick at another, earning a shake of the head from both Mai and Beau. But the guard didn't get up. The Swede closed the gap between themselves and Webb.

"Time to pay up, you Pythian bastard," he said. "Time to meet your fate."

Then something screamed toward them.

"RPG!" Drake cried thickly, throwing his body to the floor.

CHAPTER THIRTY FIVE

Hayden chased after Robert Price and his CIA entourage, hatred and payback on her mind.

"Price!" she cried, as she neared the group. "I see you. You're about to get yours, asshole!"

The Secretary of Defense swiveled his head as he ran, stumbling a little, but betrayed no emotion upon seeing her face. That had surely come when Ramses' men had led her toward certain death in the caiman pit. Now, where would he go? They had seen his face.

"Be careful now," Kinimaka said from behind. "Guy's a snake. He'll have a plan as slippery as himself."

They followed the same small path as Price and the four men who shadowed him, their number now complemented by two of Ramses' own guards. Hayden expected one of them to drop and start firing at any moment, but they continued arrow-straight on their path. After a few more minutes Kenzie spoke up.

"I know where they're going. The same village I used as a base. Maybe they have some hidden transport around there."

Smyth nodded. "I don't know who the hell you are, but that makes sense. Out of interest, do *you* have any transport?"

"Fuck you, dude. That'd be telling."

Smyth raised his eyebrows in surprise but said nothing. Hayden reflected that a heads-up from Drake or Alicia would have been nice, but understood events had happened much too fast. They would have to be careful with this Kenzie. It was somewhat telling that she'd chosen to run with the group that didn't know her.

Hayden saw the trees thin out up ahead, and a pair of localized buildings appear. Two trucks and a ruined bus gave more insight into Kenzie's camp. She raised her gun as Price and his sentinels ran straight through the middle of the wide clearing.

"Stop, I have a shot. Stop right there."

Now, one of the guards did drop and turn, rifle already aimed. He squeezed off a bullet that whickered by Kinimaka's girth, and disappeared into the forest. Smyth fired back on the run, bullets spraying the ground around the prone man. Rolling, he discharged another round, but this went awry, tearing toward the clouds. Smyth picked him off with two well-placed shots. Hayden lined up Price in her sights, deciding not to warn him again.

A CIA agent flung himself at the boss, displaying great instinct, just as Hayden pulled her trigger. Both men went flying across the rutted ground. All the other agents now turned and began to lay down cover fire. The SPEAR team scattered.

Lethal, tiny missiles crisscrossed the clearing, thudding against ancient bark and clanging off rusting metal. Hayden popped her head up and kept firing, sure that Price would be ordering the agents to keep moving. There was nowhere for him to go anymore but forward for the rest of his life.

Agents scrambled back as they fired, kicking up dirt and leaves, their faces made even harsher by the black designer sunglasses they wore. Kinimaka crawled away to the left, looking to flank Price's position, but then their quarry started running again, away from Kenzie's camp.

"Where are they going?" Hayden asked the black-haired woman.

"Don't know and don't really care." Kenzie looked bored.

"Well, how did you get to here?"

"Jeeps." Kenzie nodded at the ruined trucks. "Which your Drake kindly blew up."

Hayden once more wondered how on earth she'd somehow saddled this pony. Drake had to be laughing up his sleeve.

"Okay guys. Move."

They took off again, hampered by the dangerous forest floor. Ruts, knotted trees and waterlogged earth lay everywhere. As they ran, the single remaining guard turned and hurled an object at them, something he'd no doubt purloined from the bazaar.

"Grenade!" Smyth shouted.

Into the undergrowth they leapt, head first. A great tree stump offered protection. Scrambling around it they sought cover, and the metallic bomb exploded. Fragments shredded the vegetation, ripping through the jungle and shredding all in their path. Hayden held her breath as the blast went past then, feeling no wounds, rose to her feet.

"We okay? All right, c'mon. That bastard's still running."

As they closed in on Price's group they reloaded and regrouped, forming a tight position. Even Kenzie stuck with it, seeing the best chance of success. Price himself continued to glance over his shoulder, eyes wild and rolling. Hayden nodded with grim satisfaction. *This is what justice looks like.*

Then they passed a high rock cluster, a trickling waterfall and leapt over a wide stream. As Price was practically carried around a smooth rock the man abruptly vanished. Then the next CIA agent performed the same disappearing act and finally the guard. Hayden pulled up short and approached the area with caution.

"An entrance," she said as they crouched among the trees. "See? Behind that rock."

Kenzie let out a low whistle. "Before I came here, on receiving the invite, I researched this area, as you know. Something I am very good at. There were whispers of a hidden CIA station, a cave system where they're stashing an incredible cache from weapons to drugs and stolen works of art. Even I doubted it was real. But this . . ." she tailed off.

"Cave system?" Smyth eyed the hole dubiously. "Any idea where it goes?"

"Down," Kenzie said. "Definitely down."

"Wiseass. So c'mon, what are we waiting for?"

Hayden eyed the seemingly unguarded entrance. "Relax, Smyth, and let's take this steady. I've seen one too many traps on this trip already."

Kenzie now rounded on the ex-CIA agent, a challenge in her face. "That reminds me. How did you people end up getting caught? The Alicia bitch didn't look too happy about it and Drake and the beautiful Swede seemed mighty upset."

Hayden hefted her rifle and cinched tight her belt. "Communications surveillance," she said quietly. "It's superior to what we imagined. I placed a call to DC—they traced the call back to me."

"It's everywhere these days," Kenzie agreed. "Imagine *my* dilemma, having to smuggle stolen artifacts around the world."

"That's what you do?" Lauren asked, then shrugged. "Nice."

Yorgi stared at her. "I'm quite sure I have heard of you," he said. "Didn't you cross the Samoan Cartel once? And they're still looking for you?"

"Ha. The Samoan Cartel couldn't find their way out of Mexico if they found a map to Tijuana. They're old school."

"But stone cold killers."

Kenzie shrugged it off.

"We underestimated these people and we paid the price," Hayden said. "Maybe the CIA were involved in monitoring the airways and reporting to Ramses. From what we've seen so far, it wouldn't be a stretch."

Kinimaka rose carefully, a great shadow and now a legend of the rainforest. "I can't see jack inside that entrance. We're losing valuable time here, guys."

Hayden walked ahead. "Don't worry. One way or another Robert Price and all his cronies are gonna be on a plane to DC tonight. Whether it's in cuffs or a black bag is entirely up to him."

CHAPTER THIRTY SIX

Drake loped along in pursuit of Tyler Webb and Ramses, colleagues at his side. The RPG had whistled harmlessly by, exploding against a cluster of trees. Dahl looked like he was out for a Sunday morning jog, tongue lolling happily. Alicia and Mai ran shoulder to shoulder, just like old times. Beau trailed them carefully, a deadly, inscrutable panther.

The river ran to their left, wide at this point and scattered with barges. Early afternoon sunshine dappled the water, an image that utterly belied the intensity of the crazed human torrent that streamed toward it. Drake was not only at the heart of a mad rush for the barges, but a furious sprint for the air transport and an annoyed race toward ground vehicles, and thus unable to make much progress toward Webb.

Human fury seethed all around them. On the plus side, Webb ran alone and scared, out of his comfort zone, with no bodyguard and no obvious route of escape. Drake struggled to keep the man in his sights, knocking people aside at every twist and turn. Dahl formed the point of their wedge, happy to plow the human fields. There was even a surreal moment when the Swede spotted a vile foe he'd first encountered ten years before, caught him in a headlock on the hoof, and snapped his neck. Dahl had never looked happier.

Drake fought hard to lock away his new rush of feelings for Mai. *Less of a rush,* he thought, *more a chaos.* Questions bombarded him like missiles, and he was sure Alicia would feel the same, but for now the old training was all that he could utilize—focus on the battle and lock everything else away. He watched the surge of people empty out into a large clearing like a stream flowing into a wide ocean, most of the flood heading toward the narrow, makeshift dock. Caimans and other predators started showing an interest on the far banks. Webb ran headlong for a few seconds, head spinning so wildly Drake wondered if he might be experiencing an *Exorcist* moment, then pulled up short. Drug kings and arms smugglers poured around him. Webb clutched the satchel held at his side.

"Ramses!" he screamed. "Ramses! You owe me! You owe me *now!*"

Drake made out the terrorist leader, the man so mythical they didn't even know which or how many organizations he ran, as all seven feet of him turned and stared at the Pythian king. Whatever he said couldn't have been particularly nice, for Webb turned white and then backed away.

"A dozen legionnaires," Drake heard through the tumult. "That's all I can spare you."

Men peeled away from Ramses, forming up around Webb as the terrorist prince walked away, not in the direction of the docks but following a narrow trail into the rainforest. Drake didn't have to check to see what would happen next.

"Ram 'em," Dahl breathed.

The four-person SPEAR team backed by Beauregard smashed hard into the wall that had formed up around Tyler Webb. Dahl head-butted his opponent and ducked under a fountain of blood. Drake dropped his shoulder as he rammed into his, then lifted the man over his back. The stock of a rifle slammed down onto his neck, sending a ripple of pain toward his brain. The man crashed to the ground but before Drake could turn to re-engage, Beauregard had already ended his life.

"Beauregard!" Webb's piercing shout resounded. "What are you doing?"

Drake staggered as one of Ramses' legionnaires came at him, a knife flashing from an open palm. The blade jammed into his stab-vest then fell away, but put Drake off guard. The whole team were suddenly dealing with two to three opponents at once, and the scene got ugly very fast. Mai danced through two as speedily as ever but the second managed to snag her ankle on the way down, unbalancing even her and sending her sprawling across a pile of organic matter. When she rolled, leaves coated her entire front. Alicia defeated her first man and then nearly choked as Mai came up.

"Beautiful," she muttered as she returned to the fight. "Best Bigfoot disguise in a long while."

Drake fell again, his opponent more than capable of using legs and arms. A small pistol appeared in the man's hand but Drake slapped it aside. The terrain hampered everyone, brim-full of unseen dangers. Dahl fell hard against a tree and then almost cringed as several unsavory creatures fell all around him.

"Pussy," Alicia said with a side grin.

Beyond the battle, Webb had retained two legionnaires and was making good his escape. As they left the dock area, Webb seemed to stop and start attempting manual labor. He began to throw leaves and fronds into the forest and shouted at both men to help.

Drake fought and kept an eye on the man who soon uncovered a sturdy four-wheel drive vehicle and jumped behind the wheel. Drake finally threw his man aside and looked to the others. Mai had successfully beaten hers and was trying to scrape away excess vegetation. Dahl lay on top of two men, trying to smother both at the same time. Alicia and Beau were dealing with two more in tandem, a sight that didn't help Drake's mood. Two more legionnaires turned to run.

"Hey, they're legging it! Whoa!"

He gave pursuit, leaping from rut to rut and then finding a strip of flat land to help close the gap. Ahead, the two legionnaires stopped and then both surprisingly dropped their weapons to begin scraping branches away to reveal a second truck. Webb's vehicle roared into life, gears grinding as he tried to ram the stick-shift. Drake attacked without mercy, thrusting with his knife again and again into the first man's chest. The other whipped a small handgun from his belt and fired. Drake shifted the dead legionnaire into the line of fire, holding tight as bullets thudded into his hefty frame. At the same time he ran forward, closing the gap.

More bullets and then the shooter stepped around. Drake flung his shield as hard as his tiring muscles allowed, then followed the dead body's bulk as it collided with the other man. The gun fell away. Both legionnaires fell. Drake withdrew his own pistol and ended the fight. Fifteen meters ahead now Webb was still struggling with the stick-shift. One of his men tried to help but Webb pushed him away—the Pythian's egotistical nature unable to accept aid after he'd taken charge—and stamped on the gas pedal as if that might solve the problem.

Drake had a fast choice to make. Try to cover the distance, or start up the second truck. A quick check showed Alicia, Beau and Dahl heading his way, Mai lagging a bit behind. From the lead truck came a burst of gunfire. Bullets peppered Drake's surrounds, most of them whizzing high above his head. He didn't flinch but turned to give the shooter an icy stare.

In that moment Webb finally found success. The truck lurched forward, revving its engine loudly enough to scare local wildlife out of the trees. Both legionnaires fell into the rear of the vehicle, flung out of their seats. Webb bounced the truck onto the track in an enormous cloud of mulch.

Drake jumped into the second truck, locating the keys already hanging from the ignition for ultimate readiness. The engine roared to life just as Beau streaked past, a black panther at full pelt. Alicia panted in his wake and then climbed in behind Drake.

"Fuck that. I ain't wearing my streamlined bodysuit today."

"More's the pity." Drake smoothly engaged first gear.

"Hey." Alicia slapped his scalp resoundingly. "None of that."

Drake eased the truck onto the track. Dahl and Mai jumped in and then he floored the gas pedal in pursuit of Webb, the forest at last manageable. To his credit, Beauregard had already caught the lead vehicle—just as its legionnaires regained their seats. Several wild shots were fired. Webb eyed the Frenchman in the rearview mirror.

"Kill him! Blow that man's head off!"

Beau zigzagged. Bullets tracked his movements. It was only a matter of moments before one would tag him. Drake urged the engine as violently as he could, speeding up behind Beau and Webb. Dahl, who had taken the passenger seat, rose and rested his rifle atop the frame of the windshield. One shot obliterated the glass in the front of the lead car, a second rattled off the framework. Beau made a leap for the rear of the vehicle, catching hold of the metal, but his feet jounced painfully from furrow to furrow. Drake rode up right behind the lead vehicle, almost touching its back end as Beau jarred and weaved to the left. Alicia craned her neck to stare at the tightly clad figure.

"Wow, it's like a porn show."

Drake ducked as one of the legionnaires fired. A bullet

shattered their own windshield as Dahl let loose a volley, taking a man out. Webb urged his truck to go faster, but shouting wouldn't cut it this time—guiding a Jeep at speed through the Amazon required skill. Alicia waved frantically at Beau.

"Climb in or get the hell off!" she cried. "We've got this."

The Frenchman exhibited his unrivaled skill, slamming both feet on the floor as he hung off the truck and using the momentum to somersault his body right into the empty back bed. Drake then carefully pushed against the offside tail lights, forcing Webb to slew to the left. Putting his foot down, he impelled more impetus into the swerve and then Webb was heading for the trees.

Dahl pounded the framework. "C'mon Yorkie. Drive it like you fuckin' stole it!"

Drake buried the gas pedal. Webb's truck spun hard, broadsiding as it smashed into the jungle. Contact with a tree whipped it back around and the surviving legionnaire found out the hard way just how dangerous it could be to fly. His journey was ended abruptly by another tree and a resoundingly wet slap.

Drake jumped on the brakes, but at that moment their own truck hit a deep trough, bounding downward, then upward and to the side in the space of half a second. Everyone jolted to and fro, heads coming into contact with unyielding metal, and then the vehicle ground to a stomach-churning halt, tipping over onto two wheels.

Drake clung to the wheel as it crashed over onto one side. Dahl hugged his limbs, making sure they were inside the car. The windshield's frame pushed hard down, ooze seeping over the top. Mai cursed in Japanese, once again covered in rotting leaves.

Alicia, now at the top of the overturned truck, fished around in her back pocket. "Wait, just wait," she shouted at

Mai. "I have to get a picture of this."

Drake waited for Dahl to crawl through the broken windshield before unbuckling his seat belt and falling down into the passenger seat. It took only moments for all four members of the SPEAR team to crawl free and then meet at the back of Webb's crashed Jeep. Drake immediately saw Beauregard, nursing a gashed forehead, and then hurried around the front.

"Bollocks," he said.

The driver's seat was empty, the churned-up ground offering no clues, and the surrounding forest was empty. Quiet.

"Flung out?" Dahl wondered.

"Maybe," Drake said. "But this place is too big to start searching now. And we have Ramses to take care of."

"Best be quick," Alicia cocked her head at the sound of engines. "I think this party's about terminated."

Then Beauregard rose and jumped down from the bed of the truck. "I will hunt Webb," he said. "You return to the bazaar and stop the others."

Alicia frowned. "On your own?"

"It will be faster. And he is no warrior."

"That's an obvious point, pal," Dahl said. "But we hardly know you. In fact, everything we have ever gained from you turned purple and then black and blue very quickly. I mean, we don't know if you're going to help that man escape."

Beauregard's face turned ugly. "Then *you* deal with that. This man—this Tyler Webb—he is the worst human being I have ever encountered. He is vile. He is evil. No morals, no conscience, just a container for devilry. I will make sure they never find his body."

Drake turned away. "We don't have time for this. Beau, do as you like. The rest of you, follow me. Ramses first, and then Price and New York."

The team sped out.

CHAPTER THIRTY SEVEN

Drake returned to the dock area and a hellish scene of battle.

Barges and large boats fled the docks, scattered all across the river and at all angles underneath a sky darkened by the smoke from many fires. Rockets were being loosed between vessels and into the surrounding jungle, either as an attempt to destroy rivals or for interference. The jungle was starting to burn. Grim-faced men stood on decks, RPGs pressed to their shoulders. Others held machine guns with bullet belts wrapped around them. Still more had their entire decks lined by gun-toting guards. Upon another a deck-mounted missile launcher swiveled for a target. One more was the scene of a party, the guests oblivious or uncaring of what surrounded them.

“It’s all gone to hell,” Dahl said. “But then what do you expect of terrorists, drug runners and arms smugglers?”

“The prize.” Drake pointed their way through the ferocious extravagance.

Ramses stood poised on the wooden dock, men with weapons stationed at his back and the bodyguard, Akatash, at his side. He surveyed the fiery scenes with impassive regret, probably wondering where he’d gone wrong. Even the jungle area where he’d sited the bazaar itself was under fire now, flames and explosions erupting from the place and the sounds of buildings and trees collapsing reverberating through the jungle. Flames climbed the trees like fiery apes, crackling along the timber despite its wetness.

"The Crown Prince of Terror doesn't look so smug about it now, eh?" Alicia grinned.

Mai picked foliage off her clothing. "His reputation exceeds all. Be very careful how you handle him."

"You know about this guy?" Alicia asked. "Why didn't you mention him before, ya damn Sprite?"

"I have been away," Mai said matter-of-factly. "Out of the loop. You have no idea what I have had to endure."

Drake gave Dahl a speculative look. "Oh, I dunno. We all have our burdens to bear."

The Swede grunted. "Yeah, and Northmen being one of them. Shall we stop the chat and finish this?"

Drake slapped his friend on the shoulder. "After you, Agnetha."

Dahl started forward and then stopped, turning even as an RPG streaked past them and exploded high in the trees. The team marched together, side-by-side, four abreast along the dock, raising weapons and taking aim as fires surrounded them. It took a moment but Ramses finally saw them . . .

And recognized them.

Loathing burned from those eyes, almost of a depth to burn everything to a crisp.

Ramses stood head and shoulders above the rest of his legionnaires, and he strode through them straight at the SPEAR team, Akatash at his side. Surprise made Drake question this confrontation, but his face and body betrayed no doubts. Ramses tried to come at them first, but Akatash squeezed past his master, suddenly to be blocked by Mai.

"I know of you," the Japanese woman said. "Better than Beauregard Alain? Better than Mai Kitano? Let's see, shall we?"

Akatash moved faster than a viper, fists, elbows and knees all striking in rhythm. Mai matched him move for move, a blurry, reactionary speedster. Akatash clearly sought to retain the momentum as he pressed forward without relenting. Mai slipped a little Aikido into her fighting, allowing Akatash's pure force to work against him, but he countered almost instantly with a similar method, holding back on the power and trying to read her moves. The dock's timbers shivered beneath their feet.

Drake felt Dahl and Alicia pass him to either side, taking on Ramses' goons as the prince himself stopped only meters away. His size was quite literally shocking, and his eyes and facial expression right then could have quashed a volcanic eruption.

"The reprisals for this will never end." His voice resonated with a depth equal to the Mariana Trench.

"Bollocks." Drake laughed easily. "You megas . . . you're all the bloody same."

"Megas?"

"Megalomaniacs," Drake said. "Dictators. Tell you what, bend over, ask somebody to snap a picture of your asshole, then take a look at your mirror image."

Ramses frowned, clearly stumped, but at least it stopped him spouting the self-important expletives. In the end though he reverted to type. "Your cities are already in ashes and they don't even know it."

"Not yet they aren't. Not yet. Now, you gonna flap yer mush at me all day or are we gonna tangle?"

Ramses swallowed flies for a second before Drake became bored and attacked. His right fist struck first, impacting with Ramses' chest. It was like hitting concrete protected by brick wearing a sheet-metal coat. "What are you *wearing*?"

Ramses boomed out a laugh. "Virtuousness," he said shortly and then flung a K-rail in the shape of a fist at the Yorkshireman's head. Drake ducked thankfully, and skipped out of range. To add to the problems Ramses was fast and closed the distance almost instantly. Drake gave it a one-two punch, but barely made a dent. Time to start looking at more vulnerable options.

To his right Mai slipped on the moist decking and Akatash leapt upon her. Only flinging her head hard from side to side stopped him from breaking her cheek bones as his fists rained down. She rolled and flung him aside but a side-kick caught her in the ribs and doubled her over. Damn, the damage she had been subjected to over the years was finally starting to take its toll.

Akatash rose.

Drake leapt away from Ramses, covering Mai. Alicia dropped to one knee, firing bullets into two adversaries who fell into the river. Dahl flung a man over his shoulder and then wrestled another over the edge of the dock, but found himself tottering on the edge.

"Oh shit!"

Dahl lost his battle with gravity, but Alicia jumped and grabbed the front of his jacket, jerking him back to stability. By that time Akatash had signaled Ramses and the two were swopping vengeance for prudence and hotfooting it toward a waiting, bobbing speedboat. As the SPEAR team rose, regrouped and evaluated, half a dozen choppers rose like black predators from the trees all around.

"Hurry," Dahl said. "He's getting away."

Drake eyed the swooping, pitching, soaring choppers that blocked out the majority of the light.

"I don't think so," he said. "This battle's just getting started."

CHAPTER THIRTY EIGHT

Hayden squeezed through the cave entrance first, hyper-alert for ambushes or booby-traps. She held a small torch in the same hand as her gun, slightly above the barrel, borrowed from Yorgi who had secreted many essential jungle supplies within the folds of his robes. Lauren took the other torch, as she and Smyth brought up the rear. Quieter than thought, they advanced.

Inside, the cave broadened and then narrowed at the far end, a simple space. Footfalls echoed from some unseen passage, telling Hayden all she needed to know. “They’re running,” she said. “We have to keep up.”

Discarding a good portion of vigilance they sped up, filing through another passage and following its many nuances into the heart of a hidden mountain. The rocky floor angled downwards and the torches picked out slick, black walls and a jagged ceiling. Creatures scuttled out of their way, the slower organisms crunching underfoot. Presently, they passed through another small cavern, this one illuminated by a discarded, faltering torch and then pressed on through an even narrower tunnel.

“The CIA uses places like this?” Kinimaka whispered at her back. “Nobody ever told us.”

“It is standard procedure, as you say,” Yorgi said, “for CIA to have stash.”

“In comic books and Hollywood studios.” Hayden huffed.

“Dah,” Yorgi agreed. “And in real life too.”

Kenzie also voiced an opinion. “Never met a spook who didn’t have a secret account.”

"Actually," Kinimaka said. "You've met two. Ex-spooks."

Hayden heard noises up ahead and slowed dramatically. They were closing in. A disembodied flickering light showed them the way and, within a minute, they were creeping toward the jagged edges of a clearly man-made hole. Beyond lay a much wider cavern.

They crouched, studying the scene.

About twenty paces ahead Price, the four CIA agents and one of Ramses' legionnaires paced around the edges of a large-diameter pit. Hayden could see parts of the rim had crumbled away to reveal a hard, serrated border. With more illumination Hayden was also able to view a large collection of boxes, crates, documents, scattered weapons and other paraphernalia within the cavern. It was immediately clear to her that the agents were headed for the weapons.

The decision was instant.

"Stop right there!" She ran out into view, expecting and knowing her colleagues would be at her side. Price twitched appropriately and his guards turned with calculated looks on their faces. Kinimaka, Smyth, Lauren and Yorgi fanned out to Hayden's flanks, guns up, covering the cavern.

"Kenzie, isn't it?" Price stared insolently at Hayden and then flicked his eyes past her right shoulder. "I know of you. Two million dollars to switch sides. Right now."

Hayden kept her gun steady, but sidestepped to include Kenzie in her range of perception. "She's part of the team, Robert. Didn't you know?"

Price chuckled. "Yeah. She sure looks it."

Kenzie drew her katana, allowing the blade to catch the quivering lights. "Two million? Can you put that in writing?"

"Not until later."

"Ah. So you want me to trust you?"

Hayden walked carefully forward, shadowed by her teammates. The CIA agents twitched uneasily, the legionnaire looking very lonely stood on his own. Price switched his attention to Hayden.

"When did you know?"

"Robert Price," she said. "Secretary of Defense? Fuck you. You're a damned traitor, a terrorist and probably a murderer. So fuck you, on behalf of the *real* American government."

"Down on your knees." Kinimaka motioned. "Everyone. Hands behind your heads. One twitch toward those guns and we'll leave you down here."

Hayden paused, momentarily surprised as she saw the depth of the pit that dominated the room. Its circumference had to be twenty feet, its depth fathomless. A fetid stench blew up from below accompanied by an eerie whistle.

"Bottomless," Price said quietly. "The pit is bottomless."

"Now I do like certain things bottomless," Kenzie said. "Blondes and redheads normally, with rock-hard abs and sparkling baby blues. But pits? Nah, not my scene."

Price stared. "Are you going to use that sword or not?"

Hayden flinched, then a moment later berated herself. Kenzie was close, but not threatening. But Price had bought himself and his agents an instant in time.

The next few moments passed in a terrible blur. Hayden fired and Price ducked. Two agents fired and Kinimaka dropped his pistol as a bullet tore through his sleeve. Smyth and Lauren fired and two more agents fell. Yorgi squeezed his trigger and the legionnaire tottered on the edge of the pit.

"No!"

Hayden ran hard but nothing could save him from toppling over the side. His scream echoed for some time, but would it echo forever? Hayden forced the notion aside and ran at Price, the Secretary struggling to aim his own sidearm.

Around the other side ran Kinimaka and Kenzie. Smyth dropped to one knee and made sure both fallen agents were of no further danger as the Hawaiian and the Israeli engaged the two remaining suited men. Both the Hawaiian and the Israeli emitted grunts of surprise as they were charged hard by their adversaries, and then both realized exactly why.

Pushed toward the edge of the pit, they struggled to remain upright. Kenzie dropped her katana, holding onto her enemy's Armani sleeves with both hands. Kinimaka planted both feet, an unwavering, unbreakable tree, stopping the force that drove against him. At their backs the malodorous pit beckoned, mouth hungrily agape.

Hayden subdued Price with her fists, the man bleeding from lips and cheekbone, and then made a secure binding with his tie and one arm of his expensive suit. She didn't look him in the eyes once; sickened, dismayed that this man had tried to fill the shoes of Jonathan Gates, one of the best people she'd ever met.

"You'll never get me back to DC, Jaye."

Hayden twisted his arm. "I don't intend to. First you're headed for New York with me."

"What? Why? What's in New York? The whole place is a cesspit of corruption."

Hayden bit her tongue. Clearly, the people who knew about the suitcase nuke were fewer than she had realized. It wouldn't do now to broadcast any facts. She finished tying off the Secretary and then held up the remaining bunch of material.

"Talk again and I stuff this in your mouth. Understood?"

Price nodded.

Kinimaka and Kenzie held on tight to their opponents,

engaged in a peculiar combat which involved standing still and striking carefully with one arm. The Hawaiian grappled to and fro, finally wrenching a fist free and stunning his man with a full blow to the middle of the face. Still, this was one of the CIA's hardened field operatives and he blew blood from his mouth and nose and grabbed Kinimaka again, low about the chest, trying to heave his hulk over the edge of the pit. At that moment Hayden stopped worrying about Mano. You might as well try to move a water buffalo.

Kinimaka spun the man around and then broke his hold, knocking him out at the side of the pit. The sides broke away, crumbling slightly, and the comatose body started to slip. Hayden watched as, instinctively, Mano reach out to save him, knowing the opposite courtesy would never have happened. She then trained her gun on Kenzie's struggle, hoping to help the woman.

Kenzie gritted her teeth, matching the agent blow for blow. His head butt struck her quickly lowered skull, his viciously raised knee hitting only empty space. Kenzie spun around, tripping him as she went and impelling his body as hard as she could. The last agent sprawled to the ground, hands out as he tried to stop himself falling. Kenzie drew a deep breath and then crouched down to look in his eyes.

"All the fucking same," she said. "Those in authority. Those with power. Question is not *if* you're corrupted—it's how much."

She struck him a blow that sent him falling, screaming, over the edge.

Kinimaka ran up to her. "What are you doing?"

"Keeping it real, asshole. Staying on objective. I'll have full vengeance for my family before I die. Believe me, I will."

Hayden turned and shook Price by the lapels. "What is this place? And why are the CIA running it?"

Price looked deflated. "Black site. Safe house. Stash site. Black bag op. Call it what you will. All the clichés and more exist down here. They exist out in the field, Jaye, by necessity. But what would you know?"

"You're talking to me about the *field*?" Hayden asked incredulously. "I've seen more field than a friggin' thoroughbred. So you people run black bag ops from here? Through Brazil, Panama, all the other countries. And what? You keep the winnings?"

"I'm a patriot," Price said. "This isn't about money. It's about furthering American interests overseas."

Hayden kicked Robert Price into motion. "So get moving, *sir*. Or as God is my witness you'll be answering to *her*."

She pointed.

Kenzie hefted her katana, pure wickedness flickering by torchlight along the contours of her face.

CHAPTER THIRTY NINE

Drake evaluated the scene as the jungle shuddered.

Black choppers with bristling rocket pods hovered to left and right, ascending slowly, their engines roaring. Men hung out of the open doors, searching it seemed for any target to take a pot shot. One whirling bird let loose a missile which streaked among the trees and exploded, sending gouts of flame toward the wavering canopy. Drake saw the pavilions falling; shards and larger beams of timber erupting and tumbling in every direction.

The river's surface was utter chaos—every predator known to man battling to take a bite out of the other. Caimans lined the far banks and floated dangerously just above the water. One dragged out a man as Drake watched, its jaws clamped around his midriff, his pin-wheeling arms punching the ground in agony. Skiffs and barges, speedboats and dinghies raced every which way, many colliding, most hampering the getaways. Ramses' own speedboat started to nudge around to find an angle.

Drake and Dahl met each other's eyes.

"Is it time?"

Drake grinned and set off fast, the Swede struggling to catch him. Alicia gave chase too, her muttered comment only just reaching their ears.

"Oh shit, what now?"

The pair pounded down the length of the dock, timbers bouncing and fire at their backs, terrorists with automatic weapons all around them. Drake fired his Glock again and again, dropping guards where they stood and making a beeline for the end of the dock.

Mai loped along with them. "No boat for us out there," she said. "Just gators."

"They're not gators," Dahl observed as he ate up the ground. "They're caimans."

"Oh, excuse me. So why are we running straight at them?"

Dahl shrugged. "Drake made me do it. *Geronimo, motherfucker*!"

Both men hit the end of the dock and then jumped, sailing out at full stretch over the churning waters. Alicia and Mai, also running at full tilt, could hardly pull up and followed.

Drake came down hard on the foredeck of a drifting speedboat, scrabbling for a handhold. Dahl landed inside the craft, the white leather seat cushioning his fall. Within a second he was reaching over the windshield for the Yorkshireman.

"Need a hand?"

Then Alicia arrived, knocking him aside, and Mai hit the back end. Drake slithered and slipped across the polished prow, finding a grip for his fingers inside an ornamental venting. An enormous barge spun them around as it bashed their front end, its guards staring across the waters and not even seeing them below deck line. Alicia found herself in the driver's seat and rammed the vessel into gear. A jerky instant take-off sent Drake skidding up the prow to within Dahl's reach. He clambered into the boat and then they were threading through heavy traffic.

Alicia guided the craft in pursuit of Ramses, piloting them between barges and skiffs lined by desperate men. Bullets whizzed between them and wreckage burned on the river. Bodies and boats floated alongside, flames licked at their hull as they parted blazing debris. Alicia opened the throttle again, lifting the prow and churning water at their backs. An avenue opened ahead. The Englishwoman spun the wheel, aiming the speedboat left and right. An overturned dinghy blocked her way.

“There.” Mai pointed at another gap.

Alicia steered the speedboat through. Ahead, Ramses’ men were similarly impeded. The enormous figure stood facing the front, not even deigning to take a look back at his burning epitaph. Akatash watched Drake.

As they powered down the river, Dahl and Drake took up rifles and loosed some major firepower into the escaping barges. Large caliber rounds blasted through windows, portholes, door and bows. Guards fell sprawling to their deaths. Drake ducked as a volley was returned.

“What the hell?” Alicia cried out. “You’re attracting their attention.”

But Mai knew what they were doing. “This is about what’s right. We do this for free, any day of the week. A dead terrorist can’t plot a bombing now, can he?”

Alicia slowed the craft as it passed a larger barge. “Good point. Give ’em a hundred or so slugs for lunch, boys.”

Drake and Dahl peppered the boat with lead, then threw grenades through the holes. Huge explosions erupted behind them and detonated over the width of the river, reverberating back and forth and causing the trees to shake. Caimans slid into the water and other river creatures gathered to feast as the barges began to sink. Cheers went up from surrounding boats a moment before Drake and Dahl turned their weapons on them.

Two RPGs streaked by overhead, exploding out of sight. A whirling chopper screamed away, banking sharply and rising toward the gap in the canopy that snaked above the river. Another dogged their movements as if trying to get a bead on them. A third set down hard on the far bank, disgorging men who appeared to have been ordered to obliterate a particular barge. Alicia cursed them for their greed and viciousness and then turned her attention back to Ramses' escape and rapidly began to close the gap.

Drake saw a figure amid the tumult, a running black streak on the opposite bank and knew that Beauregard ran with them. The Frenchman approached the recently set-down chopper, a slice of darkness sent out of the forest to grab a little retribution. As they approached Ramses' craft Akatash shouted orders and then simply wrenched an RPG from the hands of a legionnaire, aimed it at their speedboat and fired all in the blink of an eye.

The rocket flew unerringly, straight at them!

CHAPTER FORTY

They reacted instantly and as one. Even under fire, guiding the boat and picking off the enemy the team were fully aware of their surroundings. Drake had already spied a third racing speedboat and knew it approached them from the right-hand side. Without a second's hesitation he threw himself off their boat and into the other, holding his breath as he fell through thin air and hoped he'd gauged the distance correctly.

The team came down hard, smashing the new speedboat momentarily beneath the waters and making it spin around. At that moment their old speedboat erupted, destroyed timbers arcing all around. One of the men who'd occupied the new boat fell out; the other faced the Mad Swede.

"Jump," Dahl growled. "Or die."

The man chose the former, and maybe the latter too depending on his luck. Dahl jumped on the throttle and increased the engine's revs at the same time as assessing the state of his teammates.

"We all okay?"

Drake rubbed bruises and Alicia flicked away blood. Mai traced the new scar mostly healed on her face, a new chapter to her story, and one she hadn't yet told Drake. The speedboats again closed together as Ramses' pilot hit even worse traffic.

"See that?" Drake pointed out the jam ahead. "Like York at bloody rush hour. Nothing's going nowhere."

Alicia raised her own gun. "And for once—that's our gain."

Akatash was trying to load another rocket, but then came under increased fire. Seeing the crush of vessels ahead, Ramses yelled into a handheld radio.

Almost immediately the hovering chopper banked and zoomed overhead, settling above Ramses' position. Two rappel lines flickered down, harnesses strapped to ends that brushed the deck.

Dahl glared at Drake and Alicia. "What are you waiting for? Shoot!"

The Yorkshireman fired, but then Akatash ordered his own men to lay down some cover. Bullets impacted dangerously close and Dahl spun the wheel in an evasive maneuver. Then, both Ramses and Akatash secured the harnesses around them and began to be hauled up toward the chopper. The bird itself rose fast as they came up, escaping the river and any danger.

Drake stayed low. "There," he said. "Go there."

Dahl wrenched the wheel in the direction of Beauregard and the chopper that had put down earlier. "Your boyfriend," he said to Alicia, "must work on some kind of telepathic link. Either that or he's an android, programmed to think laterally."

"He's not my boyf—" Alicia began.

Drake interrupted. "You really think he anticipated this?" He gazed up at the escaping Ramses as they approached the muddy bank.

Dahl shrugged. "Doesn't matter now, because one thing's for sure—that Prince of Terror is about to meet his match."

Drake paused as their radio crackled to life. "You all okay?"

Hayden shouted down the line. "We have Price. Do you have Ramses and Webb?"

"Not really, no."

"Not *really?* What the hell does that mean?"

"It means it's a work in progress." Drake flashed on the fact that when he'd seen Beauregard running along the riverbank the man had most definitely been alone. *Maybe he's stashed Webb in a tree or something?* A baboon's den, hopefully.

"Drake," Hayden asked. "Where do we stand?"

He explained quickly as they approached the waiting chopper. Dahl, Mai and Alicia ran ahead to help Beauregard mop up the remaining terrorists. "We're about to set off in pursuit," he said. "Can you grab some transport?"

Back along the docks, he remembered, two separate choppers out of many remained untouched, as their owners fought and died alongside them or became caught up in the conflagration, searching for another way out.

"Damn right we can," Hayden snarled. "Get that bird up in the air now, Drake, and chase Ramses down. If he escapes the world will pay. Once we're airborne I'm going to have to speak to the President."

Drake clambered aboard the commandeered helicopter. "We're on our way."

CHAPTER FORTY ONE

Hayden settled back as Smyth piloted the chopper into the skies. Still not safe, a missile arced up toward them but mercifully fell short. Gunfire clattered off their underside. The chopper was top-heavy, but it was sturdy and new and bore the extra weight without complaint. Through thc cockpit window she saw Drake's chopper rise fast, an enemy combatant clinging to the landing skids until he lost his grip and fell away. Mai leaned out of an open door and picked off would-be snipers on the ground below. Hayden looked over the expanding scene–shocked and saddened by what she saw.

Raging fires littered the forest floor and climbed trees. Branches sizzled as the flames passed from tree to tree. Figures ran to and fro, groups and individuals seeking refuge or trying to escape. Several four-wheel drive trucks sped down various trails, bouncing and flinging around their occupants in their haste. The snake of the river was a battle zone, almost blocked out by plumes of black smoke, cluttered with sailing craft and warring parties. Hayden realized that some of the locals might have helped ignite the fuse down there, but it was a massacre nevertheless. The site of the last bazaar was now a searing ruin, all of its structures destroyed and its tents ablaze.

Hayden turned to her sat-phone, aware innocents might still be hiding down there. Slaves from all walks of life had been bartered for and traded at this travesty, some might have been in servitude for a while but others had almost certainly been recently kidnapped. Local vermin might soon move in so Hayden called the authorities who could aid them first, reeling off coordinates as fast as she could.

Smyth chased two helicopters above the jungle canopy. An excess of blue skies stabbed at her eyes.

Hayden keyed in another number. Three minutes later she was on the line to the President of the United States.

"Sir," she said with fear, with trepidation, but mostly with regret. "I have some terrible news."

"Is it Price? Did you get the bastard?"

"We did, sir. He's here now. But that's not the bad news."

"All right. Go on."

Hayden closed her eyes, trying to tear her mind's-eye away from the horrific scenario she was about to describe.

"The last Pythian, Julian Marsh, purchased a suitcase nuke at the bazaar. He's on his way to New York with it, he thinks as a means of blackmail. Ramses has ordered all of his terrorist sleeper cells to find Marsh once the bomb is inside the city—and set it off."

Coburn didn't respond for almost a minute. Hayden didn't question it, she knew why. There was no easy way to digest this information.

"Does he have the capabilities to smuggle the weapon in?"

"We're talking the Pythians, sir. Look what they have done so far."

"What's the timescale?"

"Sir," Hayden sighed. "It may already be there."

"Oh, good God."

"But nothing will happen without Ramses' say so. And we're in pursuit right now. We'll deal with him, sir, and then head straight to New York."

Coburn sighed loudly. "I'll make sure we're prepared at this end. Where are you headed now, Jaye?"

Hayden glanced at the instruments. "On a course for the coast, sir. Probably Peru."

CHAPTER FORTY TWO

Drake sat beside Beauregard as he piloted the chopper in pursuit of Ramses. Behind them, Hayden had been concentrating solely on starting some kind of mobilization among the US government rather than their quarry. Perfectly understandable since the nuke remained an unknown and they had Ramses in their sights. An endless canopy of green terrain passed beneath, trees as far as the eye could see. Beau informed them that they were flying in a straight line toward the Peruvian coast, but beyond that they had no clear idea where they were headed. The team took the time to relax and reload, though their stores of ammunition were starting to dwindle.

An hour passed, and then Hayden came back on the line, explaining that she'd done all she could to protect New York. They simply had to bag Ramses and then hightail it immediately to America's east coast to aid in the hunt. She also told them she'd contact the nearest friendly airbase and arrange whatever backup she could to help them deal with Ramses.

Hayden began to sign off, but then stopped. "Oh, and Drake? One day you'll have to explain Kenzie's story to me and why she chose to run with me rather than you."

"She's still with you?" Drake was shocked.

"Umm, yeah. Is there a reason she shouldn't be?"

"Just be careful," Drake said. "Watch her."

The jagged shadows of mountains appeared ahead and Ramses' chopper started to descend.

"We're in business," Drake told Hayden. "He's headed down."

"And he knows we're here. Be careful, no heroics."

Dahl tapped Drake on the shoulder. "Was that directed at you? Or me?"

"Both. Why?"

"Well, it's my normal state. Does she really want me to change this?" He stared at his own figure in the window's reflection.

Alicia was gazing at Mai. "That's a helluva scar you have there, Sprite. What did you do—lose a battle with your shaver?"

"Is that a way of intimating that I have facial hair?"

Alicia shrugged. "It's not a criticism."

"Well that would be a first, coming from you."

The team quieted as Ramses' chopper suddenly swooped toward the oncoming peaks. Winds buffeted them, attacking from both sides and shrieking like Valkyries. Beauregard weaved between peaks, following Ramses' line to perfection. Drake experienced a little nausea as the close proximity of the mountains revealed just how high they were much more theatrically than flying across a roof of green leaves.

The lead chopper dived hard and then leveled out, still falling down the side of a vertical cliff face. Peering hard, Drake finally saw their terminus, a sprawling gray structure that sat upon a lower peak, overlooking the valley below.

"A castle," Drake said. "The man's full of surprises."

Beauregard sent their own chopper hot on the heels of the first. As the castle walls grew clearer and the highest tower approached Drake saw men positioned along the battlements.

"Evade!" he shouted. "Now!"

Legionnaires fired up from below, automatic weapons chattering as Ramses landed in the small courtyard. Beau pulled hard on the cyclic stick, wrenching the chopper aside, but the combined force of gravity and heavy shells sent the helicopter into free fall. Drake gripped the sides of his seat and braced his entire body. Dahl breathed heavily. Another flurry of fire and holes appeared in the metalwork. Beau worked hard to haul up the controls, trying to bring the nose up. The engine suddenly cut out and a terrible silence filled the cockpit, accompanied by the whine of free fall.

Beau's last movement was a shuddering heave on the cyclic stick.

Drake grimaced as the rock came up fast and the chopper crashed against the walls of the castle.

CHAPTER FORTY THREE

Drake held his body as firmly as he could when the impact came. Against Hayden's original wish, Beau had done a heroic job—practically leveling the chopper off as it crash landed. Its underside struck the castle walls, shattering them, rubble raining down inside and outside the structure. A new hole appeared right next to the front gates and the drawbridge that spanned a house-sized ravine. Everything juddered as they broke through the walls, then shook and bounced as the helo wobbled and vibrated its way down and into Ramses' inner courtyard.

Drake stayed still as the world spun. Then, steeling himself, he launched into action, checking the others for wounds.

"Sound off."

Affirmatives rose very quickly and clearly, the best sign that nobody was injured. Drake pushed at the door, cracking it open a little before it wedged. Beau shoved at his side, creating a gap large enough for them to squeeze through. The Frenchman went first, drawing his weapon, then Dahl and Mai. The chopper wheezed and coughed around them, glass trickling to the floor and metal shrieking as its weight shifted. Alicia paused a moment to grab more ammo and Drake gave her a shove.

"Hurry, the others are clear."

"You'll thank me later. And quit poking me, it's friggin' freezing out here."

"It would be. You've just spent days in the Amazon." Drake spoke before feeling the chill draught of the mountain air roll into the cabin. Alicia was right, it was actually "friggin' freezing", but at least they were well below the snow line.

Drake compressed his frame to fit through the small gap, gasping a little. *Bacon butties,* he thought, *will be the bloody death of me.* The sound of gunfire erupted from somewhere, shots being fired at his comrades. Drake looked up to see a swarm of legionnaires bearing down on them from the inner courtyard and more scrambling down the wreckage of the walls. Ramses stood in the center of it all, directing men, and Drake could hear the deep timbre of his voice.

"Bring me any memento you like. But make sure they're dead."

A price on our heads? No change there then.

Dahl had topped the rubble pile and was now scrambling over it, heading away from the castle and toward a stand of trees some way off. Mai and Beau quickly followed. Drake urged Alicia along as legionnaires bore down on them from three sides.

"We good?" Drake heard Dahl call.

"Go, go, go!" Alicia cried back, running so fast her legs, slipping on the shifting rubble, suddenly went out from beneath her.

Drake caught her under the shoulder, spun and rammed a fist into the first attacker. He lifted Alicia. The blonde fired instantly, two men dropping to their knees. Together, they attacked the rubble pile again, nearing the top, but they had already fallen far behind.

A whistle, and the sound of a streaking missile made his heart skip a beat. *Are they firing RPGs at us? No*, he decided a second later, *they're firing at the rubble pile!*

The rocket hit and exploded, shifting heaps of mortar, stone and rock, a percussive blast ringing around the mountains. The large mass relocated, swelling and rippling and becoming as unstable as melting ice. Drake tried to catch Alicia as she fell, but failed, for he was already tumbling himself.

Back down into the courtyard the two soldiers fell. Back down toward Ramses.

CHAPTER FORTY FOUR

Drake struggled as the bonds bit hard.

Surprisingly, they had been well treated so far. They were seated on a deep, plush red sofa, hands tied behind their backs and feet strapped together. The sofa faced a picture window that stared out over towering peaks and down into the valley. A meandering lane led from the gates of the castle, over crumbling hills, through both thick and sparse stands of trees that eventually led to a rolling, grassy floor, many hundreds of feet below. Drake guessed they had been waiting there for an hour before a door opened.

Ramses stood behind them, out of sight.

"I could use assets like you," he was saying. "Somebody willing to take a risk, put themselves on the line to make a difference. For me. Yes, I have many already but I could use people with brains. With instinct. With initiative. You would be very well reimbursed for your efforts."

Alicia shuffled. "Untie me first. Then we will talk."

"You would be willing to switch sides?"

"I've done it before."

Ramses walked into view, standing like a mountain himself before the picture window. His frame blocked out all but a little light. "Then we shall talk." He nodded behind Drake.

A gun barrel pressed against his temple. *Akatash,* he thought. The swift, silent assassin. Alicia blinked in shock, not having sensed the bodyguard's presence.

"He's good, isn't he?" Ramses said. "I am good too. I used to believe I could take care of myself, against any opponent." He sighed. "Then I met Akatash."

Drake winced as the barrel pressed deeper.

Ramses studied Alicia. "You want to kill me. You want to be free. You hope your friends will come to save you. It is understandable. Well, none of that will happen. First, we will talk."

"Torture will get you nowhere," Alicia snapped. "You will never break us."

Ramses looked affronted. "Torture? That is not what I do. I am a prince, madam. No, we will talk between ourselves and then, when dawn arrives, we will throw you from the battlements. That is all."

"That's *all?*" Drake repeated. "Easy for you to say."

Alicia was shaking her head. "Madam? I thought you said you *wouldn't* torture me?"

Ramses let out a deep booming laugh that fairly rattled the windows. A moment later a servant arrived, dressed in white, carrying a silver platter. Ramses chose three separate hors d'oeuvres and a proffered napkin. He waited whilst the servant poured him a chilled glass of white wine.

"Conti Montrachet," he breathed, savoring the taste. "A vice, I am afraid."

"Oh, wow," Alicia retorted. "We're so alike."

Drake winced at that. If they had until morning to fashion an escape there was hope. But a pissed off terrorist prince might very quickly change his mind.

"So," he stepped in fast. "What do you and Tyler Webb have in common?"

"Webb?" Ramses chewed slowly, contemplatively. "The Pythians were his brainchild, his new cabal. The man is a psychopath, deranged, unhinged, and was always meant to fail. He is alone now, searching for something he will never find. A myth. A fable. He will not last long."

"But he is alive?" Drake pressed.

Ramses hollered out a laugh. "Of course. He escaped the

Amazon as did I. There were many fail-safes around that camp and Webb, I'm afraid, insisted on knowing all of them."

"Can I ask," Alicia put in, "why the hell you're still here? You know the rest of our team are out there, probably calling on the Peruvian Special Forces for help." She squinted. "If they have one. But nevertheless, they're coming for you, big boy."

Ramses frowned a little. "I think you will find I own most of Peru's authorities, along with Brazil's. Nobody is *coming for me*. And as for your friends—let them come." More laughter.

Drake enjoyed the bullishness, but not the underlying confidence. "What is Webb searching for?"

"Truly, I have no idea. Saint Germain or some such. Perhaps he wants to grind bones to make his bread. The man is a true monster."

"How can *you* say *that*?" Alicia sat up. "Having ordered a nuclear detonation."

"Our definitions differ." Ramses stared right into her eyes. "But I see you are going to be of no use to me. This conversation will now end and enable me to turn to more pressing matters."

Drake felt the gun barrel dig in a little harder before being pulled away. Yes, Akatash was a sadist No surprise there.

"I've changed my mind," Ramses said as he walked out. "No mercy for them. Slit their throats now."

CHAPTER FORTY FIVE

Hayden chafed as they waited for the backup she'd hastily arranged but it soon arrived in the form of two big military choppers, sent swiftly from the nearest airbase and consequently equipped to fly in the Peruvian mountains, both filled with the requested backup in the form of military men. Other forms of swift transport were on full alert, ready to whisk the SPEAR team anywhere and, in particular, to New York. Over half an hour had already passed since they realized Drake and Alicia had been taken captive, but the newly arrived choppers had lifted off some time before that, during the chase, tracking Hayden's chopper through GPS and attempting to rendezvous in the air. When Dahl, Mai and Beau realized Drake and Alicia were lost they had headed quickly toward the area they saw Hayden had landed. The team were distressed and consumed with guilt, but wise enough to remember that time was the issue. They wasted none of it, going over options for an assault at the same time as hoping they were far enough away for Ramses not to consider initiating an attack of his own.

Smyth favored the full frontal. "I call it, 'the Miley approach'," he said. "Attack the castle walls, the gates, the bridge, take the fuckers out."

Hayden looked up at the mountains from their hideaway deep within a stand of trees about a mile from the castle. "Well there's no way of getting in through the back entrance," she said. "That's a sheer rock face behind the castle."

"Tunnels?" Dahl suggested. "All castles have them.

Caves. Concealed entrances. I bet Ramses has several escape routes."

Hayden nodded. "A good bet."

Kinimaka studied the castle and its environs through powerful field-glasses. "Nothing obvious up there."

Kenzie snorted, shaking her head. "As if they would stick a label on it—'secret entrance three hundred yards'."

Lauren laid a hand on the Hawaiian's shoulder. "Keep looking, Mano. You will get nowhere if you don't at least try." She shot a hard gaze at Kenzie.

Beauregard then walked up to the group. "I could infiltrate the castle. Alone."

Dahl glared. "How? It's all rock up there. No trees or hills or wooden barricades. They have guards every few feet, spotters and snipers too."

"I have my ways. I can get inside. Alone."

Hayden checked her watch. "Beau, do it. Go now. You're our backup, and please hurry."

The Frenchman slipped away, just another shadow among many.

Dahl bit his lip. "They'll be waiting for him. I don't like it. They know we're coming."

"And that is our answer," Yorgi said. "It is. We have to do the thing they least expect. It is a thief's maxim. His . . . um, slogan. What is it that they don't expect?"

Hayden again stared at the sheer cliff face that towered above the rear of the castle. "That we would come straight down that."

Smyth growled. "That's because it's impossible."

"Yesssss . . ." Hayden turned. "But maybe there's another way."

"We don't need all these men," Dahl said suddenly, eyes wide with adrenalin. "The unexpected already landed right in our laps."

*

Five minutes later the soldiers were ready to move out and attempt one of the most dangerous rescues of their careers. Both Lauren and Yorgi would be left behind, since this was considered a full-on combat mission, and they still had Robert Price to guard. The newly arrived big birds whirled and roared, no doubt seen by those watching from the castle, but that worked in nicely with the plan, as they would see only what initially happened. Dahl fine-tuned it, much to Hayden's dismay—to allow the Mad Swede to tweak any plan was adding an infinite amount of danger to it, but at least he did check that the local choppers were fully equipped with all they needed before setting off.

Dahl looked toward the castle once more before they started. "Hold on, my friends," he said. "We're coming for you."

Then he joined Hayden, Kinimaka and Smyth in a fast sprint toward the whirlybirds. They clambered on and tried not to notice the deep concern written across the pilot's face.

"He doesn't speak English apparently." Hayden confirmed. "I'm actually quite pleased about that. The guys who came with him are convinced we're gonna die."

Kinimaka frowned. "And why don't you want him to speak English??"

"He might be able to talk me out of this."

Kenzie squeezed in next to Dahl. "The soldiers don't sound too happy with your plan."

"Just buckle up and hold on. These choppers are used for this kind of thing all the time. Drill and repeat. Drill and repeat. Those guys will be here when we get back."

Without wasting a moment the pilot took the chopper into the air, lifting vertically and then swooping away. Up toward the clouds he climbed and away from the castle, making a show of it. After those on the ground would have watched the chopper heading away, he disappeared behind a peak and then rose further before banking sharply back in the direction of the castle a third of the way up its own mountain.

Dahl was already on his feet. "Chutes," he said. "Buckle in. Jumping from a chopper is only a little different than jumping from a plane. The pull string is attached to a line, so instead of pulling manually, the line will do it for you. We're gonna set it to open low, you understand." He took a breath. "Very low. Do not miss a beat or you will die."

Kenzie punched his thigh. "Playful bastard, ain't ya?" She looked around. "Don't we need oxygen masks, or something?"

"Nope," Dahl didn't look over at her. "That's essentially for television."

Kinimaka tripped over his straps as he danced around with his parachute, having fought hard to adjust it to maximum girth. Hayden steadied him with a strong hand. Smyth glanced out of the only window.

"Crap, that still looks a long way down."

"Like taking any chance," Dahl said. "Once you've learned how, it just comes naturally."

The pilot turned, face creased with worry, and indicated they had risen far enough. Dahl wrenched open the door and let in a frigid, howling wind. With a quick nod he was the first out, pulled downward by gravity and forced even harder by the rotors' downdraught. Hayden came next and then Kinimaka, Kenzie and Smyth. The chopper waited for a moment, a steady sentinel praying for their safe deliverance.

Hayden plummeted through the air, horizontal with arms spread, and with an urgency in her heart. Air pressure slammed her ears and a buffeting wind tore at her clothing. Below, the castle grew quickly from a speck to a dot and then a blotch. Very soon she was able to make out the crenelated battlements and ruined chopper.

At their backs the vertical cliff face shot by, hard impenetrable rock offering cruel death in response to the slightest slip. Dahl's chute shot open, material billowing past Hayden and then she felt the hard wrench as her own chute filled upward. A violent deceleration to their descent and then they were falling much more agreeably, guiding themselves onto the top of the oblivious guards.

The inner courtyard rushed up. Hayden took out her guns a moment after Dahl and sighted on half a dozen legionnaires. At the very last second all five descendees opened fire. The next few minutes were a total rout; the victims not comprehending where the bullets were coming from and consequently being caught out in the open. Ramses' legionnaires sprawled across the castle's courtyard and battlements, clawing for weapons or just lying still, some groaning, others falling to their deaths, dozens of them.

Hayden increased the velocity of fire as she neared the ground, knowing their greatest advantage was almost at an end, and determined to take as much of it as possible. They landed one after the other, and hit the ground running, each clicking a button to free their chutes the moment they touched down to leave the drop zone clear for the next. Hayden felt only a brief exhilaration before turning her mind to their friends and where they might be.

"Inside." Dahl started off, then almost tripped over an injured, crawling legionnaire. "Wait." He reached down and grabbed the man by the ankle, three inches beneath his bullet wound. "Where would Ramses take prisoners?" he snarled.

The soldier grimaced and shook his head. Dahl shook the leg hard. "Tell me!"

Then Smyth stepped in. "Their lives are in danger," he

roared and kicked out at the man's leg. A scream rang out and some wheezing. Seconds later they had a close approximation of where they needed to go.

Hayden ran ahead, weapons primed and aimed. Three times she squeezed off shots and three men fell, dead. Smyth and Kinimaka also picked guards off. They approached a thick wooden door, wrapped around with studded straps, and kicked it open. Inside, the castle was cold and unwelcoming, the narrow passage constructed of simple rock and unadorned. Hayden concluded it had to be the servants' quarters and ran ahead. Kenzie appeared at her side.

"Watch the head count." Hayden nodded at the ever-present katana. "We don't want to be branded criminals over this."

"Yes, your President has had to grease enough balls as it is."

"I wouldn't quite put it that way but, yes. Yes he has."

A service elevator took them to the highest floor, where they walked out onto a plush landing. The lights were golden, throwing burnished hues across the entire area and the walls were lined by immense works of art. Hayden led them down a connecting corridor and then they started checking rooms. Legionnaires appeared from three directions, initiating a firefight.

Hayden dived headlong into a room, came to her feet, and found herself facing a beautiful, picturesque window—the whole wall a piece of thick glass. Sofas, divans, eighteenth century desks, wall-fittings and statues filled the room, but Hayden's attention was drawn to the sofa nearest the window.

She would recognize those two heads anywhere.

Drake and Alicia.

But it was the way they were perched on top of the head rest that terrified her.

CHAPTER FORTY SIX

Her involuntary gasp of fear brought the heads around, and Hayden almost cried in relief. It had been an optical illusion, contrived by the sofa's odd design. As she watched, Akatash lurched over the sofa, landing hard, making Hayden even more confused. Then Beauregard appeared, a black ghost, and the scene made sense. At her back the rest of the team held off the legionnaires so Hayden made a move toward Drake and Alicia.

Beauregard glanced at them. "You took your time, SPEAR team. I infiltrated the kitchen and became tired of waiting for your entrance."

Hayden crouched down. "You good?" she asked Drake, withdrawing a knife and slicing through his bonds.

"I'll be better once we catch up to Ramses and neutralize his ass."

Alicia held her feet up in the air. "I'm fine thanks."

"You think I would flee?" A deep, baritone voice filled the room. "You think I, being royalty, would scamper away like a frightened dog?"

Drake turned his head. Ramses stood in a nearby doorway, filling it, ducking down to pass through.

The Yorkshireman rose. "There are no dogs in this room," he said. "Only wolves."

A moment passed in which there was no sound, no movements save for the erratic spinning of dust motes through tapering shafts of sunlight. And though the room was huge, the presence of those who filled it felt infinitely larger.

And none greater than the Mad Swede. "Excuse me,

boys and girls, but is this a fight or a staring contest?"

Pure mayhem erupted. Drake dove at Ramses and the terrorist prince ran straight back at him. They met at full pelt, smashing into each other, neither giving any quarter. Beauregard fell atop Akatash, firing down fist after fist like pneumatic hammers, but Akatash deflected every one whilst exhibiting an utter calm. Hayden and Alicia vaulted the sofa to see the rest of their team engaged in various types of conflict.

Kinimaka and Smyth crouched by a far L-shaped corner, and held off any legionnaires who sought to enter the fray. Mai, with lightning fast reflexes and Kenzie with her katana fought those already in the room, the Japanese woman having slipped over the battlements after the aerial assault. Dahl plucked bodies from the throng and threw them through nearby walls.

Beauregard staggered as Akatash slipped away and then delivered a series of vicious kicks. The two opponents met as one, evenly matched, battling hard. One assault was blocked and then another, a counter assault deflected and quickly punished. Bones broke, blood flowed, but neither man gave an inch. Standing up to one another they weaved and snaked, broke choke holds and fell apart. When one fell he instantly pounced back into the fray, neither prepared to lose face.

Alicia saw how evenly matched they were, peeled away from Hayden and charged in to help. Akatash flinched under Alicia's spry assault, jumping away beyond her reach. Drake bounced off Ramses one more time but continued to use him as a punching bag, slamming punches into kidneys, gut and chest, ignoring the pain in his own wrists. Ramses wasn't good enough to stop every blow but what he lacked in skill he more than made up for in muscle and pain resistance. The two blows he had managed to deliver made Drake see stars.

Kenzie danced around Mai, the two women facing six to one odds, but clouding that in a whirl of violence and precision. Dahl jumped in to help them. The sword flashed twice, back and forth, and four men fell dead. Mai glided between bodies, slipping and sliding at every turn and never offering a stationary target, senses attuned to all sides and to everything around her, bending and breaking limbs, throwing huge men with ease, and landing lethal blows. Mai was so good, would-be killers still came at her before realizing they were already dead. Kenzie's eyes filled with a new respect. Dahl kept his eyes on the sword as if desperate to ask for a loan.

Drake slid under Ramses' arm and punched three, four times. Not even a flinch touched the man's eyes or body. He moved around the back, floating like Ali, and tried three kidney punches. Ramses swung around, a haymaker coming to take Drake's head off, but it was easily avoidable. The Yorkshireman ducked and then tried Ramses' face but striking those cheekbones was like striking foundation blocks.

Drake stood back. "What the fuck are you made of?"

Ramses guffawed. "Royal—"

Drake drew a knife and sliced across the man's throat. "Blood?"

Luckily for the terrorist prince it was a shallow cut, leaking only a little red. But the pain incensed him, as Drake hoped it might. Bending down he swayed and swung. Drake concentrated on the vulnerable spots, knowing constant pain would soon wear him down.

Alicia, Beau and Akatash flowed past the expansive picture window; bewitching, eternal views to their left, violence on a whole new level to their right. Beau engaged almost all of the bodyguard's attention whilst Alicia darted in and distracted him. The Frenchman's expression said it all.

I can handle this.

Alicia checked on Drake and saw him head-to-head with Ramses. Could she help both men? The notion was relatively fresh to her—until recently she'd only cared for one person in battle—one feisty, hard-assed heroine with an attitude on the wrong side of bad. Now though . . .

Hayden saw Smyth and Kinimaka were starting to struggle at the bottleneck. More legionnaires were coming and some were slipping through. She drew her gun and ran to help, picking them off one by one.

"Dahl!" she cried.

"Low on ammo," Smyth rumbled, face like riven paving. "And no end to these fuckers."

Hayden threw him an extra clip. She didn't need to explain further. At this rate they would be using their knives soon. She scooped up the few discarded enemy weapons and piled them at Smyth's back.

"This should help."

Dahl clobbered those nearest to him and then ran among them, smashing left and right, using his gun only when there was no alternative.

Drake raised an arm as Ramses picked up a lamp and smashed it down on him. Pieces shattered everywhere. Drake grabbed the flapping cord and looped it around the giant's neck, then physically leapt behind him, pulling hard. The cord tightened and the man screeched, the first sound of pain he'd made as yet. Drake leaned back as far as he could, hauling with all his strength and using every pound of weight. Ramses pushed the other way, veins bulging, hands scrabbling to get under the cord, feet planted as if they had taken root there.

Drake leaned as far back as he dared, shocked at how hard Ramses fought. An errant bullet split the air between them, fired by a sprinting legionnaire who then collapsed dead after being cleaved by Kenzie. It seemed that both she and Mai were almost finished with their knot of legionnaires and would soon be free to help. Drake hung on, heaving, and then Ramses faltered. Falling to one knee, he put a fist on the ground, gasping for breath. Drake knew that to let up would be to risk losing his advantage, and kept on pulling although the strength was draining from his muscles. Realizing he was close enough to reach Ramses with his boot he introduced it to the man's spine, and then his lower back bone. Keeping the cord in place he then leapt high, coming down on Ramses' exposed neck as hard as he could with an elbow.

The prince collapsed, groaning. Mai ran up. Drake panted and glanced at her.

"Great timing, love."

The Japanese woman reached out a hand to help him up. "Been a while."

"The best of friends don't need to talk every day," he said. "They pick up just where they left off. Even if it's been years."

Mai's face turned speculative and Drake realized she might be reading a little too much into that. Ramses seemed to get a second wind then though, and kicked out. Drake knelt on his back and quickly tied his hands and legs with cord.

"See how you like it, asshole."

Alicia kicked at Akatash's legs as he jabbed away at Beauregard. One of her strikes caught him across the knee and buckled his leg, causing him to groan in pain. He fell to one knee, catching a shin across the face as Beauregard doubled his own efforts. Blood marked the bodyguard's features. Akatash took another blow to the face without flinching and then struck out at Alicia as he rolled across the polished floor. Alicia felt a massive pain in the thigh, nerve clusters exploding, and collapsed in agony. Akatash was on top of her in an instant.

The grinning face was pressed up against her own, sweat and blood mixing. Alicia could barely twitch, let alone move, as he bore down, hands free and thumbs driving deep into her most painful pressure points. Alicia felt agony like never before, screwing her face up to scream, and every ounce of energy fled her system. Akatash reared back to deliver a devastating blow that would snap her neck.

Beauregard couldn't stop him.

Even Drake, watching the extreme struggle and sensing its outcome, diving for a knife and flinging it end over end, was too late to save her.

Akatash struck.

CHAPTER FORTY SEVEN

Alicia stared up at the face of death, unable to move.

Her final thought: *Oh, Drake, we missed—*

Then, the killing blow came and the pain struck her heart and brain and soul, but it was not Akatash's blow. It was Beauregard, unable to stop the blow but managing to insert himself between Alicia and Akatash, taking the punch on his shoulder and then screaming with agony. Something snapped. Bones broke.

Beau whirled away from Alicia, leaving her groaning, grabbed hold of Akatash with one hand and slammed him up against the enormous window. The bodyguard tried to recover from his shock, flailing and kicking.

"So help me . . ." Beauregard said.

"Hey, Beau!" Kenzie shouted. "Does this help?"

She threw her great katana with full force, end over end, the long sword slicing the distance apart. Aimed high, it impacted above Beau's head at the very center of the picture window. Akatash flinched. The glass cracked in the middle, crazy little lines running away from the impact point and bolting toward the edges. A piece fell, just a shard, and then a larger piece. A wedge the size of a paving flag crashed down into the room, shattering. Akatash was suddenly aware of the screaming wind at his back and the endless drop.

Beauregard tightened his grip. "One more who will not be missed."

He smashed Akatash again and again into the cracking window until his body weight made it shatter completely, glass showering in both directions all across its vast expanse. The deep, lush valley suddenly felt a great deal closer.

Dahl stepped in. "Need help?"

Beau glared into Akatash's eyes. "Not today."

He flung the bodyguard into high, thin air, the vast drop yawning below.

The problem was, Akatash had not given up. His flailing arms and hands had caught hold of Beauregard's suit and taken hold with a death grip. As the Frenchman thrust with all his power, Akatash held on, and Beau went with him.

Through the window they went, Alicia now sitting up and screaming, Drake much too far away to help but sprinting anyway with Mai a step ahead. Akatash fell and took Beauregard down.

It was only the Mad Swede who stood close enough to help, and Dahl didn't bat an eye nor hesitate a moment. He dived after Beau, straight through the shattered window and toward the longest drop he'd ever seen. With floundering hands he managed to grab hold of Beau's legs before any kind of momentum took hold, then lay there, helpless. A second later and Alicia landed on his lower body, pinning him to the floor.

Beau prized Akatash off his bodysuit. The man fell away with steel in his eyes, holding Beau's gaze until he began to tumble.

Dahl held on, still sliding forward, but Alicia was joined by Drake and Mai and between them they gently began to haul both men to safety. The glass scraped Dahl's jacket and bare arms but he'd take that over a free fall any day. Minutes later and the group were sat in a tangled heap, sweating, panting and trying to recover.

Kenzie drifted over. "Looks like my kinda party. Can I join?" She reached down for her katana and then surveyed the other part of the room. Hayden, Smyth and Kinimaka had used the last of their bullets and were now down to knives. Luckily, Hayden found two grenades among their attacker's bodies and managed to whittle their number down. The explosion caused a wall to collapse, further hampering the aggressors.

"Don't you guys get it? Your boss has run away," Hayden called to them. "Go home."

Drake crawled over to the struggling Ramses and fashioned a gag for him. With a worried look he turned to Hayden.

"We can't hurt, kill or lose this man. By his order the nuke goes off."

Hayden let out a long, deep breath. "That I know, my friend. That I know. I think it's time to call in the reinforcements and get the hell outta Peru, don't you?"

"Maybe they have already found it?" Kinimaka suggested. "The nuke?"

Smyth grunted. "Not friggin' likely."

Ramses rumbled into his gag as if in affirmation of the angry soldier's comment.

"We'll put him on ice. Nobody knows we have him. Right?"

Nods all around. Beauregard was sitting up by now and Alicia along with him. Kenzie wondered if Dahl needed anything massaging and Drake eyed the distances between himself and Mai, Beau and Alicia.

Talk about complications.

But urgency stabbed at his heart. "We have no time to waste." His muscles ached, his joints groaned, his blood dripped onto the floor. He forced himself upright. "If New York . . ." He faltered. "I can't even think like that."

Hayden took out her sat-phone and informed their back-up choppers to be prepared for a flight to the nearest friendly airfield where the Jetstream was already fueled and waiting. Dahl removed Kenzie's hands and gently placed them onto her own knee.

"With all these infuriated terrorists running around with their newly purchased mega-weapons, dozens of cells fretting and waiting for Ramses' order to push the button, and the certainty that America will strike back, we're looking at another Armageddon scenario," the Swede pointed out.

Drake patted himself down. "Then we'd best be on our way."

Mai nodded. "I'm with you."

The rest of the SPEAR team walked through bodies and blood to stand together. Far away, through the picture window, a civilian-heavy city never slept and never closed down. It thrived now and built on the foundation of its past, growing stronger in the face of those who sought to bring it down, the bastion of the free world.

It had no idea what was coming. And neither did its population.

Drake, the soldier, and his team made ready. There would be no down-time this time, not even a minute.

Next stop, he thought. *New York.*

THE END

Please read on for more information on the future of the Matt Drake world.

I hope you enjoyed *The Last Bazaar*, which offers a break from the archaeological treasure hunting and presents a new style to the Drake stories. Next up—*The Edge of Armageddon (Matt Drake 13)*—will do the same whilst hopefully becoming the fastest-paced book I have ever written. At least, that's the sight I have set. It will release early April, so not too long to wait. I'm planning a stand-alone Torsten Dahl novel for the middle of 2016 and already working very hard on the details. After that it's Alicia 3 or Drake 14.

Beyond that look out for regular, signed paperback giveaways on my Facebook page: https://www.facebook.com/davidleadbeaternovels/

As always, e-mails are welcomed and replied to within a few days. If you have any questions please drop me a line.

Check my website for all the latest news and updates—www.davidleadbeater.com

And give your favorite author a hug:
Reviews are everything to an author and essential to the future of the Matt Drake, Alicia Myles and other series. Please consider leaving even a few lines at Amazon, it will make all the difference.

Made in United States
Troutdale, OR
08/29/2023